The Righteous Rakehell

Also by Gayle Buck

Gayle Buck

<u>Regency Love Duets</u>
Cassandra's Deception & Belle's Beau
The Hidden Heart & The Desperate Viscount
Chester Charade & The Fleeing Heiress
The Waltzing Widow & Hearts Betrayed
Lord John's Lady & The Magnificent Match
The Holybrooke Curse & Cupid's Choice

Chapter 1

Upon his arrival, Justin Avery, Viscount Kenelm, was ushered into the library, a somber room lined with books and furnished with several pieces of handsome furniture. A fire crackled on the hearth, adding a touch of warmth to the chill atmosphere.

The graying man seated at the mahogany desk that commanded one side of the library gave no sign he had heard his eldest son announced. He continued to give his entire attention to the sheaf of papers before him. He picked up a pen, dipped it in the inkwell, and leisurely made a notation.

The viscount, after eyeing his lordship for a moment, went to the grate and spread his fingers to the heat. The firelight silhouetted his face. His profile was stern, almost forbidding, a circumstance made more noticeable by the thinning of his lips. He was not best pleased to be summoned by his father, the Earl of Belchester. He did not anticipate a pleasant interview.

A rustling caught the viscount's ears and he turned quickly.

The Earl of Belchester neatly shuffled his papers and laid them aside, looking toward his son as he did so. His expression was one of weary boredom. "Well, Justin?" There was a sardonic twist to his lips. His gold-flecked eyes reflected mild cynicism.

"I am here, sir, as you see," said the viscount, slightly angered. The earl had not invited him to seat himself, and as a consequence he felt not unlike an erring schoolboy being brought to task.

"As I see," agreed the earl gently.

Silence fell. The viscount became increasingly restless under his father's dispassionate gaze. Unconsciously he put a hand to his cravat as though it were suddenly tight. His gesture amused the earl.

"I believe you realize my reason for . . . requesting your company, Justin," said the earl.

"As to that, sir, I am not certain. You have never before interfered," said the viscount. He leaned against the shoulder-high mantel and thrust his hands into the pockets of his fawn breeches.

"This time, as I am certain you will agree, is different. The lady in question is the wife of a very powerful man. In short, Justin, the lady has been indiscreet and her husband is reputed to be out for your blood."

"Gad, sir, surely you do not believe such hearsay," exclaimed the viscount scornfully.

The earl imperturbably flicked open a gold snuffbox with one finger and took a pinch. "On the contrary. I sustained a visit from the tearful lady herself. I was not amused, Justin. However, I found the lady's tale illuminating and I judge that she has cause to fear for your safety."

The viscount stared at him a moment, disconcerted. Then he gave a crack of laughter. "That's just like Charlotte. Surely you do not credit her bird-witted prattle."

"She is, isn't she?" agreed the earl. "Nevertheless, I do credit her with some sense. I wish you to terminate your entanglement with her ladyship."

"That is easily done. She was beginning to pall on me in any event," said Lord Kenelm with a shrug.

The earl did not appear to hear and continued smoothly, "Also, I wish to hear of your approaching nuptials very shortly."

The viscount stared at him, stunned.

"Your ears did not deceive you, Justin," said the earl, allowing a hint of amusement to enter his suave voice.

Flushing, the viscount straightened. "Why this sudden interest, sir? 'Tis complimentary, I swear," he said, assuming an air of lightness.

"Very likely. However, my feelings are quite the reverse. I do not enjoy the task of forcing you into wedlock."

"Then why do you do it?" asked the viscount with sudden savagery. His eyes flared a strange yellow color.

"You are nine-and-twenty, Justin. Yet you behave with no thought of moderation. For years your excesses have been a constant source of gossip for the curious and the vulgar. I have held my peace over your gambling and your string of mistresses. I even managed to restrain my annoyance at news of your Cyprian ball. Out of a mild curiosity, Justin, did you indeed hold an 'auction' of the most infamous 'untouchables' to the highest bidders among your drunken rowdy guests?"

The viscount bowed, unsmiling. "It was a rare evening's entertainment, sir."

The earl grimaced. "Quite so. Justin, you have made my point for me very well. I flatter myself that I have withstood all with an admirable composure. But I must draw the line when the ladies begin to call on me."

"I beg your forgiveness for the inconvenience, sir. Your disgust is obviously such that it is a wonder you have not cast me off," said the viscount.

"My dear Justin, I have indeed toyed with the notion of making your younger brother my major heir. While it is true that William is a bit thickheaded at times, he is at least respectable," said the earl. There was a hint of steel in his soft tone. "I do hope that you will abide by my wishes in this delicate matter, Justin."

The viscount stared into his father's suddenly hard brown eyes. His own eyes seemed to gleam a brighter yellow. "It seems I have little choice, sir. You will read of my engagement in a twelvemonth," he said, controlling his fury.

"Then that will be all, Justin." The earl smiled pleasantly, the sardonic twist to his lips more pronounced.

"With your permission, sir, I will return to London tonight. I must make my adieus to the fair Lady Albion," said Lord Kenelm, bowing with grace.

"Of course," the earl agreed. He fell to contemplating the engraved design on his snuffbox as his son strode to the door. His gentle voice stopped the viscount with his hand on the knob. "Justin, how do you rate such devotion? I never did."

The viscount's tightly-held lips relaxed. He laughed. "It is my eyes, sir. The color fascinates the female sex!"

He was gone on the words, but both men felt they understood each other very well.

A carriage drew up at the door of an imposing residence of red stucco. The postilion jumped down from the carriage to let down the iron step and open the door. A well-built young man descended to the walkway. He waved the equipage away and walked up the stairs to ring the bell. A porter peered out, recognized him, and immediately ushered him inside.

"Is her ladyship in?" asked Lord Kenelm, handing his beaver and cane to a footman.

"Yes, milord, in the salon," said the footman. He was newly assigned to his post and committed the faux pas of leering slightly.

Lord Kenelm raised a mobile brow. His brown-gold eyes fixed upon the footman's countenance and under his stare the footman paled slightly. "Exactly so," said Lord Kenelm softly. He smiled, dispelling the uncanny likeness he bore to an unblinking lynx, and strode to the salon with the air of long familiarity.

At his entrance a pretty young woman in a long-sleeved round dress of semi-transparent blue muslin glanced up. She cast down

The Lady's Magazine, whose pages she had been languidly turning. "Justin!" She ran to him on satin-slippered feet.

Lord Kenelm received her with amusement as she flung her exquisite figure into his arms. "My dear Charlotte, such an affecting welcome," he drawled.

"How can you tease me so, Justin, when you know how deeply attached I am to you," said Lady Albion. She raised reproachful violet eyes to him, and her rosebud mouth trembled.

"I am persuaded that you are. Certainly, you persuaded my father of it as well. I must thank you for apprehending him of my doubtful future," said Lord Kenelm dryly, releasing her.

"Oh, Justin, pray do not be too angry with me. I am just so very much afraid that he will call you out. That would be too horrid for words," said Lady Albion breathlessly, clasping her hands before her low décolletage.

"You need not fear, Charlotte. I shouldn't kill him, only wing him a little," said Lord Kenelm casually.

"Justin, I was thinking that he might kill you and then be forced to flee the country, leaving me destitute," said Lady Albion. She gave an artistic shudder.

Lord Kenelm stared at her, astonished. "Well, I hope that he don't call me out then, Charlotte, if that is how he means to conduct the affair. I'll be dashed if I let some cow-handed whipster who hasn't a particle of talent with pistols show good against me. I should have to kill him," said the viscount bluntly.

"Justin!" Lady Albion's bosom swelled becomingly and her eyes flashed. "He is not cow-handed."

The viscount was startled by her vehemence. He looked searchingly at her indignant face, and as her color rose under his scrutiny, he said very softly, "Charlotte, I believe I understand. You have fallen in love with him." Her blush deepened and she nodded almost shyly. The viscount bowed. "Then I most certainly apologize and I give you my sincere felicitations."

"Thank you, Justin," said Lady Albion, smiling waveringly.

"But why didn't you tell me this at the outset rather than pretend that he was making dark threats at me? My father was none too pleased by your story, Charlotte," Lord Kenelm said sternly.

Lady Albion turned the gold wedding band on her finger. She glanced up at him, half-fearfully. "I rather thought it might hurt your pride," she said timidly.

The viscount sternly suppressed a quivering lip. The lady had always been a vain little creature. He said gravely, "I see. You were right of course."

"Yes." Lady Albion nodded, satisfied.

"I believe it is time I take my leave of you, Lady Albion," said Lord Kenelm, raising her fingers to his lips.

"You aren't angry with me, Justin?" asked Lady Albion, glancing at him anxiously.

"Do I look it?" asked the viscount, amused.

Lady Albion shook her head. She began smiling. "Your eyes haven't turned that queer yellow."

Lord Kenelm smiled back. He said softly, "You are a silly widgeon, Charlotte." He shut the door of the salon behind him and left the house.

The velvet curtains across the connecting door to the library stirred and a tall man stepped out from behind them. He caught Lady Albion's startled hands. "Did you have to cast yourself upon him, Charlotte?" he inquired quizzingly.

Lady Albion quickly recovered from her surprise and defiantly tossed her head. Dusky curls bobbed on her neck. "Certainly, I did. The viscount's pride is very high. He knows he is attractive and he expects females to throw themselves at him."

Lord Albion's fingers tightened on his wife's hands. "Do you still find him attractive, Charlotte?"

"Yes, Edward, but I much prefer you. His eyes are so unsettling," said Lady Albion, dimpling.

"I believe Lord Kenelm was correct, Charlotte. You are a very silly widgeon," said Lord Albion gravely.

"Edward!" Lady Albion gasped, affronted. She attempted to free herself.

"Yes, Edward!" Her husband mocked her, laughing down into her indignant violet eyes. Suddenly he caught her up into his arms, heedless of the danger to his beautifully tied cravat. Her squeal of surprise was cut short.

After a long moment Lady Albion sighed ecstatically. "Oh! I really do prefer you, dear, dear Edward!"

THE VISCOUNT, JAUNTILY swinging his stick, repaired to Jackson's Saloon for a couple of hearty rounds and thence to Watier's for nuncheon and a rubber or two of whist. During the game he looked up from his cards and met the quizzical eyes of Lord Albion. "I fear I must throw in my hand, my friends," said Lord Kenelm.

The viscount rose from the table amid mild protests. "Kenelm, dear boy, give me a chance for revenge," pleaded one acquaintance, striking a tragic pose.

"My dear foolish Howard, you have attempted to revenge yourself upon me for the last hour, and try as I may, my luck is in and I can't seem to lose to you," said Lord Kenelm, sighing in mock sorrow. Good-natured laughter greeted this sally.

The young man with riotous gold curls flung up a hand. "Kenelm, you profoundly wound me," he said sadly.

"I trust not," said Lord Kenelm with a smile. He approached Lord Albion and bowed. "I hope you can bear me company to

Tattersall's, Lord Albion?" he asked, flicking open a gold enameled snuffbox.

Lord Albion hesitated for a moment. "Certainly, my lord." He was curious as to why the viscount had singled him out. He was not left long in suspense.

Scarcely had the two gentlemen left the portals of the club when the viscount said abruptly, "I called on Lady Albion this morning. I suppose her ladyship told you?"

"I was present," said Lord Albion blandly.

"The devil you were!" The viscount was momentarily disconcerted, then his strange eyes narrowed in amusement. "I think I should have expected that." Lord Albion merely glanced at him and Lord Kenelm grinned. "I must beg your pardon for my insulting words, then."

"Your apologies have already been made to her ladyship," said Lord Albion disinterestedly.

"Ah, but I must tell you the reasoning behind my somewhat unflattering description. I called on Lady Albion to sever any relationship between us. I thought that by insulting you, I would kill any lingering interest her ladyship might harbor for me." Lord Kenelm paused and satisfied himself that he had gained Lord Albion's attention. He said deliberately, "I realized almost instantly that my precaution was unnecessary. Lady Albion was more than usually adamant in her defense of you."

Lord Albion's eyes held an intent, startled expression. "Her ladyship defended me to you?"

"Indeed, and quite often. I realized very early in our . . . friendship . . . that your wife only turned to me out of loneliness. She very much needed someone to confide in, and it was my sympathetic ear rather than my charm which interested her. It is a lowering reflection for me, is it not?" asked the viscount, his keen eyes scrutinizing Lord Albion's face. He was satisfied with what he saw and he was content to allow silence to fall between them as they walked a few steps.

"Forgive my curiosity, my lord, but how is it that you could abandon such a young and naive bride to the preying wolves?" asked the viscount casually, swinging his walking stick.

Lord Albion's lips twisted. "I believed what I thought to be evidence that she was forced into marriage with me. She once vowed in the hearing of a younger sister that she would never marry an older man no matter what her father decreed. Her sister let drop the remark immediately after Charlotte and I had married. It was too late then, and fool that I was, I thought the least I could do was to make of our match a marriage of convenience. Once she presented me with an heir, I made it clear to her that I would leave her strictly alone to lead her life as she chose. Even when that meant turning a blind eye when she took a lover."

"You astonish me, my lord," said the viscount, throwing a look at his companion.

Lord Albion laughed with a touch of bitterness. "Yes, I own that it was astonishingly thickheaded of me."

"Frankly, my lord, Lady Albion was bird-witted to believe that a matter of—you are two-and-thirty? —that twelve years makes that great a difference in marriage," said Lord Kenelm.

"She had seen me but once before I asked permission to press my suit, and she believed the age difference to be much greater," said Lord Albion gently.

Belatedly the viscount recalled a tale of Lord Albion's twin brother, who had died on the guillotine for the crime of aiding the hated *aristos* escape from France. It was said that Lord Albion's hair had turned white overnight when he received word of his brother's death, and as a consequence he appeared several years older than his actual age. "I see," said Lord Kenelm slowly.

The gentlemen's steps by now had carried them into the subscribing room of Tat's. The viscount suddenly announced, "I shall be leaving town for a few days. Otherwise I would ask you to share my hospitality at Belchester. My father would be pleased to make your acquaintance."

"My lady wife and I would have graciously declined," Lord Albion said formally. Laughter had unexpectedly lighted his eyes at the viscount's impulsive behavior.

"It would delight me if your lordship would put a halt to these stuffy conventional phrases and tell me to my head to go to the devil," said Lord Kenelm, a pained expression on his face.

"Certainly, my lord. You may freely go to the devil," Lord Albion obliged.

The viscount laughed. "Be damned to you, then."

The gentlemen parted with an underlying understanding, much to the dissatisfaction of some of those about them. It was well-known that Lady Albion and Viscount Kenelm were a pair, and it would have been a piece of choice gossip to have been able to say that Lord Albion had publicly acted in defense of himself as the cuckolded husband.

Chapter 2

The viscount made an appearance at two engagements that evening, staying for only an hour at each. Boredom finally drove him to Brooks's, where he spent an agreeable time among acquaintances at the faro table. His luck was in and his companions were congenial, so Lord Kenelm remained until the early hours of the morning, an often-emptied brandy glass at his elbow.

Finally, he threw down his cards. "All for me, gentlemen. I am devilish tired," he said, cracking a yawn.

"'Ish the bran-brandy," pronounced a bleary-eyed gentleman thickly. He gave a wise nod and promptly fell over onto the table, beginning to snore.

The viscount laughed softly. "No doubt. I will see you next week, my friends. I leave tonight." He swept up the vowels and guineas before him and carelessly dropped them into his coat pocket.

"You're never leaving tonight, Justin," exclaimed a gentleman, bolting upright in his chair.

The viscount put up a brow. "My dear Hugh, why should I not?"

"You must be mad. You've drunk brandy all night. You're certain to overturn," said Hugh Crofton, his eyes fever-bright but clear.

"Your concern for my safety overwhelms me, Hugh," said Lord Kenelm.

"Damn yours eyes, my lord! I have bet a pony on you," said Hugh in exasperation.

The viscount laughed.

"I say Kenelm ends in a ditch," hiccupped one of their tablemates who had fuzzily followed their conversation.

"Hear, now! Drunk as a coach wheel, Lord Kenelm drives to an inch," objected a second gentleman strenuously.

"Thank you, Sheffield," said Lord Kenelm.

His friend managed a wavering bow in his direction before offering odds on the outcome of the viscount's race. The betting book was called for and the odds were duly recorded. Despite a last plea from Hugh Crofton, the viscount left amid the sleepy inane bickering with the intention of driving his race to best the time record between London and Dover.

Lord Kenelm waved away the services of a chairman, electing to walk the few blocks home and cool his fevered brain. Despite his assurances to Hugh Crofton, he was mildly aware that his mental powers were a trifle hazy. The observation amused him. "I must be boskier than I thought," he said aloud, and laughed.

Swinging his cane at a jaunty angle, the viscount continued down the darkened street with admirable equilibrium. A flickering movement caught the corner of his eye. He whirled, instinctively dodging the club of a businesslike footpad. He delivered a hard blow to the man's middle.

His assailant grunted, then bored in with his cudgel flailing. The club struck its mark. The viscount staggered, shaking his head to clear it. Desperately he sprang at the footpad, trying to close with the man. The viscount knew instantly that his timing was off. He had moved too slowly. His fingers barely grasped tattered cloth when the club struck harder than necessary. His skull seemed to explode. The viscount fell heavily, a shout dimly penetrating his consciousness. As he hit the hard cobbles, a blackness rolled over him.

There was another shout. The footpad cursed his luck and took to his heels. Two men raced after the footpad while three others with a lantern stopped beside the viscount. The silver-haired man gently rolled him over and felt for his heart. A steady beat reassured him. "He is alive," he said, looking at his companions.

The thin youth with a cap pulled low over his face let out his breath in a sigh of relief. He brought out a handkerchief and knelt to wipe the blood away from the gash in the injured stranger's forehead.

"It would have been a pity for a game 'un like him to stick the spoon in the wall," said the other man cheerfully, retrieving the viscount's chapeau bras.

"Yes, but Father, what are we going to do with him?" the youth asked quietly.

The older man's thin brows rose in surprise. "Do with him?"

"We cannot simply leave him here, after all," said the youth, smoothing a lock of the viscount's tumbled hair. Over his head his companions exchanged a quick glance.

"Cat, the gentleman is not one of your strays," said the larger man. He was thrown a look of blazing scorn.

The silver-haired man was scrutinizing the viscount's lean face. Though abnormally pale, there was yet a reckless set to his features. He said slowly, "We need another hand and this fine buck looks to me as would enjoy it."

"You cannot be serious, sir!" exclaimed the larger man, aghast.

The silver-haired man grinned suddenly. "Aye, Christopher. Cat has the right of it. It would be unchristian to leave the poor gentleman injured and helpless. And we cannot hail the watch on the gentleman's behalf, for reasons you are well aware of. So we shall shanghai him."

"Thank you, Papa," said the youth quietly.

"God help us all," said the larger man, still shocked but resigning himself to the inevitable.

The last two members of their party reappeared, breathing heavily, to report with disgust the footpad's cowardly disappearance. They were informed of the decision made about the injured gentleman's future and cheerfully took up the viscount's long body. The youth picked up the lantern and the group continued on their way to the wharves.

Rounding a corner, they came face to face with the watchman. The larger man groaned a soft curse and the youth sucked in his breath. Holding his lantern high, the watch advanced toward them. "'Ere, wot's this?"

The silver-haired man stepped forward. "Eh, you may well ask! The master's had too much. He's tripped and cut his head open," he said bitterly, pointing out the sluggish trickle of blood on the viscount's lolling head.

The watch shook his head, clucking. "'E looks proper bad, 'e does. These quality ain't got no 'ead for it."

The silver-haired man agreed and spent a comfortable time enumerating the faults of his master to the watch. Before they had parted with every show of amiability, the larger man had broken into a nervous sweat.

The watchman continued his round, cheered by the reflection that a gentleman's servant, one of a group who were notoriously superior, had admitted to the follies of the quality.

The thin youth gave a gurgling chuckle, and that set off the others in hard-repressed laughter. The silver-haired man admonished them halfheartedly, but finally allowed himself a wicked grin. "It's an actor I am," he said modestly.

Reaching the wharves on the Thames River, the group cast off in a waiting rowboat. The unconscious viscount was wedged upright between the larger man and the youth so that he wouldn't slip over the side into the water that slid by dark and silent.

When the rowboat bumped gently against the side of yacht, the silver-haired man let out a low whistle. A rope came slithering down from the side of the yacht. Three of the oarsmen in the rowboat docked their oars and scrambled nimbly up the rope, followed by the youth. Then the rope was tied about the viscount's body and he was pulled swaying into the air.

A few moments later the rope once more descended. The larger man waited while the silver-haired man handed the remaining oarsman a small pouch that clinked. "We will see you again next time," he said softly, clapping the man on one broad shoulder.

"If your luck holds, ye mean," said the oarsman dourly.

The silver-haired man laughed and clambered up the rope, followed by the larger man. The oarsman skillfully maneuvered his boat away from the yacht and disappeared into the dark.

Viscount Kenelm groaned and put a hand to his aching head. His thoughts ran blearily. He had never awakened with such a bad head in his life. He must have swallowed more brandy than he remembered. He thought he would be able to withstand the pain and rise, if only his head would stop spinning. Slowly Lord Kenelm became aware that the motion he was experiencing was not in his head, and he opened his eyes, his brows drawing sharply together.

The well-furnished cabin of a small yacht lit by two lamps met his questioning gaze. Of a sudden he remembered the footpad's attack. His eyes began to gleam yellow as he looked at the unoffending red hangings and the richly polished wood and brass which reflected the shifting lamplight. His glance came to rest on his coat and chapeau bras laid across a chair. On the carpet beside it were his top boots and cane. Above the chair was a liquor cabinet built into the wall of the cabin.

The viscount sat up and his head pounded from more than the bludgeoning. Cursing softly, he made his shaky way across the cabin in stocking feet to the liquor cabinet. Inside it he found a decanter of port. He poured out a glass and tossed it down. The port burned, but almost immediately Lord Kenelm felt his head begin to clear. Once again he took survey of the cabin and his anger smoldered.

The cabin door opened and the viscount stiffened. A slight youth dressed in breeches, an overlarge woolsey shirt, and coat entered with a soft tread. The boy's green eyes widened at sight of the empty bunk. His hand stole instinctively to the knife at his belt. At the sound of an amused chuckle, he whirled.

The viscount put down his glass and leaned against the cabin wall, his hands thrust deep into his pockets. "I assume that I was not yet supposed to be awake. However, I am known to have a fairly hard head," he said conversationally.

He curiously inspected his visitor and received a distinct shock. The youth's wary green eyes stared unblinkingly at him, giving Lord Kenelm a taste of his own feline gaze, but that was not what he found so incredible. The youth was half-crouched, one slender hand clasped on the hilt of his knife. Short blond curls brushed the youth's high cheekbones and fell to his collar. His face was regularly featured and almost delicate in appearance, except for a determined chin. Lord Kenelm's eyes narrowed. No amount of misshapen clothing could truly disguise that face and form, and he knew with certainty that his first instinctive impression was correct. The youth was actually a young woman.

"Must you stare at me with such ferocity? It is most unnerving, I assure you," Lord Kenelm said with a slow smile. When he chose to be at his most charming, his smile never failed to elicit a response from the ladies. But the green eyes did not waver, and the notoriously attractive Viscount Kenelm received his second shock.

The young woman turned her head toward the door, yet the viscount had the feeling that he was still under the surveillance of those magnificent green eyes. Suddenly his ears caught sounds which the young woman obviously had already heard. The faint shout had been in French, Lord Kenelm realized incredulously.

Before Lord Kenelm had recovered from his astonishment, the young woman had slipped quickly out the cabin door. Lord Kenelm sprang toward the door, but he was too late. He heard the bolt shot home even as he wrenched on the handle. The viscount's smile turned grim. His eyes gleamed yellow. He was a prisoner, then.

Several moments later the door was again unbolted. The young woman entered, followed by a silver-haired man and a tall bronzed seaman. The seaman kicked the door shut.

Lord Kenelm waited, his face a mask of utter boredom. He leaned negligently against the bunk, seemingly totally at ease. Only the blazing yellow of his eyes betrayed his rage.

The older man dropped into one of the chairs around the small table in the middle of the cabin. The lamplight emphasized the hollows in his cheeks, making him appear older than his spry five-score. He sighed as his gaze rested thoughtfully on the viscount. A twinkle came into his eyes. "Supremely bored, of course, but ever polite as you wait to be told why you happen to be on this yacht."

The viscount felt a reluctant respect for the man's insight, but he brushed it aside. He'd had time to think and he believed he knew who was responsible for his present predicament.

"I believe I may guess why I find myself here. What remains to be seen is how you mean to deal with me," said Lord Kenelm in a hard tone.

Lord Albion had been wily to seem so accepting of his young wife's indiscretion, he thought. Otherwise Lord Kenelm felt he would have been on his guard. Certainly, he would never have left Brooks's alone and half at sea with brandy. Now he could but count himself the fool. Obviously, Lord Albion did seek revenge, and he had chosen a complicated means to achieve it.

"Allow me to explain, then. We had a rather pressing engagement with this vessel, but Christian charity being what it is, we could not abandon a gentleman with a broken head to the gutter. That is how you happen to find yourself on board," said the silver-haired man. He paused, only to meet the viscount's disbelieving stare. He smiled. "I see that you are wary, and well you should be. We have two propositions to lay before you. One, you may agree to be ransomed for a good deal of currency. We have use for king's gold."

Lord Kenelm was startled. Surely Lord Albion would not wish his henchmen to ransom ... his eyes suddenly narrowed. Of course—the Earl of Belchester would find such a position humiliating. Lord Albion would know from his wife of the friction between the Earl of Belchester and his heir. Lord Kenelm could recall mentioning it to Lady Albion once after a particularly blistering meeting with his father. Perhaps Lord Albion hoped to achieve a permanent breach between the earl and his son, one that would bring public shame to the family name. Lord Kenelm thought he would rather face any fate rather than subject his father to ignominy. "I fear you have the wrong man," said the viscount in a controlled voice. "My father would not pay ransom to have me back."

The silver-haired man raised his brows. "You surprise me profoundly. According to the calling cards in your coat pocket, you are Viscount Kenelm, therefore the heir to the earldom."

The viscount made an impatient gesture, and the older man sighed. "It is a true pity you will not agree to be ransomed. However, I shall not repine on it. The second proposition I make for your consideration is that you join with us in bedeviling the French patrols. You see, we do a bit of smuggling, and now and again we chance to run afoul of a patrol. When we return to England, we shall set you safely on shore so you may make your own way back to London."

The viscount stared at him in astonishment, then glanced at each of his companions. The young woman's grave eyes gave no indication of her thoughts. The seaman's gaze was openly challenging.

"Do you know Lord Albion?" asked Lord Kenelm abruptly.

"Albion?" The silver-haired man appeared genuinely puzzled.

"It is of no moment," said the viscount with a shrug. He was somewhat disconcerted to find that Lord Albion was not responsible for his present circumstances, after all. He addressed the silver-haired man. "I have little choice but to accept your second proposition. May I know who I am dealing with?"

"Certainly. This young cub is Cat and the tall one is Christopher. I am the captain," said the older man suavely.

The seaman whom he had called Christopher chuckled. "That's all you need know, my lord."

The viscount smiled faintly. The silver-haired man's evasive caution was warranted. He must know that his educated accents betrayed him, and certainly Christopher was also no ordinary smuggler. Lord Kenelm had a shrewd idea that onshore these smugglers masqueraded as members of respectable families. His glance fell on the young woman. He wondered even more what she was doing dressed as she was and part of this dangerous enterprise.

Her green eyes were steady as she met the viscount's frowning gaze. She seemed to partially read his thoughts. "We cannot trust you."

"I return the sentiment. You are not what you would have me believe," said the viscount. The young woman's cheeks flamed suddenly as she caught his meaning. He casually transferred his attention to the silver-haired man, who was chuckling over his words.

"Aye, I shall not deny it. But for the moment it's best as it is. As Cat says, we cannot completely trust you," he said. He stood up. "You'll want to get up on deck, of course. Christopher will find some breeches and a shirt for you that will be more appropriate than your evening clothes. In the meantime, I will have someone bring you some food." The silver-haired man nodded at Lord Kenelm, then he left the cabin with Christopher and the young woman, Cat. The door was gently closed. Lord Kenelm was pleased that this time there was no key grating in the lock.

Chapter 3

It was not long before Lord Kenelm climbed up on deck. A stiff breeze was blowing and he breathed deeply after the close air of the cabin. He went to the rail to look out over the fog-laced water. Cold salt spray dashed his face. The viscount felt a sudden exhilaration. The creaking of the sails, the dull boom of the choppy waves against the side of the yacht, the soft occasional mutters of the crew left his senses tingling.

He looked up at the clouded sky. There was a grayish half-light to the horizon. Lord Kenelm judged the time to be just an hour short of dawn.

Christopher joined him at the rail. "I see that you already have your sea legs. It would have been your misfortune if you were made sick by the sea."

"I am not so poor a creature," said Lord Kenelm, his smile thin. Their gazes met and locked, each man seeking but not finding weakness in the other.

Christopher smiled and nodded in acknowledgment. He turned his gaze out to sea, only to stiffen. An explosive curse escaped him. Lord Kenelm swiftly turned his attention seaward, where he saw the outlines of a French sloop. "Now we're in for it," said Christopher softly.

"Why not simply let them board?" asked Lord Kenelm, though he suspected the answer.

Christopher flashed a grin. "Our hold is stocked with prime French goods, my friend. And those fellows there know it. We slipped past them earlier, but the fog is too thin now to hide us. If we cannot outrun them, it shall come to a fight." There was heightened activity around them, proving that others had also seen the sloop and knew what it meant.

"I have no quarrel with the French," Lord Kenelm said slowly. With his sharp eyes he had discerned the guns mounted on the sloop and he wondered just what he had fallen into.

Christopher laughed. "My dear viscount, do you honestly think that you will be believed when you claim to be only an innocent passenger? No, it will be your neck as well as ours if we are taken."

"I am forced to concede the point," Lord Kenelm said with grim amusement.

Christopher pulled a long-barreled pistol from out of his wide belt and offered it to the viscount. "You might have use for this, my lord."

Lord Kenelm's hand closed on the butt of the firearm. "Dare you to trust me this far, Christopher?" he asked softly.

Christopher grinned with the air of devil-may-care that Lord Kenelm was beginning to associate with him. "I trust when I must, my lord. If I have made an error, I shall correct it." Though Christopher's expression remained amiable, there was a hardening of his eyes.

Lord Kenelm nodded. "Good enough." He deftly checked the pistol and was satisfied. Then he stood in silence beside Christopher to await the outcome of the cat-and-mouse race that the yacht played with the menacing sloop.

It was soon apparent that the yacht was sailing faster than the pursuing French. The yacht began to put some distance between her and the sloop. "They won't follow much longer. We are too close to England and our own patrols for their comfort," murmured Christopher.

Lord Kenelm became aware that the young woman had joined them at the rail. He turned his head to watch her intent expression. He idly wondered what she could be thinking. A young woman who exhibited such calm when faced with danger was totally outside his wide experience with the female sex; his curiosity was piqued. Suddenly there was a boom, followed closely overhead by a frightening whoosh of sulfuric air. Instinctively he ducked. "What the devil!" he exclaimed.

"The bastards are shooting at us. They have decided to sink us rather than allow us to escape!" Christopher shouted as another shot whistled too near. There was a splintering crash and slivers of wood showered the air. Beside Lord Kenelm, the young woman gasped. Christopher started away at a run. "I must see the damage!"

The viscount started to follow, then realized that Cat was slowly sliding to the deck. He turned and in the cold clear light of dawn he saw the stain that was swiftly darkening her coat. "Dear God!" He bent and scooped up the young woman in his arms. His one thought was to get her out of the confusion and danger. He made for the cabin that he had so recently vacated.

Lord Kenelm kicked shut the cabin door and strode over to the bunk to deposit the young woman. She lay unmoving, her lashes still against pallid cheeks. He pulled back the coat and ripped open the bloodied shirt, exposing her white camisole and above it the ragged edges of the wound. A huge splinter had entered the point of her shoulder and made an ugly, bloody tear.

Lord Kenelm fetched a bottle of spirits from the liquor cabinet and after a swift search he found some linen napkins stowed away in one of the drawers built into the cabin wall. With the pocket knife he always carried he carefully extracted the wood splinter, then poured raw wine over the open wound. He used the linen napkins as a folded compress and tied it on securely with the neckcloth that he stripped from around his own neck. When he was done, he was relieved to see that the young woman began to show signs of consciousness.

Her lashes fluttered briefly, then her eyes snapped open. She started to sit up but immediately she fell back again. "Oh!" she said in surprise.

"You have been wounded. I shouldn't wonder if your shoulder won't be rather tender for a few days," Lord Kenelm said. He was unsurprised by her startled glance or the sudden flush in her face as she realized that he had tended her. He had already decided that this was no slattern immured to a gentleman's scrutiny. The fine embroidery that edged her camisole as well as her previous conduct bespoke some education and breeding.

"I suppose I must thank you, my-my lord," she said in a low voice. Her green eyes held an expression at once uncertain and vulnerable.

Lord Kenelm matter-of-factly pulled the coat gently over to cover the soft swell of her camisole. The young woman flushed vividly. "I am only glad that I was at hand to offer my assistance," he said. He was about to ask her a few home questions when the cabin door was thrust open. He turned and found himself confronting a grim-faced Christopher and the captain, the latter of whom hurried to the bunk.

"Daughter, are you all right?" asked the older man with concern.

"Your daughter!" Lord Kenelm was stunned. He had guessed that the young woman was probably related to one of the people in the old gentleman's service and he had disapproved of it. But to find out that the captain had selfishly exposed his own gently nurtured daughter to the dangers of smuggling made him furious. "Sir, I should like a few words with you," he said tightly.

The captain, having assured himself of the young woman's welfare, turned toward his guest. He raised a brow in surprise at the viscount's blazing yellow eyes. "Christopher, pray help Cat to her own cabin. I should like to be private with Lord Kenelm," he said quietly. He waited until Christopher and Cat had left the cabin before he looked inquiringly at the viscount. "Well?"

"Sir, I find it inexcusable that you have deliberately exposed your daughter to this outrageous undertaking. No man of decency could ever countenance it," Lord Kenelm said in a harsh voice.

"I do not believe we are so well-acquainted that you may take the liberty of criticizing me, my lord," said the older man frostily.

"Nevertheless, I do take the liberty, sir. I am admittedly a rake and at times a frippery fellow, but I would never permit a lady of my acquaintance to participate in pursuits likely to end in her harm," said Lord Kenelm heatedly.

The viscount's ingenuousness appealed to the older man's sense of humor and served to dispel his anger. "I see. I understand your chivalrous feelings, and they do you credit. Indeed, I had qualms in including Cat in our enterprise, but my daughter is a headstrong young woman when she wishes and it is at times impossible to gainsay her. This trip she simply would not stay at home."

The viscount impatiently brushed aside this poor excuse. No young lady of his experience would be able to withstand parental dominance. "As her father, you could have forbidden her."

The older man smiled faintly. "Of course. But I do not believe that you need concern yourself over the matter any longer, my lord."

Lord Kenelm looked at the older man. He realized that the matter had been declared closed and he acknowledged it with a nod. He had said what he felt must be said, and there was nothing more he could do. More than ever he was curious why this extraordinary man would stoop to smuggling, which went against both English and French law. "Sir, I have been made curious. You are obviously a gentleman. Why are you involved in this sordid business? Surely it cannot be solely for gain, or even for a sense of adventure."

"There you are wrong, my lord. Those are precisely my motivations," said the older man. He sighed and shook his head. "I shall be glad to let well enough alone, believe me. This episode with Cat points it up all too clearly."

"Then why, sir?" asked Lord Kenelm quietly.

The captain's eyes suddenly blazed with a purposeful light. "The mortgages, sir, the mortgages! I am mortgaged to the hilt, the results of a misspent youth. But I wish to leave my son a clean inheritance and for my daughter a decent marriage portion. And I shall do so! It is nearly within my grasp."

The crippled yacht made its way safely to port, dropping anchor in a shallow deserted cove. Rough-dressed men in a longboat appeared seemingly from out of the rocks bounding the small lonely cove and rowed out to meet the yacht. The cargo was unloaded and disposed of in a swift, tense manner that spoke volumes. Lord Kenelm was amazed by the practiced and almost silent efficiency of the operation. He aided in the disembarkation of the several barrels, and though he did encounter one or two unfriendly stares, no one openly questioned his presence on the yacht. The urgency of the atmosphere was such that even Lord Kenelm was affected. He found himself casting frequent glances toward the farther reaches of the cove for any sign that the excise men were creeping up to catch the smugglers in the act.

When at last the longboat men had returned to shore and melted from sight, Lord Kenelm turned to find the captain's dispassionate gray eyes on him. There was something in that gentleman's measuring gaze whch made the viscount stiffen. It crossed his mind that he was the outsider here and therefore could be viewed as a potential danger to the smugglers. He could well have an end put to his life and his body neatly disposed of in these very waters.

The captain smiled, as though he could read the viscount's thoughts. "It is time for trust between us, my lord. I am Lord Thomas

Talbot of Ravensclaw. I hope that you will accept a few days' hospitality from us."

Lord Kenelm felt a wave of unexpected relief wash over him. "I would be honored, sir," he said, bowing. He realized that he spoke in all sincerity. His curiosity was too strong to allow him to bid good-bye to the captain, or Lord Talbot, without knowing any more than the gentleman's name. And there was the matter of the intriguing daughter, Cat. He wished definitely to pursue his acquaintance in that direction, at least until the novelty of her unconventional taste for adventure had worn off.

"Good! Ravensclaw is but around the promontory. We shall arrive in time for breakfast," said Lord Talbot.

The yacht's passengers were welcomed at the shore by a small wiry gentleman, who asked a soft sharp question of Lord Talbot. "Devil a bit," said that gentleman cheerfully. "We have seen a worse crossing. The yacht can be mended, never you fear."

"It hain't the yacht I am concerned for, my lord. I have eyes in my head," he said, and he jerked his chin at the white sling that held the young woman's arm immobile across her chest. She was being helped into the saddle of one of the mounts which the small man had tethered close by.

"Aye, you've reason to be cross. It was a mistake not to be repeated, I promise you," Lord Talbot said quietly.

"Glad I am to hear it," said the small gentleman sourly. He stumped away.

Lord Talbot realized that the viscount's eyes were on him. He smiled, dispelling his frowning expression. "It is sometimes a disadvantage to keep around old and trusted family servants. They have a distressing tendency to speak their minds," he said with a chuckle. He gestured at the horses. "Shall we, my lord?"

Lord Kenelm accepted the invitation and swung himself into the saddle. Christopher and Cat had already disappeared from sight when he started at a fast trot after Lord Talbot.

Ravensclaw was a neat small mansion tucked among old trees. The estate was bounded on one side by the sea and by well-kept fields and meadows on the other three. The headland that the yacht had rounded offered protection from the worst of the winds from off the sea to manor house and lands alike. Lord Kenelm was shown over it all in the first two days by an enthusiastic Christopher Talbot, who not unexpectedly had turned out to be the scion of the house.

On the third day at dawn the gentlemen set out from Ravensclaw for a day's hunting carrying flintlocks and accompanied by three liver-spotted spaniels to flush the game. At last pleasantly wearied by their sport, they returned across the fields and meadows.

"I would not willingly give up Ravensclaw," said Mr. Talbot, looking across the meadow toward the manor house in the distance. Smoke rose lazily from its chimneys into the gray evening sky and light beckoned welcomingly from its windows.

"I envy your sense of place, my friend. I am myself too restless to settle for any one place or, indeed, any one woman," said Lord Kenelm with a laugh. He lifted the brace of pheasants he carried. "We've enough birds here to ensure our welcome. What say you to an indolent evening basking before the fire with a glass of fine French brandy and the comfortable conversation of his lordship and the ladies?"

His companion readily agreed and the gentlemen continued on to Ravensclaw.

The pheasants made a surpassing dinner and afterward those at the table gathered in the drawing room. Lord Kenelm was at first engaged in conversation with Lord Talbot and his son, but he soon sought the company of the ladies. Miss Henrietta Talbot was a spinster cousin of Lord Talbot's, a rather gooseish lady whom everyone appeared to hold in fond disregard. In contrast, the viscount had discovered that Miss Catherine Talbot had a keen intelligence and a decided sense of humor. He was still amazed that the self-possessed attractive lady seated on the settee could be the same young woman who had attired herself in a youth's clothing and participated in a smugglers' run.

Henrietta Talbot was just rising as he approached. "My lord! I was about to sit down to the pianoforte. Is there anything you particularly wish to hear?" she asked.

"I will be pleased with whatever selection strikes your fancy, Miss Talbot," said Lord Kenelm, bowing to her.

"Such a nice gentleman," Henrietta said, gratified, and she bustled away. Soon the strains of an old air softly pervaded the sitting room.

"May I join you, Miss Talbot?" Lord Kenelm asked, indicating the settee.

Catherine inclined her head, not once faltering in the embroidery stitching that she worked. "Certainly, my lord. I always enjoy our conversations," she said graciously.

Lord Kenelm glanced at her. "Forgive me for touching on the recent past, but the thought crossed my mind just now that it seems incredible that I first met you on a smugglers' boat. One would have expected that to have been the trick of a regular hoyden, but I have seen in the past few days that description could never be ascribed to you, Miss Talbot. On the contrary, you bear all the appearance of a lady who is content within the bounds of convention."

Catherine laughed. "And so I am, up to a point! But it is difficult to be left out of an occupation that consumes so much of the interest of those one loves. I wished to experience it just once so that I knew what my father and my brother were undertaking. I do admit, however, that I encountered more than I bargained for when I was wounded."

"I hope the wound is not still troubling you, ma'am," Lord Kenelm said quietly.

She shook her head. "It is healing nicely. I have only a little stiffness, but that too shall disappear." There was the faintest touch of rose in her cheeks. With his inquiry the conversation had crossed over into an intimacy which created an odd breathlessness in her.

"I should thank you for your kindness since that time, my lord. My masquerade was surely an astonishment to you. It could not have been wondered at if it had given you a permanent disgust of me," she said in a low voice.

Lord Kenelm smiled. The expression in his eyes was peculiarly warm. "It was not such a surprise as you assume, ma'am. I had time to adjust to the thought, and even to wonder a little."

Catherine's gaze flew to meet his. "You knew from the moment that I entered the cabin! I was not certain, but then later—" She felt herself blushing furiously as she recalled the circumstances. She finished working with the gold thread and snipped it, giving herself time to recover her equilibrium. "What are your plans now, my lord? Do you stay a few more days?"

"Are you so eager to be rid of me, Catherine?" asked Lord Kenelm, amused by the change of conversation.

"My lord!" She was shocked by his use of her Christen name. It was a breach of social convention. Then Catherine saw the wicked light in his dancing eyes and realized that he teased her. "You are abominable, sir. Take care that you do not ask too much, for I promise you that I shall air my opinion," she warned.

"Indeed, well I know it," Lord Kenelm said, laughing. He was aware in that moment that he had rarely met a woman with whom he was so comfortable. Miss Talbot's personality combined a touch of the unconventional with warmth and grace in a way which was entirely pleasing. He thought in all honesty that he would regret losing her friendship when he returned to London.

Chapter 4

L ord Kenelm returned to London on a crisp Monday morning, happy with the world. He had been gone nearly a fortnight and he'd had a rare adventure. He thought he would long remember his time with the Talbots, not the least of which had been the excellent hospitality shown to him at Ravensclaw. All in all, he had rarely spent a more pleasant time outside London.

He walked up to the door of his town house and let himself in. He scooped up the cards and invitations which lay in the tray on the occasional table in the hall and started up the stairs, calling out for his valet. He met Simmons at the top of the stairs.

The valet's eyes had widened at sight of him and he pressed a hand to his heart. "My lord!"

Lord Kenelm paused to study the valet's extraordinary expression of astonishment and then glanced back down the stairs. He was annoyed to see that the porter was staring up at him. "Simmons, perhaps you might explain the matter to me. Have I suddenly grown warts on my nose? Or perhaps I have become a hunchback?"

The valet recovered sufficiently to usher his master into the bedroom. "Oh, no, milord. My lord's countenance is as comely as ever, though perhaps a shade browner than before, but certainly not what one would call swarthy. As for my lord's physique, I assure you, my lord, that I have yet to see a finer set of shoulders or turn of leg on any other gentleman."

Lord Kenelm was momentarily taken aback, then his eyes took on a sudden gleam. He said hollowly, "Then it can only be one thing. I admit it, Simmons, I do admit it and I sincerely beg your pardon."

"My lord?" stammered Simmons uncertainly.

Lord Kenelm struck a dramatic pose in front of the mirror. With all appearance of loathing he ripped the neckcloth from his neck and tossed it to the floor for the benefit of Simmons' astonished gaze. "I have wantonly damaged your reputation as a gentleman's gentleman. I have trampled your professional pride underfoot. In short . . ." He paused, and the valet stared at him, holding his breath in dread. "In short, I am wearing the same clothes that I set out in a fortnight ago."

"My lord!" A certain look of relief crossed the valet's face. "I assure you—"

Lord Kenelm interrupted him with an upflung hand. "Pray do not stop me now, Simmons. Confession is good for the soul, so they say. I must abase myself further. I am compelled to tell you that other hands than yours have laundered and pressed these wretched rags. And so you see me today, quite sunk beyond reproach." He began to shrug out of his coat and the valet rushed to assist him, making haste as well to reassure.

"Certainly not beyond reproach, my lord. The pressing is not as well done as I should like to see for your lordship, and the shine is quite gone from your boots, but—" Simmons recovered himself and blurted the thoughts uppermost on his mind. "My lord, this is quite off the point. We all took your lordship for dead. It naturally came as quite a shock to see you well and healthy a few moments ago. Indeed, my heart gave such a palpitatious leap that—"

Lord Kenelm had unbuttoned his shirt and began to pull it off, but he stopped with one arm still in its sleeve. "Did you say dead?" he asked incredulously.

"Indeed, my lord! As I was saying, it was a shock to see your lordship walk in. Why, we have received callers for the past three days desiring to know the truth of the rumors," Simmons said. He brushed off the viscount's coat and picked up the abandoned neckcloth and shirt from the floor.

Lord Kenelm threw himself into a chair to pull off his boots. He was highly amused. "I am touched by your concern, Simmons. But why should you or anyone else think me dead if I drop out of sight for a few days? I have done so many times before."

The valet gave a discreet cough. "Your lordship's reasons for those disappearances were well-known in several quarters. If your lordship will pardon my saying so, the ladies in question were always extremely well-favored."

"Damnation! I always thought myself to be acting with discretion." Lord Kenelm eyed his valet. "I am not certain I wish to hear in which quarters my trysts created such interest."

"No, my lord," said Simmons.

"So, there was no rumor of my having a current ladybird and therefore some of my acquaintances concluded that I must be at death's door. I shall like to see their faces in the club tomorrow," Lord Kenelm said. He threw back his head, hooting with laughter. After a moment he recovered and dashed the tears from his eyes. "And who were the long-faced callers who came to tender their respects, Simmons? I tell you I shall fairly rib them for it."

"Their cards are in the tray in the hall, sir. But their main purpose was to discover his lordship's direction," Simmons said.

Lord Kenelm bolted upright in the chair, all feelings of amusement gone. "Do you mean to tell me that my father has been receiving condolences on my unexpected demise?" At the valet's unhappy nod, Lord Kenelm's eyes began to gleam with a familiar yellow. "Damn the meddlers. And damn this idiotic household of mine. My God! His lordship will be demented with rage when he learns that it was all a mistake. Did no one stop to think that I might possibly be alive? Why did no one question such a nonsensical notion?" He stared accusingly at his hapless manservant.

"But we had no word of you, my lord," said Simmons.

"Well?" Lord Kenelm asked, a hint of steel in his soft voice. His eyes glowed dangerously.

"When your lordship did not appear for the race, and then we had no word of you..." The valet gestured expressively.

Astonishment, followed almost immediately by rueful acceptance, crossed his master's face. "Of course. I had forgotten the race. Lord Kenelm would never willingly forfeit a race, would he? And since I did not show, it was thought by all and sundry that I had met with an unfortunate accident."

"Not quite that, my lord," Simmons said with a meaningful look.

Lord Kenelm raised his brows, then sighed. "No? If I did not meet with an unfortunate accident, pray tell me how my demise was effected, Simmons."

The valet was plainly unhappy. "There have been loud whispers of foul play, my lord, and in particular connection with Lord Albion."

The viscount's mouth dropped open. He stared at his valet for several unnerving seconds. When at last he spoke, it was in an uncharacteristically grim voice. "It is worse than I thought possible. Simmons, I shall want my valise packed for a few days' stay in the country. I will be paying a call on Lord Albion this morning. When I return, I will want my phaeton."

Simmons hurried to the wardrobe and dressers to bring out the proper afternoon attire for a gentleman about town. "I understand, my lord. Shall you need my services on this journey?"

In the act of shrugging into a clean shirt. Lord Kenelm glanced at the valet. "Indeed, Simmons. His lordship will be choleric enough without adding fuel to his wrath by appearing at dinner in an unpressed coat."

"Yes, my lord."

Within the hour, Lord Kenelm entered the portals of Brooks's and paused while he became the focus of all eyes. There was a flurry of whispers which died into stunned silence. Lord Kenelm glanced around and then leisurely made his way across the room to a small card table where a solitary gentleman sat. There was a noticeable circle of emptiness around the gentleman, as though the other club members had deliberately set him outside their ranks. Lord Kenelm's eyes gleamed yellow as he took note of the deliberate isolation of Lord Albion. He stopped at the table and placed a hand on the empty chair across from Lord Albion. "May I join you, my lord?"

Lord Albion looked up, his expression at once hopeful and weary. When he recognized Lord Kenelm, there was an instant of startled relief in his eyes. He said quietly, "Your company would be most welcome, my lord."

Lord Kenelm's smile was a shade grim as he glanced about at the avid gazes turned on them. He sat down in the chair. Deliberately he did not lower his voice. "I have had the most extraordinary adventure these past two weeks, Albion. When I last left this club I was set upon by a footpad. The rascal had little trouble from me, since I was awash with brandy, and I was knocked out cold. Imagine my feelings when I awoke to the ministrations of a beautiful angel!"

Lord Albion's lips twitched and his gray eyes gleamed with quiet amusement. "I can imagine that my own reaction would be one of pleasurable surprise."

"Quite, my lord. I was in a perfect daze by my good fortune. The lady is as sweet as she is comely. She insisted that I remain quiet until she was certain I did not suffer a concussion and my weakened state was such that I was compelled to agree," Lord Kenelm said. He seemed to notice for the first time the gentlemen who had drifted closer to hear his tale, and he singled one of them out. "Forgive me,

Fergy. I know that you placed your bet on me. I assure you that I would not have willingly forfeited the race."

"You devil, Kenelm! Give you a peek of a pretty face and every other obligation flies out of your brain," the gentleman said cheerfully. The others grouped around laughed.

Lord Kenelm smiled and spread his hands in a helpless gesture. "What would you, gentlemen? My sweet angel insisted on ministering to me. It would have been intolerably rude to have rushed off."

The gentlemen laughed louder, harder. One of them bent to address a jocular remark to Lord Albion, whose tension eased with the increasing warmth he felt in the group toward himself.

Lord Kenelm watched as several gentlemen made a point of addressing Lord Albion. Briefly, his gaze met Lord Albion's eyes. The older man acknowledged his gratitude with a slight nod. Lord Kenelm's attention was claimed when a friend urged him to reveal the name of his "angel of mercy." The viscount laughingly declined, invoking respect for the lady's honor. He spent a half-hour with his cronies, appearing at ease and amused, but inwardly he was eaten with impatience. When he thought that enough time had elapsed where he could make his escape, he made his excuses and left the club.

Lord Kenelm returned to his town house and immediately went upstairs to change into his driving attire. The valet noted his master's frowning brows and abstracted gaze. Long familiar with the viscount's moods, he maintained silence as he assisted him to shrug into a greatcoat and handed him a pair of kid driving gloves. Before many minutes had passed, Lord Kenelm and his valet climbed into the phaeton waiting at the door.

Simmons took firm hold of the seat railing and gritted his teeth, preparing himself for the viscount's mode of driving. Unaware of his valet's private dread, the viscount expertly flicked his whip at the tip

of his leader's ears and the team of four moved smoothly and swiftly
into the afternoon traffic. More than once Simmons squeezed shut
his eyes as the viscount guided the phaeton with hair-precision skill
through the streets crowded with dray wagons, curricles, coaches,
and pedestrians.

Simmons breathed a little easier when the outskirts of London
were reached, but it was a momentary respite. Lord Kenelm touched
the whip to the horses and the phaeton picked up speed until it
positively flew behind the thundering horses. Simmons snatched at
his hat when the wind threatened to tear it from his head. He
moaned unintelligibly.

"What was that you said, Simmons?" Lord Kenelm shouted, not
taking his eyes from the swiftly undulating road.

"N-nothing at all, my lord," gasped the white-faced valet. The
hedgerows whipped by on either side with sickening rapidity.
Simmons sent up a fervent prayer that his fingers would not slip from
the seat railing and that the viscount would not overturn into the
ditches.

The drive from London to Belchester was a distance of three
hours. Lord Kenelm covered it in slightly more than two. He leapt
down from the phaeton as soon as the grooms had run out to catch
the horses' heads. Simmons was still clumsily descending to the
ground as Lord Kenelm bounded up the steps of the family seat into
the hall.

The butler was patently astonished to see him and his usual
imperturbability was ruffled. "Lord Kenelm!"

The viscount stripped off his driving gloves. "My father. Where
is he?"

The butler regained his equilibrium and now felt alarm. "His
lordship is in the sitting room, my lord, but—"

The viscount brushed aside the butler's attempt to stay him. Gloves in hand, he strode across the hall to the sitting room and opened the door. "Sir!"

At the viscount's impetuous entrance, the Earl of Belchester and the two ladies who were with him looked up. One of the ladies squeaked and turned pale, and both fixed Lord Kenelm with a concentrated stare. At sight of his son, alive and well, the earl's eyes blazed. His expression smoothed to bland politeness as he turned his head to address his callers. "As you can see, the viscount is alive and whole. I hope that you may do me the favor of aiding me in scotching these entirely unfounded rumors of his untimely death."

"Well. Well!" The larger lady surged to her feet. She quivered with embarrassment and indignation. "Indeed, my lord. I shall certainly see that a bug is put into the ear of a particular personage who led us so far astray. I do apologize to your lordship for our unwarranted intrusion."

"Yes, indeed. Your lordship has been wonderfully patient. We shan't bother you further," said the other lady, also getting to her feet.

The earl bowed to the ladies and ushered them toward the door. "I can but thank you both for your well-meant concern," he said.

His son stepped back a pace to allow them to pass and bowed to the ladies. He was startled by the frosty, resentful stares that they gave him in return.

When the Earl of Belchester returned from showing his callers to the door, he shut the door to the sitting room with a snap. The earl's forbidding expression did not register overmuch with his firstborn son.

"I believe those two good ladies would have preferred that I had staggered in to expire my last at their very feet rather than to discover that I was alive," said Lord Kenelm with a laugh.

"The thought is not altogether an unpleasant one," said the earl, his voice cold.

Lord Kenelm's smile faded and at last he recognized the blaze of temper in his father's eyes. "Sir, I came as soon as I learned of that ludicrous rumor of my demise and Albion's supposed villainy. I came at once to relieve your mind."

"I was hardly prostrated, Justin," said the earl. He sat down on the sofa. "Quite the contrary. I am actually invigorated by this latest escapade of yours."

The viscount had flushed at his father's ironic tone, but now he took a hasty step toward him. "Sir, my disappearance was not what you obviously think it. Believe me, I would never willingly have put you through such anxiety."

The earl threw up his hand. "Pray spare me any explanation, Justin! I am wearied beyond death of speculation and explanation. I have sustained numerous visits from the curious; in the same breath that they expressed their condolences, they each put forth their own peculiar theories for your mysterious disappearance. Curiously enough, it occurred to none of them that you had come to a peaceful end. I found that to be particularly amusing."

"I am happy that you were able to find amusement in this ludicrous coil," said Lord Kenelm. It stung his pride that his father rejected any explanation from him even before it was given. As he matched his father's implacable gaze, his mouth set in stern lines. He would not now, or ever, explain the past fortnight to his father.

"We agree on the one point, then. Indeed, ludicrous is but the mildest term I would put to the result of your thoughtless actions." The Earl of Belchester examined his son's countenance for some sign of contrition, but the viscount's cold expression did not change. The earl took out his snuffbox and absently fingered the gleaming gold lid. "I must tell you, Justin, that my patience is at an end. I have thought that I have been generous with you. I have been willing to allow you time in which to readjust your habits to better suit your position as my heir. But I can no longer tolerate scandal of this sort in this family."

"Do you mean to disinherit me, then, in favor of my brother?" asked Lord Kenelm in a hard voice.

The earl sighed. "Pray do not rush me, Justin. Even as a boy you were so unnervingly impetuous," he complained. "William will return from his grand tour of Europe in a matter of weeks. If you hope to retain your position as my main heir, you will post the announcement of your engagement in the *Gazette* and set a wedding date before your brother sets foot on English soil."

Lord Kenelm gave a bark of unamused laughter. "I hope that you are not prejudiced against a lower sort of daughter-in-law, then. My reputation damns me. I cannot think of one respectable maiden whose family would agree to rush their daughter to the altar in a manner certain to arouse gossip."

"I have been told that when you choose to do so, you are able to exert a certain amount of charm. I advise you to make the effort, Justin," said the earl gently.

"Is that all, sir?" The viscount felt his teeth grate with the effort to maintain a respectful tone.

"Not quite, Justin." The earl looked up from contemplation of his snuffbox. "If you have not become affianced to a respectable girl in that time, I shall strike through your name in the family Bible. It will be as though your dear mother never penned it. Do you understand my meaning, Justin?"

The viscount turned white under his tan. He stared down at his father, understanding all too well. The loss of his substance was naturally of concern, but what the Earl of Belchester now threatened struck at his very soul. Stripped of his identity, he would become a man without inheritance or family or even a name to call his own. It was unthinkable. Without a word Lord Kenelm turned on his heel and wrenched open the sitting-room door. He strode out.

The Earl of Belchester heard the hard rap of his son's boots in the hall and his shout for his phaeton. Then the front door crashed shut. The earl sat unmoving, a curious expression in his eyes.

"My lord!" The butler had rushed into the sitting room upon a fleeting glance of the viscount's blazing yellow eyes and now paused at sight of the earl's haggard appearance. "My lord, is—is there anything that I may do for you?"

The Earl of Belchester pulled himself together, his customary controlled expression back in place, and shook his head. "Nothing at the moment. Thank you, Humphries."

Chapter 5

L ord Kenelm had no very clear idea of where he was going. He simply drove as fast as his team would run. His strong hands instinctively guided and controlled his horses. His eyes were unseeing of the few wagons and coaches that he passed. But their passengers did not soon forget the madman who passed them in a fury of thunder and billowing dust.

It was not until his team was nearly blown that Lord Kenelm came out of his black fury long enough to realize what he was doing to his horses. He cursed himself for his stupidity and slowed the team to a near walk. The breeze freshened and gradually Lord Kenelm began to detect the slightest hint of salt on the air. He glanced about him, his attention suddenly sharpened to his surroundings. He thought he vaguely recognized the locale, but he was still unsure of his exact location. Presently he came upon a small inn and he directed the phaeton into the yard. His stomach rumbled and he was reminded of the lateness of the hour. He had had kidney and eggs for breakfast but nothing since, and he had been driving the greater part of the day.

The inn appeared to be respectable and clean, and Lord Kenelm made a sudden decision to stay the night. He was expected nowhere since his household in London had been told that he planned to spend a few days at Belchester, and at Belchester it would be assumed that he had returned to London. He had well and truly disappeared without benefit of valet or baggage. The thought unaccountably cheered him, and he was able to reply to the innkeeper's welcome with every sign of affability. He made clear his desire for dinner and lodging for the night.

The innkeeper was well-pleased. It was not every day that the inn attracted the business of a true gentleman. He assured his lordship that all would be done to his satisfaction, and ushered the gentleman inside. Before he shut the inn door, he cast a knowledgeable look at the clouding sky. "Ah, but this season is a treacherous one. See, the wind has freshened a bit. I'll not be surprised to find we have frost in the morning. Some nights the wind blows so cold off the sea that a man's bones quake with ague. It makes for illness in man and beast alike."

He mistook the gentleman's startled glance. "But don't be worrying over your cattle, your lordship, for the stable is as snug as you please. Built proper of stone, it is, and with a fine layer of grasses in the stalls." The innkeeper continued to bend the gentleman's ear with a rattle of local trivia and comfort as he showed the way to the inn's best parlor. He left the gentleman alone after a last promise to make certain that his lordship's dinner would be all that he could wish for.

Lord Kenelm sat down to a supper of roasted duck, slivers of ham and roast, the remainder of an excellent cottage pie, and peas and new potatoes. After the waiter had removed the dishes and lighted the chamber fire, he sat at his ease in a chair with his feet to the grate and a glass of French brandy in his hand. On the small table beside his chair was the half-full bottle of wine that he had requested the waiter to leave with him. Lord Kenelm felt much more content with his lot than he had a few hours before. It was amazing the difference that a filling meal could make in one's perspective, he thought.

However, there was still the earl's ultimatum hanging over his head. The thought of it kindled a fresh gleam of anger in his eyes, but he was able to view it with more objective consideration than before. He had no choice but to bow to his father's wishes and marry as swiftly as possible, but Lord Kenelm hoped that he was not one to be bullied into fitting a pattern not of his making. The stuffy confines of marriage and its attendant obligations were not for him. He liked his freedom too well. There was now a stern set to the viscount's lean face. He would definitely marry, but the wife of his choosing would not be allowed to interfere with his pleasures. Nor, once he married, would his father have the same hold over him, for Lord Kenelm knew him too well to believe that the earl would cast him over when there was the obligation of wife and family to be met.

The viscount's smile was one of grim satisfaction. Indeed, the more he thought over the thorny issue, the more it appeared to be the key to his freedom. However, there still remained the problem of settling on a suitable bride and of persuading her family to agree to an uncommonly short betrothal. There would undoubtedly be objections raised by the family to the length of the engagement he intended to request, but Lord Kenelm hoped that he had wit enough to smooth down fears of any whisper of scandal. After all, he and the family need only say that there had been a private agreement of long standing. Not one gossip could say otherwise when the Earl of Belchester himself smiled on the betrothal. As for objections to himself personally, Lord Kenelm believed that his reputation could be overcome. His circumstances and his aspirations to the title were too well-known for any truly ambitious parent to refuse the hand of his daughter.

Lord Kenelm swirled the excellent brandy in his glass and the probable origin of the wine caused him to smile. Earlier he had smelled salt on the air and he had not missed the innkeeper's comfortable reference to the sea. Undoubtedly the French brandy had found its way to this quiet inn on a smuggler's packhorse. His thoughts made a natural leap to the Talbots and the hospitality they had shown him. He had spent some very pleasant hours at

Ravensclaw, and not the least of that pleasure had been due to Catherine's quiet wit and straightforward speech. He grinned suddenly, remembering a particularly entertaining conversation, and sipped his wine to pleasant thoughts.

It occurred to Lord Kenelm gradually that Miss Catherine Talbot was a surprisingly comfortable female. She put on few airs and her glance was open and honest. He knew her to be an unusually daring young woman, unafraid to take on new experiences, yet she had also given him the impression of being content within the confines of her quiet life in the country. Her intelligence was such that he felt certain she would understand and accept that another individual might choose an entirely different mode of life. Indeed, thought Lord Kenelm idly, Miss Talbot was herself just unconventional enough that she would in all probability not require the usual sort of social attention and courtesies from a husband that another lady might expect as her due.

Lord Kenelm straightened suddenly in his chair. He wondered why he had not thought of it before. Miss Talbot was obviously in temperament the perfect wife for him. Moreover, she was of good family and she was educated in the social skills necessary to uphold the position of his wife. She would also understand the advantages of a marriage of convenience. It was unlikely that she would kick up a dust at being ensconced in the country for the greater part of the year while he made several trips to London during the Season. As for her family's possible reluctance to an immediate announcement, he thought it could be dealt with easily enough. He had the advantage of knowing about the mortgage on the Talbot estate. The offer of a very generous settlement should quiet any objections, he thought complacently.

When Lord Kenelm conjured up Catherine's image in his mind's eye, he was pleased to recall that she was not uncomely. And though her figure might appear a trifle thin to some, he had had the advantage of having seen her in breeches. The viscount grinned lazily, for Cat's figure had been entirely satisfactory.

The viscount stood up, swaying a little. He had come to a momentous decision. He was going to offer for the hand of Miss Catherine Talbot. He made his way to the writing desk, which was set against one wall of the parlor, and sat down again abruptly in its chair. He took out paper and inkwell to pen a short note to his valet, requesting that Simmons join him at the inn with all the baggage necessary for a gentleman who planned an extended stay at a country house.

Catherine knew almost the instant that Lord Kenelm arrived. She was in the garden snipping blossoms from the rose bushes for the hall table when a phaeton and four swept up the drive toward the house.

Catherine shaded her eyes, curious. Two men occupied the high seat, but her gaze was instantly riveted by the driver. His beaver was set low on his brow against the wind and his greatcoat swathed his form, but in that fleeting instant she recognized him. "Bother, bother! I look a fright," she exclaimed. She was acutely aware that she was wearing her oldest dress and her short hair was rough and windblown.

With the basket of roses over one arm and her muslin skirt caught up in her hands, Catherine flew across the garden and over the lawn to the house. She left a trail of yellow roses to mark her path. She was gasping when she threw open the French doors to the study and entered with precipitate haste.

Her father's cousin, an amiable lady of indolent habits and indeterminate age, glanced up from the latest copy of *The Lady's Magazine*. "Dear Cat, how did you know that I was thinking of you? Do but look at these gorgeous gowns. Do you not think—"

Catherine thrust the basket of blooms at her. "I am sorry, Henry, but I've no time. These are for the hall table. Now I must go and change at once." On those words Catherine ran from the study and up the hall stairs.

"How extraordinary." Miss Henrietta Talbot blinked at the spot her young cousin had vacated with such undue haste. She glanced down at the basket in her hands and with decision said, "A vase and water is what is required, I see. Come along with me." She bustled away on her errand.

Catherine entered her bedroom calling urgently for her dresser. "Sadie! Sadie, I wish to change at once."

The dresser rushed in from her own adjoining room. "Why, Miss Catherine! Whatever can be the matter?" She relieved her impatient mistress of the task of undoing the row of tiny buttons down the back of the old muslin gown.

"Lord Kenelm has arrived. He must be with Father now. Oh, do please hurry, Sadie," Catherine said breathlessly. The last button gave way and the gown fell to her feet. She stepped out of its folds and turned to the washstand to splash tepid water on her face and arms.

The dresser sent her mistress a knowing glance as she went to the wardrobe. Miss Catherine had never paid the least heed to any of the local gentlemen who called so hopefully. But Sadie had noted that during the viscount's last visit, Miss Catherine had been unusually fussy about her appearance. The dresser thought she knew which way the wind blew, and it was not out to sea. And just as well, she sniffed. Her young mistress had no call to involve herself in that dark business. Sadie drew forth from the wardrobe a new gown that had been finished by the seamstress only days before. "It is near enough to nuncheon to wear the leaf-green day dress, Miss Catherine," she said.

"Oh, yes! It is perfect, Sadie," exclaimed Catherine, finished with her toilet. She ran her fingers through her tangled hair. "But do hurry, Sadie."

"Yes, miss."

Within a very short time Catherine stood dressed and freshly coiffed before the mirror. She stared anxiously at herself in the cheval glass. Her blond curls framed a face slender and fine-boned. The soft-green gown set off her large green eyes and clung softly to her rounded bosom and the sleek line of her hips. She made a face, wondering if she would ever have aught but a boyish build. She had the unhappy suspicion that Lord Kenelm probably preferred ladies of voluptuous proportions.

Unaware that he was the source of such dismal thoughts, Lord Kenelm made known his request to see Lord Talbot and was immediately ushered into that gentleman's study.

Lord Talbot came from around his mahogany desk to offer his hand to the viscount. "My dear Lord Kenelm! I had thought we were well rid of you. Come in, come in, and take your ease. Jeffrey, take his lordship's things so he can be comfortable. And bring us a bottle of the best cognac." The footman obediently took charge of the viscount's beaver and gloves and his greatcoat, then gently closed the door. Lord Kenelm accepted the chair in front of the hearth to which Lord Talbot directed him. "You will enjoy the cognac, my lord. It is really the finest year," said Lord Talbot, seating himself in a wingback chair opposite the viscount.

"It is certain to be the best out of France, in any event," said Lord Kenelm dryly.

His host laughed, acknowledging the truth of his hit with a bow. "So, tell me, to what do we owe the pleasure of your visit so soon after our little adventure?" Lord Talbot asked curiously. The footman returned with a bottle of wine and glasses on a silver tray which he set down on the occasional table at his master's elbow.

"I have come on a bit of business, actually."

Lord Talbot's mobile brows rose, but he waited until the footman had once more left them alone before he pursued the viscount's quiet statement. Lord Talbot poured the wine and handed his guest a glass. "I assume it has something to do with the stocking of your wine cellar, my lord," he said.

Lord Kenelm, who was beginning to feel an unaccountable nervousness, was startled by Lord Talbot's conclusion. "What? I assure you, nothing of the sort. Not but what a few bottles of claret would be—" He said hurriedly, "But that is quite off the mark. On the contrary, I have come on a purely personal matter. I believe you must have formed some notion of my character during our short acquaintance, sir, and I hope that your impression of me is favorable." Lord Kenelm took a deep breath, feeling as though he were about to step into an icy bath. "In short, I have called on you to request your permission to press my suit with your daughter, Miss Catherine Talbot."

Lord Talbot blinked, but otherwise his expression registered nothing more than friendly interest. "I pride myself on my ability to read a man's character, my lord. I can tell you that I believe you to be a good-enough man, perhaps a trifle headstrong and opinionated, but nevertheless a worthy acquaintance."

Lord Kenelm was completely taken aback. It had never entered his head that Lord Talbot would actually judge him. "Thank you, Lord Talbot," he said, though unsure whether he should be flattered or insulted.

Lord Talbot brushed aside the viscount's interjection. "In regard to my daughter, however, I must take pause. I have heard of your rakehell reputation, my lord. I do not consider it reassuring when we speak of my daughter's future happiness. I would not wish to see her neglected," he said.

Instantly Lord Kenelm saw what concerned Lord Talbot. "Believe me, sir, as my wife, Miss Talbot would have nothing of which to complain. My intentions are honorable. She would want for nothing; whatever she wished for would be instantly provided. My wife's social position will be eminently respected, and, of course, one day she would become the Countess of Belchester. I give you my oath that Miss Talbot would never have cause to regret accepting my offer."

"You are reassuring, my lord. I find that I have no other reservations," said Lord Talbot, smiling. "It is only for Catherine to give her consent to your suit."

"I beg pardon, Lord Talbot?" said Lord Kenelm, startled.

Lord Talbot's grin broadened. "I do not speak on behalf of my daughter without her leave, Lord Kenelm. Catherine, as I am certain you have noticed, is somewhat independent of my authority. The final decision regarding your offer must come from her."

"I understand," said the viscount slowly. He thought it was simply another example of Lord Talbot's too permissive style with his only daughter. It was the parents' duty to make such important decisions for their young daughters, who certainly were not experienced enough in the world to make the wisest choices. However, Lord Kenelm was willing to carry out the farce for the time being. But once Miss Talbot became his fiancée, it would be his duty to make clear that she was to rely on his better judgment for her welfare.

"Do you indeed? I wonder," murmured Lord Talbot. He met the viscount's sharpened stare with a benign smile. "I give you my permission to approach Catherine on this matter whenever it may best suit you, Lord Kenelm."

He nodded his satisfaction. "Thank you, Lord Talbot. I had planned on a short visit, so Miss Talbot and I could become better acquainted."

"An excellent idea, my lord," said Lord Talbot, rising from his chair. "I believe I heard the bell summoning us to nuncheon some time ago. Pray join us, Lord Kenelm. It will be just the family—myself and Catherine and my cousin, Miss Henrietta

Talbot. I am sure that you recall my cousin. She is a bit vague at times, but I know you won't mind that."

"Is your son not joining us also?" asked the viscount as he accompanied Lord Talbot from the study.

"Christopher is away for a few days on family matters. Perhaps he will return before your departure from Ravensclaw," said Lord Talbot easily.

Lord Kenelm thought he could guess what sort of family business had called away the scion of the house, but he did not pursue the matter, preferring to know as little about the Talbots' smuggling enterprise as possible.

Chapter 6

Catherine had deliberately taken her time in going to the dining room, as though this were only an ordinary nuncheon. But it was difficult to maintain a calm expression when her heart was oddly aflutter and her breath felt quite shallow.

She was profoundly let down when she entered the dining room only to discover it empty. She glanced at the table set for four and then turned to address the footman who was setting a covered dish on the sideboard. "Has not Lord Talbot heard the bell?"

"I wouldn't know, miss," said the footman, bowing before he left the room.

Catherine was far from satisfied, but she had no choice but to seat herself at the table. As she was placing her napkin in her lap, Henrietta came into the dining room. The older lady glanced about with a slight frown.

"I thought we had a visitor. Cat. And where is your father? He is missing as well."

"The footman informs me that he wouldn't know," Catherine said shortly.

Henrietta digested this and then took her own place. "But how odd. I have often wondered how the servants always know what we are about, and now one of them cannot tell us where Lord Talbot is! The cheeky fellow must be funning with you. You must not allow the servants to take such liberties, Catherine. Do, pray, call him back and ask him again."

Catherine was spared the necessity of replying to her cousin's suggestion by the entrance of her father and Lord Kenelm. Lord Talbot smiled at his daughter, his eyes bright. "My dear Catherine, look who we have as our guest today," he said.

Catherine nodded to the viscount, her smile cool. She extended a courteous hand to him. "My lord, how delightful it is to see you again, and so soon after your last visit with us."

The two gentlemen exchanged a swift glance which Catherine could not interpret.

The viscount took her hand and bowed to her. "I am happy that my reappearance is so warmly received, Miss Talbot." He turned then to address Henrietta with equal courtesy.

Catherine watched him with an expression of cool interest. There was no indication in her demeanor that her pulse was pounding in reaction to his presence. Why had he come? she wondered.

The nuncheon was agreeably spent with good conversation and an excellent repast. During the course of it, Catherine gradually lost her initial tenseness and she was able to speak quite naturally to the viscount. As nuncheon was ending, she said with elaborate carelessness, "I have not thought to ask you before, my lord. What brings you back to us so soon? Are you perhaps seeking to restock your cellar?" She laughed at her own small joke, and the viscount smiled. Again, Catherine thought there was a quick exchange of looks between the viscount and her father, and her curiosity was aroused. She began to suspect that the gentlemen were embroiled in some scheme or other.

But she was not to have her curiosity satisfied for several days, which she did not mind in the least, for these were days that were very pleasurably spent in the viscount's fascinating company. Catherine knew that the viscount must soon grow restless and that he would wish to return to his friends in London, but she put aside such thoughts. When Catherine looked up to meet the warmth in his smiling eyes, it was so deceptively simple to forget that his attentions were mere courtesies and that he was obviously practiced in the art of flirtation. Catherine allowed herself to exist in a happy daze, content in the moments granted her.

Toward the end of a particularly halcyon day, during which she and Lord Kenelm had seemed to meet and agree with every thought, Catherine was astonished when the viscount asked permission of Lord Talbot to be private with her in the drawing room.

"Of course. I do not mind in the least," Lord Talbot said. "Henrietta will keep me good company."

Henrietta nodded graciously as the viscount escorted a completely mystified Catherine from the dining room.

When they entered the drawing room, Catherine turned to face Lord Kenelm, who was closing the door. "This is all very mysterious, sir." She was smiling, but there was a questioning look in her magnificent eyes. A young woman was rarely taken off alone by a gentleman, nor were such meetings encouraged by her parents. But Lord Talbot was quite unlike other fathers, Catherine reflected.

"Please be seated, Miss Talbot. I feel somewhat foolish to be squared off against you, as it were," said the viscount with a smile.

Catherine laughed and complied by taking her seat on the sofa. "I did not realize that we were antagonists, my lord."

"I hope we may never be that, Miss Talbot," said the viscount. He cleared his throat and absently tugged at his cravat.

Catherine was astonished by these apparent signs of nervousness. She had assumed Lord Kenelm to be a man never at a loss whatever the situation in which he found himself.

Lord Kenelm felt suddenly, queerly, ill-at-ease. It had been a minor thing to broach the subject of offering for Miss Talbot to her father, who had been completely amenable, compared to the task of approaching the lady herself. He had been surprised by Lord Talbot's request that he make known his intentions personally to Catherine, but he had agreed to do the thing. This evening had seemed the perfect time to do so; yet now, with Miss Talbot's cool green gaze on him, he found it proving much more difficult than he had imagined.

"Dash it all," he muttered under his breath, and took the plunge. "Miss Talbot, as it happens, I have come to Ravensclaw to request your hand in marriage."

Catherine turned white. For an instant she thought she might faint. The viscount seated himself beside her and took her hand, which trembled ever so slightly in his gentle grasp. "Forgive me, my lady. I have started badly."

"Oh, no, truly. But it is such a... a bald statement," said Catherine faintly.

"I have made many pretty speeches for the ladies' ears, but I have never previously proposed. I find I am incredibly gauche at it," said Lord Kenelm with a faint grin.

Catherine gave a shaky laugh. "Certainly, you have startled me, my lord."

"I hope you are persuaded of my complete sincerity," the viscount said.

Catherine looked into his eyes, her own gaze somewhat bewildered. "But I do not understand, my lord. This has come about so suddenly." If she had hoped for a declaration of undying devotion, she was disappointed.

Lord Kenelm released her hand and stood up. He moved away from her a few paces before he turned. "I shall not pretend with you, Miss Talbot. I naturally assumed that one day I would marry, but I did not give it much thought. However, recently it has been borne in on me that it is time to marry. But not having a particular affection or partiality for any one lady, I did not know how to go about choosing someone with whom I would feel comfortable. It was quite a thorny question, I can tell you. Then it occurred to me that there was a lady whose company I enjoyed and whom I did indeed hold in high regard."

The viscount paused, his gaze on her face. Catherine felt compelled to breach what was to her an unbearable suspense. "And I am that lady, my lord?" she asked with an uncustomary shyness. Her cheeks were warm and she knew that she was blushing.

"Indeed, Miss Talbot. The circumstances of our original acquaintance were somewhat bizarre, but I do not think that otherwise I would have come so quickly to appreciate your intrepid spirit. Then later I had the opportunity to observe you here at Ravensclaw in your natural setting, and I felt the appeal of the grace and comfortable wit which are a part of your nature," said the viscount. "I have felt the same affinity this second visit, especially in the last two days. So I have chosen this evening to declare myself to you."

"You have made me out to be more friend than prospective wife, sir," Catherine said with a laugh. There was a happy flutter in her breast. She hardly dared to believe her good fortune.

The viscount was relieved. In the last several days he had come to learn that she was of a quick intelligence, and he appreciated the fact now. He sat down beside her again, once more completely confident. It was going far more smoothly than he had dared to hope. "You have pinpointed it exactly, Miss Talbot. I had hoped that you would understand. A marriage of convenience could hardly be amiable without our understanding each other."

"A marriage of convenience?" Catherine repeated stupidly. She had the oddest sensation of stepping into a gathering fog.

The viscount did not notice the obvious look of shock in her eyes as he spoke aloud his thoughts. "I will naturally want an heir, but otherwise I cannot foresee that we should make any unnatural demands upon each other. We shall each be free to live our own lives. I daresay that you will come to care for Belchester as much as you do your home here, and my father isn't a bad sort once one gets used to his ways. No doubt you will now and again want a holiday from the country. I would not object, of course, as I shall keep the town house in London open all year with the exception of the hunting season, when you may expect me to join you at Belchester." Lord Kenelm stopped, realizing suddenly that he was monopolizing the conversation while his chosen lady sat quiet. "I am getting ahead of myself when you have not yet accepted my offer. What do you say, Miss Talbot?"

"What?" There was an extremely distant expression in Catherine's eyes as she looked at him, and she appeared not to have heard his question.

"I am asking you for an answer to my proposal, Miss Talbot," said the viscount in some amusement. He wondered if all young ladies entered a sort of trance when receiving an offer from an eligible *parti*.

Catherine rose abruptly from the sofa, her hands pressed together in agitation. "Oh! I cannot possibly give you an answer now, my lord. I have such thoughts! Pray excuse me!"

Though surprised by Catherine's agitation, Lord Kenelm did not hinder her hasty exit. He laughed, somewhat flattered that he had been able to fluster the intrepid Miss Catherine Talbot. He took her incoherence as the natural shock any young lady might feel at her extreme good fortune in attaching Justin Avery, Viscount Kenelm. He felt that the interview had gone extremely well. Miss Talbot had proven herself quite intelligent in her swift grasp of the nature of his proposal and she had not set forth a single objection. The viscount had no doubts as to what Miss Talbot's eventual answer would be. He left the drawing room whistling, with the express purpose of finding his prospective father-in-law and proposing a toast.

Chapter 7

Catherine sped at once to her bedroom, where she paced about in a perfect rage. "How dare he! The arrogant, blind, self-centered monster," she exclaimed, almost choking on the words.

She flounced into the chair at her vanity table and stared furiously into the mirror. Her eyes blazed bright emerald-green fire and deep color burnished her cheeks. "A marriage of convenience indeed," she said furiously. She was freshly incensed whenever she recalled each word he had uttered. Viscount Kenelm intended to assure himself of an heir; then he meant to casually stroll away to London and leave her immured in the country year after year with a growing nursery of howling infants and his crotchety old father the earl for her sole company. Catherine had little difficulty in rejecting such a life for her, and she had every intention of informing Lord Kenelm so in no uncertain terms.

Catherine stared at her reflection. Then why had she not done so while in the drawing room? "Drat the man! Why must I be in love with such a vile, arrogant creature?" she asked herself despairingly. She had loved him from the moment she had first set eyes on his stern, white face as he lay unconscious in the gutter. Her brother, Christopher, had spoken more truly than he knew when he had called Viscount Kenelm one of her beloved stray dogs, she thought, as a feather of a smile crossed her lips. But this "stray dog," lying there helpless and hurt, had stolen her heart for good and all. She had treasured each moment she had been in his company on the yacht and later those few days at Ravensclaw before he had departed for London.

Catherine had never paid the least heed to the local young gentlemen who called in hopes of winning a smile from her. For that reason, she had never taken pains over her appearance, reflecting when she gave it any thought at all that her gentlemen friends could accept her as they found her, whether she was presiding over the tea tray or had just come in from the stables. But Catherine's indifference had disappeared while Lord Kenelm had been at Ravensclaw, to be replaced by an unusual attention to every detail of her dress and grooming. Sadie her dresser had felt compelled to drop a coy observation. Catherine had thrown her hairbrush at the woman, but halfheartedly, because she was honest enough to recognize the truth in her companion's words. The dresser had pursed her lips, content that enough had been said, and had since hummed tunelessly in a knowing and irritating manner.

Catherine could scarcely credit how thoroughly her close-held dreams had seemed to be coming true when the viscount had again appeared at Ravensclaw. Then Lord Kenelm had actually offered for her and Catherine had felt almost light-headed with dazed happiness. But upon his elaboration on the type of marriage he proposed, she had felt as though her heart was dashed to the ground and cruelly trampled. When Catherine recalled that Lord Kenelm had said he held her in high regard, she could not help a shudder. He does not care one jot for me, or anyone, if he could approach a woman with such a monstrous proposal, thought Catherine with a sigh. She did not care that marriages of convenience had long been accepted and to some were even preferable to a love match. It was her heart, bruised and bleeding, that mattered and her future that concerned her.

Catherine sighed again. She knew she would not turn down the viscount's offer. After all, she had not done so while she was with him in the drawing room and at the height of her indignation. The chance to become his bride beckoned too strongly, and perhaps, too, the hope that she could possibly win his love. The opportunity would not come again if she sent him away now. "But I shall not be the meek, unassuming wife you obviously wish for, my lord. You will not ignore my existence when it is convenient to do so. On the contrary, I intend to cut up your peace until you must notice me. And perhaps, just perhaps, one day you shall come to honor me as your true wife," Catherine said quietly. Doubts and fear assailed her, but she determinedly brushed them aside. There was a growing stubborn light in her eyes. She was not one to shy at fears, but she preferred to face them boldly. In this instance, the risk was great; there was much to lose but also much to win.

She sat quite still for several moments while she thought and carefully devised her plans. When she rose from her vanity table, automatically smoothing her hair, she was prepared to convey to her father her acceptance of Lord Kenelm's most obliging offer and the conditions that she meant to insist upon.

In due course Lord Talbot conveyed the happy news to the viscount, who received it as though he had expected no other. Lord Talbot wondered what the viscount's feelings would have been if Catherine had declined his suit as she had done others in the past. He rather thought that Lord Kenelm would have expressed disbelief.

The gentlemen sat down to discuss the settlement and the stipulations that Catherine had set forth along with her acceptance. Lord Kenelm was dismayed when he heard that Catherine had set her heart on a June wedding. He was on the point of rejecting the late date when it occurred to him that he needed only to be betrothed in the next few weeks to satisfy his father's ultimatum. He therefore acceded to Miss Talbot's wishes.

"I do not pretend to understand this whimsy of my daughter's, my lord. She has not expressed a desire for a London Season before, and in fact made it quite clear when the subject was raised a year ago that she had no interest in what she termed 'frippery, shallow gaiety,' "said Lord Talbot with a smile. He was curious to observe the viscount's reaction to what must seem to him an unwarranted bias against the social world of which he was a part. But the viscount merely laughed.

"I have sometimes expressed much the same sentiments, Lord Talbot. And I believe that I understand Miss Talbot's sudden turnabout now. Most young ladies have their first taste of polite society during their coming-out, and it would be strange indeed if Miss Talbot did not feel the lack of such an experience, especially before her elevation to the status of matron," Lord Kenelm said easily. He was actually pleased to hear of Catherine's disapproval of society. More and more she seemed the perfect bride for him, he thought, one who would not make too many demands nor rip up at him when he continued to pursue his pleasures. As a consequence, he felt especially magnanimous in granting her the small pleasure of indulging in a Season. In fact, he thought it would be a fine idea to enlist the aid of some of the hostesses he knew to show his affianced bride such a whirl of gaiety that she would be quite run off her feet, which would certainly cure her for all time of all yearning for the London scene. "I certainly have no objection to Miss Talbot's request that the wedding date be set at the end of the Season. However, I do wish to place the announcement of the engagement in the *London Gazette* next week," Lord Kenelm said.

Lord Talbot's brows flicked upward in surprise. "Surely that is a bit premature, my lord, since the wedding will not take place for several months?"

"On the contrary, it will serve to discourage those blades hanging out for a wife from importuning Miss Talbot during the Season. It will also elevate her a degree above the other debutantes in that she will be freer to choose her entertainments. I wish Miss Talbot to be able to participate fully in all that a Season may offer without the usual conventions which restrict a debutante," said the viscount. He was smiling but there was a look of determination in his eyes which Lord Talbot did not overlook.

Lord Talbot was not a stupid man. He prided himself on his ability to intuit the motives of his fellow man, but he could fathom no reason for the viscount's insistence to post the banns so many months ahead of time. He was bothered by it, yet there seemed no good reason to deny his wish. Instead, he made plain his skepticism of the viscount's explanation. "Catherine must be allowed the opportunity to waltz at Almack's, after all," he said dryly.

Lord Kenelm laughed, well aware that he had not hoodwinked his prospective father-in-law in any degree. But he had no intention of describing to Lord Talbot the satisfaction it would give him that the Earl of Belchester would learn of his eldest son's nuptials in a few days by opening the paper while at breakfast. He was certain it would come as a surprise, perhaps even an unpleasant shock, to the earl that his son had obliged him so promptly. Lord Kenelm still smarted from his last interview with his father, and he thought it would do the old gentleman little harm to feel perhaps a touch of anxiety over the hastiness of his son's choice. After all, Miss Catherine Talbot was an unknown, and the earl would undoubtedly wonder whether her antecedents were elevated enough to make her worthy of becoming the next Countess of Belchester. Though thoroughly angered by his father's ultimatum, Lord Kenelm nevertheless had given thought to the lady for whom he meant to offer; it had never entered his mind to engage himself to a lady of unsuitable background. But whether the Earl of Belchester understood his son well enough to realize that remained to be seen.

Lord Talbot indicated that Catherine would have no objection to the notice being inserted in the *Gazette,* and the discussion passed on to the settlement. Lord Kenelm was agreeably surprised when

Lord Talbot mentioned a dowry of four thousand pounds, a respectable-enough portion but entirely unexpected, since Lord Kenelm distinctly recalled that Lord Talbot had once claimed to be mortgaged to the hilt. Apparently, the old gentleman's illegal smuggling enterprise was beginning to show a profit at last, he thought. He filed a mental note to point out the inadvisability of smuggling to Lord Talbot once the knot had been tied; he had little desire to have a father-in-law who flirted so dangerously with imprisonment and scandal. As for his part, the viscount mentioned a princely settlement that, if Lord Talbot but knew it, was meant to put him under an obligation of honor to his future son-in-law. Lord Kenelm had every intention of using that obligation to influence Lord Talbot to retire from his midnight enterprises.

The gentlemen closed negotiations with the greatest of amiability. Lord Kenelm indicated that his man of business would shortly be in touch with Lord Talbot's solicitor to draw up the marriage agreement, setting out the terms agreed upon, and that he meant to take his leave early on the morrow so that he could put the thing into motion with as little loss of time as possible. Once more Lord Talbot was struck by the viscount's urgency, and he wondered whether Catherine well knew what she was about to accept the Lord Kenelm's suit so readily. Lord Talbot was not unaware of the startling eligibility that an offer from one of the peerage constituted to those whom society meant much— and there was one lady in the neighborhood in particular who had stigmatized Catherine as a headstrong baggage that it would give him great pleasure to inform of his Cat's triumph—but he hoped that he cared more for his only daughter's happiness than for his own worldly satisfaction in seeing her well-established.

After dinner that evening, when the gentlemen had finished their wine and joined the ladies in the drawing room, Lord Talbot decided to broach the subject closest to his heart. He wanted to judge for himself what Catherine's true feelings were about her engagement. She had been calm and collected during their meeting earlier in the day, but showed none of the pleased excitement that he thought would have been natural to a young lady newly affianced.

Catherine had seated herself on a settee close to the hearth where the light was a little better and enabled her to see the embroidery frame that she worked on. Beside her, Henrietta was engaged in matching her yarns for her. The evening had drawn on chillier with the setting sun, and the warmth of the cheerful fire was welcome to the occupants of the drawing room. Lord Kenelm stood at the mantel, the firelight throwing up strange shadows across the stern planes of his face. Lord Talbot sat in a wingback chair from where he could observe his daughter's and the viscount's faces. He hoped to be able to discern something of Catherine's state of mind during the course of the conversation.

"My dear Cat, this has been truly a most momentous day, do you not agree? We shall have such surprising news for Christopher when he returns," Lord Talbot said idly.

"Indeed, Papa. He will be quite bowled out," Catherine said. She did not pretend to misunderstand her father. She knew him well enough to suppose that he would somehow deliberately attempt to throw her into such disorder that she would not be able to hide her thoughts from him. While Lord Talbot was a tolerant parent, he was also a loving, protective father when it came to the question of his daughter's welfare. She could have wished that he had chosen another time to play off his tricks, since Lord Kenelm was in the same room. She could not help the warmth that rose to her face when she felt the viscount's gaze, and Henrietta's too-obvious approval did not aid her countenance, but she continued to ply her needle with admirable calm.

"Miss Talbot has done me a great honor, sir," said Lord Kenelm quietly. He smiled reassuringly at his betrothed. It was easily seen that Lord Talbot's heavy-handed observation had embarrassed her and he hoped to put her once more at her ease. There was a coolness in her glance toward him, but Lord Kenelm thought it the proper reserve of a well-bred young lady. He was not altogether displeased, either, by her apparent lack of romantic fancy. She may blush at her father's allusion, but she was not reduced to stammers and giggles. Of all things he most disliked were women who clung like vines about the necks of their unfortunate swains.

"I daresay," murmured Lord Talbot, and turned the subject. He was not entirely satisfied with his daughter's reaction. She had met his gaze readily enough and had certainly carried off her consternation with aplomb, but there was still a shadow of something in her eyes that bothered him. He resolved to speak privately to his daughter and to bring his concerns into the open.

For the remainder of the evening the conversation touched on every subject but the engagement. Lord Talbot was pleased by the easy discourse between his daughter Catherine and Lord Kenelm, and the way their glances met on a shared thought. He did not think the pair ill-matched, nor did he find anything to criticize in Lord Kenelm's manner toward Catherine. The viscount was pleasant and attentive; if he were bored by a country evening's conversation, it never showed through his courtesy or flickered in his eyes.

The clock struck eleven and Catherine began to put away her embroidery in its basket, declaring herself fatigued. She begged pardon of the gentlemen and, accompanied by Henrietta, left them to go upstairs. As Lord Talbot thought he might, Lord Kenelm also expressed himself ready to make it an early evening, since he meant to leave for London in the morning. After signaling to the butler that he could douse the candles, Lord Talbot accompanied his guest up the stairs. When the viscount had taken himself off to his room, Lord Talbot approached his daughter's apartment and asked if he might enter. Upon his daughter's leave, Lord Talbot opened the door.

Seated at her vanity, Catherine was arrayed in her gown and robe and having her hair brushed by her dresser. She dismissed the dresser, who softly closed the door, and stretched out her hand to her father. "I have been expecting you, Papa," said Catherine, smiling.

Lord Talbot took her hand between both his palms. "And well you might, my girl. I confess to some anxiety over this engagement of yours to the viscount." He felt her fingers tremble before she withdrew her hand.

"I know you do. But you need not," Catherine said. She still smiled but her eyes had clouded.

Lord Talbot seated himself on the bench at the end of her bed. "Do not try to gammon me, Cat. I can sense the trouble at the back of your mind. Is it your honest wish to marry him?"

The concern in his frowning eyes overwhelmed her and her pent feelings burst forth. "Oh, Papa!" Catherine cast herself at his knees, tears springing suddenly to her eyes. Lord Talbot smoothed her golden hair, murmuring soft endearments. When, finally, she raised her head, it was to give a watery gurgle of laughter. "I do beg your pardon, sir. I am not used to dissolving into a watering pot."

"Well I know it, my girl. You were always the spirited little thing, even when your lovely mother died when you were fifteen. I have often wondered if I was wrong to encourage that natural independence in you," Lord Talbot said.

She shook her head as she dried her face with the sleeve of her robe. "I fear we should have fought far more often if you had attempted it, sir. I am cursed with a streak of obstinacy, as you well know."

"Indeed," Lord Talbot said in an extremely dry tone. Catherine could not help laughing, and seeing that she was recovered, he returned to the subject at hand. "Now, Cat, I desire an answer of you."

"I wish to marry Lord Kenelm more than you know, Papa," she said.

He peered at her keenly, and when her steady gaze did not falter, he nodded. "I understand you, daughter. But I do not believe that Lord Kenelm returns your sentiments."

Catherine bowed her head. It was painful for her to speak of it, but she was compelled to be completely honest. "He offered me a marriage of convenience, Papa. He wants a wife who will give him an heir and thereafter allow him to live as he likes. In return he would not interfere with his wife's mode of life."

For a moment Lord Talbot was still, absorbing the mingled pain and humiliation that he heard in his daughter's voice. "Damn him!" uttered Lord Talbot explosively. It wrung his heart that his beloved daughter should be exposed to the heartbreak which had obviously accompanied Lord Kenelm's offer. If he had known Viscount Kenelm had meant to propose such an arrangement, he thought, he would have categorically refused him entry to the house. His Cat deserved far better.

"Yes, I thought so, too. I was enraged, and I meant to refuse him, but I could not." Catherine looked up at her father, the troubled look in her eyes. "Do you understand, Papa? I could not refuse him. I want the opportunity to win him to me. I do not know if I can do so, but I so want the chance to try."

"Oh, my dear Cat," Lord Talbot said helplessly. His common sense told him to persuade her to abandon the hope, but he was not immune to the mute appeal in her eyes. He said slowly, "I cannot in all fairness forbid you, Catherine. You are a woman grown. But I warn you, it is a huge risk you are taking. You may find yourself in a position of misery for the remainder of your life, tied to man who at worst has learned to despise you and at best will treat you with friendly indifference. It is not a fate that I would choose for you."

"I do not intend to choose it for myself either, Papa." Catherine took a deep breath because she knew that what she said next would more than likely appall her father. "If I cannot manage to fix Lord Kenelm's interest by the end of the Season, I mean to call off the engagement," she said.

Lord Talbot stared at her in liveliest dismay. "Jilt him, do you mean? My dear! Surely ..." He was struck by a thought. He grinned suddenly and there was a hint of wickedness in his glance. "You've a wicked, cool streak, Cat, that much reminds me of myself."

"Then you do not mind overmuch?" she asked.

Lord Talbot waved his hand airily. "You must decide what is for the best, Cat. There would be a scandal, certainly, but our family has weathered worse. I will support you in whatever scheme you may propose, dear daughter." He stood up then and drew her to her feet to plant a fond kiss on her brow.

Catherine clutched his lapel briefly. "Thank you, Papa," she whispered gratefully, and kissed his cheek.

He grunted, pleased, and detached himself to go to the door. With his hand on the knob, he turned. "Er, what exactly have you in mind, Cat? It occurs to me that I have just given you *carte blanche* and the thought naturally fills me with misgiving," he said.

Catherine laughed at him. "I intend to set London and Lord Kenelm on their collective ears," she said baldly.

Lord Talbot gazed at her for a long moment. "Already I am aquiver with horror, but I do not go back on my word. I will support you, heaven help me. It is a fortunate circumstance that we are done with this smuggling business, for I foresee that I shall be required to remain respectable so I can bring you off safely from certain destruction."

Catherine laughed again and waved him a good night as he left the bedroom.

The following morning Lord Kenelm and Catherine met on the stairs on the way to breakfast. Lord Talbot was already at table when his daughter came in on Lord Kenelm's arm and was seated by him. She murmured her thanks quietly and thereafter maintained a calm, unruffled appearance while Lord Kenelm and her father talked of London. It was decided that Lord Talbot would bring up his household to London as soon as a house could be found to be rented and a staff engaged.

The viscount turned to his betrothed and said with a smile, "You must naturally be excited by the prospect of visiting the metropolis, Miss Talbot."

"I am, my lord. I look forward in particular to plunging into society. I am certain it will be vastly entertaining," said Catherine, her eyes dancing a little. She spared a sympathetic glance for her father, who had suddenly choked on a biscuit. "I hope to visit the shops and a *modiste* first thing, Papa, for I know I am sadly out of fashion. Henry will be in raptures to be able to accompany and advise me, I know, because she is forever bringing to my attention the latest mode in *The Lady's Magazine*."

"Certainly, you may rely on Henrietta's taste, my dear," said Lord Talbot hoarsely, still strangled on the crumbs. He cleared his throat at last. "And you need not concern yourself overmuch with the cost. I daresay that I shall be able to spring for it."

Catherine thanked him and assured him that she would not run him into the ground. Lord Talbot snorted and hoped that he was savvy enough to discount any vows of economy from a young female, to which Catherine took laughing exception. Lord Kenelm listened to their badinage with amusement, but he thought he would do well to draw Lord Talbot apart later and put to him the suggestion that he be allowed to contribute to Miss Talbot's debut. She was, after all, his betrothed, and he had an undeniable interest in her turnout. Lord Talbot was too sensible a man to take affront if Lord Kenelm was to point out his own responsibility, and he rather thought that the old gentleman might feel a slight sense of relief. It could not be a comforting thought that the ill-gotten gains from the smuggling were to be flung away on a Season for his already-affianced daughter when it could be better applied to the mortgaged estate.

Lord Kenelm wondered again whether Mr. Talbot was away plying the smuggler's art and decided it would probably be indelicate to inquire. He hoped, however, that once he and Miss Talbot had embarked on their nuptials, he would be able to persuade his in-laws to give up the gentlemen's trade. It was a dashed sight too havey-cavey for the heir of an earldom to be associated with, he thought, even by marriage. It never occurred to him to wonder how strange it was that he, one of the chief makers of scandal broth, should be so nice in his tastes.

When the leisurely breakfast was finished, Lord Kenelm judged it time to make his farewells. He did manage to have a few private words with Lord Talbot and he was satisfied by the result. Catherine had gone up to refresh herself, and upon her return the viscount was appreciative of her enhanced appearance, liking the glow in her cheeks. He was not to know that Catherine's dresser had made a sly comment which had made her mistress blush. He merely thought that his betrothed did him credit, and instead of shaking her hand with circumspection as he had ought to in the presence of her father and the onlooking footman, Lord Kenelm raised her hand to his lips and kissed her fingertips. Swift color warmed Catherine's face and she could not help a tiny gasp. "Good-bye, dear Miss Talbot," said Lord Kenelm softly. He turned to the door and was gone in an instant more in his phaeton.

The footman closed the door, throwing a curious glance over his shoulder at his youthful mistress. Catherine had turned away from the door, her hands held against her hot cheeks. "Oh!"

Lord Talbot laughed and drew one of her hands down to place in the crook of his arm. "Come, dear daughter. We shall take a turn about the gallery while you collect yourself. He is a fine rake, I must say."

"Papa!" exclaimed Catherine, but when she met Lord Talbot's quizzical gaze, she could not help laughing. "Indeed, sir, I may have met my match!" They walked off companionably and left the footman agog with the fervent desire to take himself off to the servants' quarters to share the extraordinary scene he had witnessed with his peers.

Chapter 8

L ord Talbot was not one to waste time once a decision was made. That same morning, he sent off a letter to his solicitor informing him of the marriage settlement and of his own immediate removal to London.

Mr. Talbot was in the metropolis making final arrangements to settle the mortgage on Ravensclaw with the ill-gotten gains from smuggling. Lord Talbot wrote him the happy news of Catherine's engagement and of her desire for a Season. He requested that his son extend his stay in London for the purpose of finding a suitable residence for rent. The post a few days later brought Christopher's hastily scrawled reply, expressing his astonishment and satisfaction over his sister's engagement. He had had a liking for Lord Kenelm from the start and thought that he would make an admirable brother-in-law. He promised to send the address of an appropriate house as soon as he was able.

Meanwhile, the preparations for the departure from Ravensclaw had grown apace and the packing was done. Some of the household servants would accompany Lord Talbot to London while the remainder would keep Ravensclaw open for Christopher, who preferred the country over town at any time. Henrietta was in her element and she bustled about with astonishing vigor for a lady who customarily took her ease. She made innumerable lists and announced that such grave necessities as liniment and hartshorn must be procured for the perilous journey. She also dashed off several letters to old acquaintances, informing Catherine that one never knew when an old friend might not prove useful to one. "When I left London so many years ago, I never thought to see my dear school friends again. But I kept up a correspondence of sorts, just to stay up with the gossip, you know, and now, I can say that I am acquainted with a good many respectable hostesses. We shall not want for invitations, I promise you," she said with a complacent air.

Catherine thanked her for her efforts, but to her father she expressed astonishment at Henrietta's unwonted energy. "It is quite marvelous. I cannot quite get over it. Overnight Henry has turned into a whirlwind." She laughed.

"I am not at all surprised, however. The prospect of a Season invigorates her. Henrietta was a popular debutante in her time and she cared for nothing better than fun and frolics. She often danced all night and then would awaken at dawn for an early-morning breakfast al fresco," Lord Talbot said.

Catherine stared at him, suspecting that he was testing her gullibility. She had known Henrietta Talbot all of her life and she had never seen that lady other than indolent. Catherine could as easily envision a flying snake as she could believe Henrietta capable of engaging on a whirl of social activity. "I can scarcely credit it, sir. Henry is the most placid of creatures. But if what you say is true, why should she change so?" she asked.

"Many years ago, Henrietta suffered a disappointment in love. The gentleman was killed in a mad curricle race. He broke his neck and Henrietta's heart at one and the same time. She could not bear the parties and gaiety after that, and your mother invited her to visit with us at Ravensclaw. She simply stayed on and eventually Ravensclaw became her home," said Lord Talbot.

Catherine was much struck by the tragedy of Henrietta's history, and when next she had occasion to speak to her cousin, she treated Henrietta with such a wealth of solicitude that the lady fixed her with an uncharacteristically penetrating gaze. "I suppose Lord Talbot has gone and told you that very old story. You need not concern yourself, dear Cat. I have quite gotten over it these several years past. Indeed, I have difficulty in recalling the gentleman's name. I daresay we should not have suited anyway. He was mad for horses and I never could abide the great horrid creatures," she said. She held up a copy of *The Lady's Magazine*. "What do you think, Cat? Should we have this ravishing morning dress made up out of that lovely blue velvet which your father kept? Really, it is quite fortunate he was always going to France, for as a consequence we have a veritable treasure room of fabrics at our fingertips to choose from."

Catherine was a bit startled to have her sympathies so effectively dashed, and allowed herself to be drawn into a lively discussion of the latest patterns offered in *The Lady's Magazine*. She agreed to accompany Henrietta on a visit to the local seamstress later that same afternoon.

The nearby village boasted a very good seamstress, a quiet lady who was said to have escaped from France's guillotine years before, and who wrought magic for the ladies of the neighborhood. Though Catherine never gave much thought to her appearance, she had always dressed in style and elegance due to the good lady's trusted needle. Catherine entered with enthusiasm into plans to enlarge her present wardrobe with several morning dresses, two pelisses to wear over her gowns when the weather was particularly cold, and a number of evening gowns. On the return walk home the magnitude of the order given to the seamstress dawned on her and Catherine said in dismay, "Poor Madame shall never have the half of it done in time. Papa announced only yesterday that he is sending the staff up to London, along with Hobson to oversee the hiring of any other servants needed, so that they may open up the house which Christopher found for us. Henry, I really feel we shall do better to cancel the better part of the gowns we have ordered from Madame and have them made up later by a *modiste* in London."

"Indeed not! Madame is quite equal to any town seamstress and very likely better. And we have given her fabrics that we would never find in London, not while those wicked laws against trade exist. I've never seen the sense in depriving people of those things they need, but there! As for the gowns, Madame will notify us when they are completed and we shall have someone bring them up to London for us. I have already arranged it with Madame, Cat, so you need not concern yourself. I have it well in hand," said Henrietta.

Catherine was silenced. That was the crux of the matter, as she admitted to herself with mixed amusement and indignation. Henrietta did indeed have things well in hand, so much so that Catherine found herself at odds in her own home. Later she recounted the conversation to her father with a rueful expression. "And so, I find myself with very little to do, Papa. Henry has quite taken over management of the household and the preparations for the journey. Do you know, I shall actually be glad to attend a few London parties, for I am bored senseless here. I am naught but a dressmaker's dummy, standing still for fitting after fitting while pins are stuck in me and Henry and Madame wrangle over the proper width of a bit of ribbon."

Lord Talbot laughed, but he was fully aware that there was an underlying note of discontent in his daughter's voice. "Never mind, my dear. We shall be gone by the end of the week. I have received another billet from Christopher. He is quite impatient for us to arrive. I suspect he wishes to return to Ravensclaw as soon as he sees us settled. He asks what keeps us so long. But here, read it for yourself. Perhaps you would like to write him a reply? I feel quite unequal to the task of describing our activities here."

He was glad when Catherine readily took up his suggestion. She expressed the mischievous intention of describing in such exhaustive detail what was transpiring that her brother would regret ever having asked.

Lord Talbot judged that she would be happily occupied for the next couple of hours. Perhaps he ought to ask Catherine to take care of some of the minor estate paperwork until they left. She obviously needed some kind of employment. He had observed for days the restless twitch that Catherine gave to the drapes as she bent her frowning gaze on the inclement weather, and her obvious dissatisfaction that decisions governing the household had been swept out of her hands. Catherine had been responsible for the running of the household at Ravensclaw for nearly six years, since her fifteenth year, when her mother had died. It was difficult now to have that responsibility taken from her, thought Lord Talbot, and especially by Henrietta, since his cousin had never before shown any inclination for assuming such duties.

The departure from Ravensclaw was smiled on by a watery sun. Catherine, who had been kept busy organizing the estate records for the last few days, was in a fine humor. "At last, Henry! It is just like the beginning of an adventure," she said.

"Indeed it is. I am all aflutter to see London again," said Henrietta placidly, taking out her knitting. The ladies rode in a carriage followed by another containing their baggage and maids.

Lord Talbot elected to ride beside the carriages even though the skies remained overcast in the distance. "I never could abide rocking about inside a box," he said.

The journey itself proved uneventful. Henrietta soon began to nod over her handiwork. Before long her head was resting against the seat squabs and a gentle snore issued from her open mouth. Catherine whiled away the hours with reading or with watching the wet countryside slip past.

When the carriage rolled into the outskirts of London, Henrietta wakened with a snort and instinctively reached up to straighten her bonnet, which had become askew with the bow riding up under one ear. She marveled at how London had changed since her day and regaled Catherine with anecdotes. The streets were congested with carriages and wagons of all descriptions that rumbled on the cobbles while pedestrians and urchins darted swift and sure among the traffic. Hawkers lifted raucous cries as they peddled their goods.

As the ladies were carried farther into the city, the loud confusing hubbub began to give way to quieter areas. Finally, the carriage drew up at a handsome residence on Berkeley Street, and the ladies disembarked from their carriage. The front door was opened to the travelers by Hobson the butler, who greeted them with a rarely seen smile. Footmen scurried to unload the several trunks and Lord Talbot's horse was attended to. The bustle of arrival precluded much in the way of conversation, but the travelers agreed to sit down to tea in the drawing room in an hour.

The ladies were shown upstairs to their bedrooms so that they could freshen themselves after the tedious journey. Catherine was well-pleased with the tastefully furnished room she was given, and her maid approved of the spacious wardrobes. Catherine changed from her dusty pelisse to a long-sleeved green stuff dress and returned downstairs carrying a cashmere shawl to ward off drafts.

Her favorable impression of the house was reinforced when she entered the well-appointed drawing room with its gilt mirror above the mantel and the velvet draperies hanging at the tall windows. The tea urn was already in place and the sideboard was loaded with a collation of cold meats, breads, and jellies. Lord Talbot stood at the sideboard and spoke quietly to a tall gentleman whose back was turned to Catherine but whom she had no difficulty in recognizing. "Christopher!" she exclaimed.

The visitor turned, putting down a plate piled generously with ham. With a swift stride he went to her and took her outstretched hands. His grin was large and sincere. "Hello, Cat! I want to be the first to offer you my felicitations on your betrothal. You have decided upon a capital fellow, you know. You could have knocked me over with a feather when I read Papa's letter, but I have heard that sometimes the attraction between two persons strikes quicker than a breath."

Catherine thanked him in a restrained manner. She slid a glance toward her father, wondering if he would say anything concerning Viscount Kenelm's offer. But Lord Talbot, correctly interpreting the question in her eyes, gave a slight shake of his head. Catherine felt easier. Not for anything did she wish to burst her brother's bubble and tell him the truth. Christopher was something of a romantic, she thought; he would not understand how she could accept a marriage of convenience. She gave her brother a warm smile. "I am most happy to see you, Christopher. But how did you know so quickly that we had arrived?"

"I gave old Hobson instructions to send a man around to my hotel the moment he saw you. For days I have been all impatience to tell Papa every detail of my dealings here in London," said Mr. Talbot. His eyes gleamed with satisfaction and pride. "Cat, we have done it. Ravensclaw is at last ours again. I have just given Papa the old mortgage so that he may have the honor of burning it himself."

"That is truly wonderful, Christopher. I know how much it means to you to have Ravensclaw unencumbered." Catherine said warmly. She was well aware that her brother's blood and bones were a part of the land in a way that hers had never been.

"Your inheritance is also safe, Catherine." Lord Talbot smiled at his daughter's puzzled glance. "There was an ample sum left after the mortgage was paid, which I have set up in trust for you. It is but a small independence, Cat, but you shall be able to draw upon it at your own discretion. It is tied up for you and any children you may have. You will never have call to feel yourself dependent upon a husband or upon either Christopher or myself."

Catherine reached out to catch her father's hand and gave it a brief squeeze. "Thank you, Papa. This means a great deal to me," she said quietly. Even if she did not marry Lord Kenelm or anyone else, she need never feel that she was a burden to her family.

"I say that we cease this discussion and descend on the repast that awaits us so temptingly. And here is Henry! A moment later, ma'am, and you would have had nothing but the crumbs," said Mr. Talbot, greeting Henrietta Talbot with a fond hug.

"Such a dear boy," said Henrietta, affectionately patting his arm. She looked up at him with a vague confusion. "But are you staying with us, Christopher?"

"Not I! I've but come for tea and then I am off. I leave for Ravensclaw in the morning," said Mr. Talbot cheerfully as he escorted Henrietta to the sideboard and then retrieved his plate.

"So soon! I had hoped we would see a little more of you before you left London," Catherine said, dismayed.

"Devil a bit! I've been too long in this confounded noisy anthill as it is. No, I shall be happier at home. But if you mean to spend Easter here, I shall make the trip back to be with the family," said Mr. Talbot.

"Then that is when I shall expect to see you next," Catherine said, smiling up at him. Brother and sister held each other in true affection and rare understanding. Just as Catherine knew of the ties that bound Christopher to the land, he knew of her restlessness of spirit. They had rarely been apart during their youth, but each was now beginning to find separate places in the world. Catherine thought, however, that there must always remain a special bond between them.

"Allow me to propose a toast," said Lord Talbot. He waited until all had a glass of wine before he raised his own wineglass, which held only ratafia. He smiled around at his family. "May I toast the successful conclusion of a bold, though somewhat unrespectable enterprise?" A general laugh was raised by his sally. He held up his hand to forestall them. "And let us also drink to the equal success of our future undertakings, whatever they may be."

"Here, here!" exclaimed Mr. Talbot heartily. He was echoed by Henrietta's "Bravo, Thomas!"

Catherine met her father's smiling, tender eyes. She nodded acknowledgment to him. "Yes, to the future," she said quietly.

Chapter 9

Miss Catherine Talbot's debut into polite society was accomplished painlessly. Henrietta's letters to London had excited friendly interest in her correspondents and consequently bore fruit. Three days after the ladies had arrived in London, Henrietta insisted that she and Catherine must call at once on some of her old friends, which resulted in a respectable number of invitations for the month. Henrietta was well-satisfied. "We shall not long sit at home, dear Cat. Once we are known generally to be in residence, we shall be flooded with invitations." Her expression was beatific as she contemplated the array of cards before her on the table.

Catherine laughed at her. "Really, Henry, you look exactly like a kitten pleased to have found a pot of cream."

"And so I feel! Alberta and Augusta have come through handsomely, and as for Harriet . . . well!" Henrietta waved one of the elegant gilt-edged cards in triumph. "Unless I miss my guess, this rout of hers will be a veritable squeeze. You will be introduced to scores of the *ton*. Your success is virtually assured. Cat."

"Oh, I hope so. I have a strong wish to make a splash," said Catherine, only half in fun. Her thoughts were never far from Lord Kenelm and her hopes of arousing his interest in her.

Henrietta looked at her in some surprise. "Would you, my dear? How odd that I should not have guessed it. But I am such a peagoose that I frequently mistake what is under my nose. You will think me a funny one, but I had thought you completely content at Ravensclaw."

Catherine colored faintly. "My interest in polite society is very recent, Henry. I should like to see what my life may be like once I marry."

Henrietta regarded her with sudden, uncomfortable sharp comprehension. "Lord Kenelm does have the reputation of being a man-about-town. I have not read the gossip sheets these many years and not learned that. I do hope you will not be very disappointed, my dear. Fixing a gentleman's interest is simple, but keeping it is quite a different thing. The male sex is notoriously wayward in their affections. Respectably married or not, gentlemen often take mistresses."

Catherine was blushing in earnest. "Really, Henry! Such thoughts never entered my head."

"Of course not, dear Cat. So silly of me." Henrietta patted her young cousin's hand. "Now, what do you think of the aquamarine satin for Alberta's little gathering? It is to be a music evening, you know, and quite unexceptional. I hope I am not put off my dinner. I have always detested harps, but that is neither here nor there. We shall go. The aquamarine gown is just elegant enough to pass, I believe."

"I quite agree. Henry. It is the very gown to wear to a recital," said Catherine, trying not to laugh at Henrietta's aside. The conversation passed on to other things far removed from Lord Kenelm, but presently Catherine found her thoughts returning to what Henrietta had remarked about gentlemen and their mistresses. She wondered if the viscount had a mistress, and she decided that he was too attractive a man not to have one. The thought was a sobering one, for Catherine was certain that the unknown woman could not be other than beautiful. At Ravensclaw, when she had decided to accept Lord Kenelm's offer in hopes of teaching him to love her, it had not occurred to her that she could have a rival. But naturally, there would be any number of ladies, and less respectable females as well, with their caps set for the viscount. Catherine's only consolation was that she had the advantage of being already betrothed to Lord Kenelm.

On Friday evening Lord Talbot escorted the ladies to the recital. As they entered the receiving hall and gave their cloaks to an attentive footman, the sound of a harp being tuned struck their ears. Lord Talbot winced visibly at the discordant notes. "I would not attend this for anyone else but Cat, Henrietta," he muttered feelingly.

"I understand perfectly, dear Thomas. Believe me, I truly do," said Henrietta with a sigh. She stepped forward, her hands outstretched, to greet a very thin lady bearing down on them. "Alberta!"

"Henrietta Talbot! How good of you to come to my little gathering. I have missed you these several years," said Lady Alberta, taking Henrietta's hands in a bony clasp. The ladies exchanged measuring, calculating looks, each comparing the changes in the other's face and figure and mode of dress. Lady Alberta smiled with a shade of insincerity. "You look perfectly splendid, Henry, though I own my surprise that you are so much plumper than you used to be. But then we cannot all keep the same waist we had as girls, can we, dear Henry? I may still call you by the old foolish name, mayn't I?"

"Oh, do. We are such old dear friends, after all," said Henrietta cordially. She paused the fraction of a heartbeat to glance at her hostess's gown. "I see that you have still a penchant for wearing puce satin. How amusing that some follies are always with us!"

Lady Alberta, whose parchment complexion was too yellow to allow her to wear purple, showed her teeth. "Indeed, puce has always been quite my favorite color."

The ladies smiled at each other, satisfied that obligatory insults had been well-traded. Henrietta drew attention to her companions. "I believe you may remember my cousin, Lord Thomas Talbot. And this young lady is his daughter, Miss Talbot."

"Of course, I recall Lord Talbot! You are distinguished as ever, my lord," said Lady Alberta. Lord Talbot murmured a polite phrase, but she was already turning from him to fix Catherine with a sharp glance. "My dear Miss Talbot! When Henrietta wrote and informed me that her young cousin was embarking on her first Season, she neglected to impart a most important tidbit of information. You may imagine my blank astonishment to read the very next day in the *Gazette of* your betrothal to Lord Kenelm! So naughty of you, Henry, to keep such staggering news to yourself. Tell me, my dear, when did you chance to become so well acquainted with the viscount?"

Catherine was taken completely by surprise by her hostess's direct question. She boggled at the thought of announcing to the lady that Lord Kenelm had met her on a smugglers' boat and dressed as a boy.

Lord Talbot smoothly interposed. "It was a family understanding of long duration. I believe I hear that the harpist is about to begin. We should go find our seats, ladies, and not keep Lady Alberta from her obligations any longer." Catherine flashed him a grateful look as without further ado he escorted her and Henrietta into the recital.

"What a horrid creature she is! We were once bitter rivals for the gentlemen, you know. It is a wonder we are still on such good terms," Henrietta said blithely.

"Indeed, I have rarely been privileged to witness such an outpouring of friendship," said Lord Talbot dryly.

Catherine laughed and could only shake her head at Henrietta's inquiring glance.

The Talbots were unable to find unoccupied chairs except close to the front of the gathering. As they took their seats, the harpist attempted a particularly daring run. The vigorous notes rippled and surged like the crashing of the sea.

Lord Talbot, pressed as far back as his chair would permit, wore an extremely pained expression. "I hope you appreciate the enormity of my sacrifice this evening," he said loudly.

Catherine was also startled by the sheer volume of the harpist's energetic plucking. She was accustomed to the usual drawing-room fare, which was a light accompaniment to polite conversation. She leaned close to Henrietta's ear in order to make herself heard. "I had never realized that a recital could prove so—so invigorating," she said. Henrietta did not acknowledge her but sat with an increasingly glazed look in her eyes.

The harpist ended her part of the program with a crashing chord. For a moment the audience sat as though stunned before a smattering of applause grew to a polite level. Lady Alberta swept forward to announce that a particular treat was in store for her guests, and she proceeded to introduce the popular and very expensive Catalani. Catherine caught the sound of a stifled groan from Lord Talbot, and she choked back a laugh. Her father was not in the least musically inclined, and she could well imagine that he was not anticipating the singer's performance. But even as she laughed, she could sympathize with Lord Talbot. After the harpist's jarring rendition, surely not even the most well-thought-of singer could salvage the evening.

But Catherine and her father were pleasantly surprised. Catalani's performance was enthralling. The audience expressed its enthusiasm with prolonged applause. Catalani bowed and smilingly declined the entreaties for an encore. Lady Alberta was flushed with the success of her offering. She graciously accepted the compliments of her acquaintances as she directed her guests to the dining room for supper.

As Lord Talbot handed Catherine into a chair at the dining table, she said with a teasing glance, "Admit it, Papa. Despite yourself you have actually enjoyed the recital."

"Quite to my surprise, I must say. But Catalani possesses a pleasingly rich and powerful voice. I do not regret the half-hour we listened to her," said Lord Talbot.

The dinner was of indifferent quality, but it was doubtful that the Talbots noticed. Several persons claimed old acquaintance with Lord Talbot and Henrietta and engaged them in conversation. As for Catherine, she was the focus of much attention due to the betrothal notice in the *London Gazette*. "The entire world seems to have read the notice. I am almost a curiosity," said Catherine between exasperation and amusement.

"Lord Kenelm is a well-known personage. It is only natural that his betrothed should excite some interest," said Lord Talbot. His eyes twinkled at his daughter. "I shall not waste a dram of sympathy upon you, my dear. I know you too well to believe that the novelty of the experience does not appeal to you."

"At this moment I feel highly disrespectful toward you, Papa," said Catherine feelingly. Her parent laughed.

It was late before Lady Alberta's guests began to take leave of her. She took time to say a particularly warm word to Henrietta and her companions before she would allow them to part from her door.

Lord Talbot at last handed his ladies into the carriage. Catherine sank back against the seat squabs with a sigh of relief. She was surprising fatigued by the evening. "I shall be asleep the moment my head touches the pillow," she said, stifling a yawn.

"Was it not a wonderful evening?" exclaimed Henrietta, who was not in the least tired. She spoke of nothing but the recital the entire trip home to Berkeley Street. Lady Alberta's musical evening was an unqualified success from her point of view. As Henrietta had initially feared, the harp music had indeed served to put her off the dinner. But she confided to Catherine as they entered the house, "I discount the discomfort, dear Cat, for you have no inkling how gratifying it is to be remembered by personages one has not seen for simply ages. Furthermore, we have been extended so many gracious invitations. We shall not spend a single evening at home for weeks. Is it not wonderful?"

Catherine agreed to it but with another yawn. "Forgive me, Henry. I am unused to the lateness of the hour. Good night, Papa. I shall see you both in the morning at breakfast." She went upstairs to her room, leaving Henrietta staring after her in bewilderment.

"Well! Thomas, did you ever? She is hardly excited at all. I am well able to recall that during my first Season I could hardly sleep a wink for the anticipation and gaiety," said Henrietta. She was a little hurt that her young cousin did not enter into her enthusiasm.

"Henrietta, you were a debutante beyond compare. You could run circles around every other young lady and you had beaux trailing you wherever you went besides. It is different for Cat." Lord Talbot smiled at his perturbed cousin. "You must be patient with her, Henrietta. It is all so very new and perhaps a little frightening for her."

Henrietta was at once flattered and had her ruffled feathers smoothed. "Oh, I do see what you mean. And especially with such attention focused upon her! I had not thought, but of course . . . Well, it stands to reason that dear Cat was quite bowled out. She is completely unused to society, and now to be betrothed to a known rakehell such as Lord Kenelm must be ever so unnerving. I shall do just as you say, Thomas, and exercise patience. Dear Cat will come around." She swept upstairs, once more in high good humor.

Lord Talbot grimaced and requested Hobson to bring him a sandwich in the study.

The following morning there were several callers. Henrietta was triumphant and even Catherine was not unaffected by the flattering notice created by their appearance the evening before. But Catherine's composure was slightly shaken when Hobson announced the Earl of Belchester.

"Oh, dear me," murmured Henrietta, unwittingly echoing her young cousin's flutter of uncertainty. Catherine had vaguely wondered from time to time what to expect of her inevitable introduction to Lord Kenelm's father. Now that the moment had arrived, she felt totally unprepared.

The Earl of Belchester paused in the door to calmly survey the four ladies seated comfortably on settees before the fireplace. Two of the ladies he recognized, and he bowed in their direction, garnering effusive greetings in response. The third lady he judged as too elderly to be his prospective daughter-in-law, and he turned his gaze on the youngest lady present. He approved of what he saw, though he was somewhat surprised that his scapegrace son should choose a lady so demure in appearance. He smiled, his eyes remaining on Catherine's face as he approached her and raised her hand to his lips. "Miss Talbot, I have long been anticipating the day that I should pay homage to my son's chosen bride."

Catherine came to herself with a start. In the first fleeting seconds that the earl had stood in the doorway she had stared at him in bemusement. The earl was a gentleman distinguished in appearance, but there was a cast of sternness to his features that intimidated. She readily saw the resemblance between father and son, but she rather thought that Lord Kenelm's countenance was not as harsh and his eyes were warmer in expression. A little flushed, she gestured to a wingback chair near her. "My lord, pray won't you be seated? I do not know if you have met my cousin, Miss Henrietta Talbot."

Henrietta murmured a polite greeting as the earl took his seat. He said suavely, "Ah, Miss Talbot. I seem to recall that we did meet once, or perhaps twice, some years ago. You appear as youthful as ever, ma'am."

Henrietta was thrown into confusion. "Yes, of course. We must have, surely. You are very kind, sir." She recalled her duty to her other guests and addressed a disjointed statement to them, thereby attracting the ladies' attention to herself.

The earl was left free to speak to Catherine. His eyes held a distinct gleam of amusement. "I see that my visit to you comes as a total surprise. But reflect a moment and you will concede that I was to be expected. Once the notice came out in the *Gazette,* I was besieged by well-wishers, all of whom desired to be told my honest opinion of my future daughter-in-law. I had no alternative but to meet you as soon as possible."

Catherine laughed, at once put at her ease by his irony. She realized that the coldness of his countenance had been greatly lightened by the strong gleam of humor in his gold-flecked eyes, and she regained her confidence. "I can appreciate that your position was an awkward one, my lord," she said, still smiling.

The earl agreed to it and he inquired after Lord Talbot. Catherine replied that her father had disappeared early that morning to visit his old club. "He has always declared himself unequal to the task of entertaining so early in the day. And indeed, at Ravensclaw he was known at times to shut himself in the study with his man of business rather than endure a morning call from the squire's lady or Mrs. Furstbee, the parson's wife. It was really too bad of him, for both ladies are very well-intentioned," said Catherine.

"But perhaps they were also a trifle busy?" suggested the earl gently.

Catherine chuckled even as she nodded. "I fear so, my lord. My father does not lightly suffer interference in his affairs, well-intentioned or not."

"Lord Talbot and I share a common trait, then. Tell me, Miss Talbot, what was his lordship's reaction when he was approached for your hand by my son, who by all accounts is a scoundrel?" asked the earl.

Catherine was taken aback by the direction the conversation had suddenly taken. "My father liked Lord Kenelm well enough, despite what he knew of his lordship's reputation. As I did," said Catherine slowly. She wondered what the Earl of Belchester could possibly be leading up to.

"Ah, yes, Justin's famed charm with the ladies," said the earl softly. The coldness had returned to his eyes.

There was a faintly mocking inflection in his voice which made Catherine stiffen. "Lord Kenelm is indeed charming, my lord. But my eyes are well open. He is also insufferably arrogant and self-gratifying," said Catherine, her gaze steady and challenging.

The Earl of Belchester regarded her silently for a moment before he said quietly, "Pray forgive me. I have made a grave error in judgment. And I suspect that my son may well be in for something of a surprise."

Catherine did not immediately have a chance to digest his last cryptic remark as he rose to take his leave.

The ladies conversing with Henrietta also chose to end their visit. When they had gone, Henrietta turned at once to Catherine. "Such say-for-nothings! I thought they would never leave. My dear Cat, I am eaten with curiosity. Whatever did you find to talk about with the Earl of Belchester for so long? He appeared so forbidding, so cold, that I would have been in a positive quake to have been in your shoes."

"I am not certain, but I think we talked about my suitability as Lord Kenelm's bride," Catherine said.

"No! Well! What was he thinking of? The earl must be a very odd man indeed. I think it the rudest thing I ever heard," exclaimed Henrietta.

"On the contrary. I found him most pleasant and oddly likable for all his top-lofty ways. Though I will admit that he does have a curious bent of mind," said Catherine.

"I should think so," said Henrietta huffily. She could not forget the Earl of Belchester's visit all the afternoon, exclaiming over it more than once, and as soon as Lord Talbot returned to the house, she seized upon him. "Thomas! You shall never guess who came to call this morning. The Earl of Belchester! Yes, and let me tell you of the insulting slant of his conversation with poor Cat," she said, and proceeded to pour the story into his ears.

"I, too, had the privilege of meeting the Earl of Belchester today, while at the club," Lord Talbot said calmly.

"Whatever did you think of his lordship, Thomas?" demanded Henrietta.

"I found the earl to be a well-spoken, personable, and courteous gentleman," said Lord Talbot.

"Oh! That's just what Catherine said, and she is the one who was insulted. I shall never understand either of you, never," said Henrietta.

Chapter 10

Though he knew the Talbots' direction in Berkeley Street, Lord Kenelm did not immediately call on his betrothed. His race to Dover had been rescheduled and he left London in a cloud of dust. He won by several minutes and put a few noses temporarily out of joint, but those who had been unwise enough to bet against his skill and his team paid up handsomely.

After the celebration with his cronies in Dover, Lord Kenelm returned at a leisurely pace to London with the intention of beginning his duty toward Miss Catherine Talbot. He would do all that was proper on her behalf to launch her into society. He thought that his betrothed would likely be very glad to see him after being in London for a week, surely a strange and frightening place for a country miss, with no one for company but Lord Talbot and the unworldly cousin, Miss Henrietta Talbot. Lord Talbot would in all probability have no fashionable friends left after keeping himself immured at Ravensclaw for so many years; the entertainment at Berkeley Street would consist at best of a series of dinners for a few fudsy old bodies that for a young lady could only seem sadly flat. As Lord Kenelm thought about it, the more convinced he became that Miss Talbot must be feeling both out-of-water and bored. She would certainly be more than happy to receive him.

Lord Kenelm rather liked the thought of himself cast in the role of generous sponsor and he repaired to his town house in an expansive mood. After changing from his driving togs to attire more suitable for making an afternoon call, he sauntered over to Berkeley Street.

The butler Hobson admitted him readily enough, but when Lord Kenelm inquired after the Talbot ladies, he was regretfully told that the Miss Talbots were not at home.

Lord Kenelm was momentarily taken aback. It had not occurred to him that he would not find his betrothed quietly embroidering in the drawing room. "The ladies will be out shopping, I expect. When they return, pray tell them that I shall call again, perhaps this evening," he said.

Hobson bowed. "Very good, my lord."

Lord Kenelm returned to his town house, disgruntled. He had planned to take Miss Talbot driving in the park at the fashionable hour of five o'clock to give her a glimpse of the tonnish set that she would shortly be associating with. The outing would also have served to introduce her to acquaintances of his that they chanced to encounter and begin the easing of his betrothed into the public notice. He was well aware that the notice of his betrothal had come out in the *London Gazette* several days before and that it would be certain to excite curiosity. He had thought it would be easier for Miss Talbot to be exposed to such curiosity in a small dose at the first. Once she began to accept invitations to various fashionable gatherings, she would be unmercifully scrutinized and discussed.

Lord Kenelm quickly flipped through the gilt-edged invitations awaiting him. Lifting one for closer inspection, he frowned. He had forgotten this particular engagement. He would not be able to call on Miss Talbot that evening, after all. He was promised to attend a rout given by Harriet Wendover. Any other hostess and he might have begged off, thought Lord Kenelm, but Harriet was a deuced nuisance when it came to ensuring that her gatherings were well-attended. Harriet Wendover was an influential hostess and one of those he meant to solicit for favors on Miss Talbot's behalf. It wouldn't do to offend the Wendover at this juncture. He would have to attend the blasted rout.

While dressing for the evening's entertainment, it occurred to Lord Kenelm that he could call in Berkeley Street while on his way to the Wendover rout. He would be more than an hour late to the rout, but he was not one to allow such a consideration to weigh overmuch with him. Accordingly, he stopped at the Talbot residence once more, only to be informed that the ladies were not at home. Balked, he stared at the butler with the faintest gleam of yellow in his eyes. "Perhaps Lord Talbot might be in to company," he suggested.

"His lordship also had an engagement, my lord," said Hobson regretfully. He supposed that he could tell Lord Kenelm where the Talbots had gone; he had no orders to the contrary. But then again, Miss Talbot nor anyone else had left special instructions concerning Lord Kenelm. It was a pity Miss Talbot had already left, as Lord Kenelm looked that fine in his evening togs that the mere sight of him must gladden any lady's heart.

"Pray inform Miss Talbot that I shall call again later in a few days," said Lord Kenelm shortly. He left Berkeley Street with his generous mood destroyed. The Talbots did not see fit to be in when he called—very well! He was not one to kick his heels awaiting someone else's pleasure. Miss Talbot would wait in vain for his next visit. She would quickly learn that if she wished to see him, then she would make herself available whenever he sent word that he might be expected.

Lord Kenelm entered the portals of the Wendover residence. The hour was advanced and his hostess had long since abandoned her post at the door to mingle with her guests, so his arrival went virtually unnoticed. Those who did espy his tall form hesitated to approach him, put off by his frowning eyes.

"Damn, the viscount must be in a mood," said one gentleman. "Oh, I doubt anything is meant by that look of his. He'll only be looking for his betrothed, I expect. But he'll have the devil of a time finding the lady in this squeeze," replied another.

The viscount's frown deepened to puzzlement when a number of acquaintances began to congratulate him on his choice of bride and commented that they had found Miss Talbot to be charming. He wondered where they could have met his country miss. Surely not at a dinner in Berkeley Street! His bewilderment was put to rest when his hostess discovered him.

Harriet Wendover tapped his arm smartly with her fan. "Justin! You are late, as usual, but I shall not scold you. Why ever did you not tell me of your fiancée? Miss Talbot is utterly charming. But you are aware of that! Come, I shall take you to her immediately," she said.

"Miss Talbot is here?" asked Lord Kenelem sharply.

"But of course. Did the minx not tell you? How delicious! You have been given a taste of your own at last," Harriet said, casting a mischievous glance up at him. What she saw did not encourage her to tease him further and she changed tack as she led him through the crowd. "Once I had dear Henry's letter that she and her young cousin were coming to London, I immediately shot off an invitation. Henrietta Talbot and I went to school together, you know. Such a dear lady, but I *shall* hold it against her that she never breathed a word of her cousin's betrothal to you. A regular sly-boots and so I told her! I had to read the notice in the *Gazette* and naturally I was made doubly curious then about Henry's cousin. I must tell you, Miss Talbot has fulfilled all my expectations. She has already collected quite a court. But you may see for yourself."

The viscount's first sight of Miss Talbot that evening stunned him. She was surrounded by gallants young and old. Her father and the elder Miss Talbot were at that moment nowhere in sight, so that she was to all intents and purposes unchaperoned. Miss Talbot was laughing and she obviously had no difficulty in conversing with the press of gentlemen about her. Her eyes sparkled as brilliantly as the emeralds around her slender neck; her hair had been cut short in the latest fashion and it curled about her head like feathers of gold. She was attired in a sea-green satin and chenille-embroidered gown that was scooped daringly low across her bosom and left her creamy shoulders bare. Lord Kenelm stared at his betrothed. She was breathtakingly lovely. She was not at all the awkward, fade away moth that he had envisioned she would be in the midst of exalted company. The fleeting thought that Miss Talbot was not what he had assumed her to be crossed his mind. Unaccountably, he felt a surge of annoyance.

"My dear Miss Talbot, look whom I have found," said Harriet Wendover, drawing the viscount to her notice.

A leap of pleasure lighted Catherine's eyes. She held out her gloved hand to the viscount. "My lord! It *is* good to see you here this evening. I am sorry to have been out this afternoon when you called, but Henry had insisted on an outing to Mayfair." She smiled warmly at him.

Lord Kenelm bowed over her fingers, but instead of releasing her, he drew her forward and firmly placed her hand on his forearm. "I believe that I may claim this next dance for myself, gentlemen," he said. There was a glint of challenge in his gaze for the circle of interested spectators.

"Oh, none of us could deny that, my lord. Though I daresay we would if Miss Talbot was not already spoken for," said one admirer. The other gentlemen laughed and were loud in agreement as Viscount Kenelm made off with the prize.

"That was very bad of you, my lord," Catherine said with a laugh.

"Was it? I did not notice," Lord Kenelm said with indifference. He glanced down into her upraised face. "You are lovely tonight, Miss Talbot. But I am certain you must have been told that a great many times already."

"But not before by my betrothed," she said. Warmth rose in her face at her own daring. She had not before dared to flirt with the viscount and it was a heart-pounding moment. She did not know how he would receive it.

Lord Kenelm was startled. Surely his betrothed was not actually setting up a flirt with him, but one glance at her blushing countenance confirmed it. He smiled at her, his annoyance evaporating. "I did not expect to find you here, you know. But Harriet informed me that Miss Talbot was a former school friend."

"Yes, Henry seems to have several old friends in London. We have already accepted a score of invitations to various functions, and she is in glowing spirits. I did not realize until we came to London how isolated she must have felt at Ravensclaw," Catherine said.

"What of Lord Talbot and yourself? Have you enjoyed your stay in London thus far?" asked Lord Kenelm.

"Oh, Papa never allows much to show, but I think that he is also enjoying himself. As for myself, it is all very new but very exciting. I am more used to spending my evenings in a quiet fashion, as you know, but I am not displeased to have attended so many entertainments," said Catherine.

Once more Lord Kenelm was forced to revise his mental image of the Talbots. Obviously there had been no boring round of insipid dinner parties at the house on Berkeley Street this past week. Again, he felt a faint annoyance. "I see," he said.

Catherine threw a glance up at his face as the movement of the dance briefly parted them. She wondered a little at the cause of his frown, and hoped she had given the viscount some food for thought. She had spoken quite honestly, but she saw now how her artless words fit perfectly into her campaign to win Lord Kenelm's sincere devotion. If he should be made to feel just the slightest bit of jealousy over her modest popularity, so much the better.

When they came together again, Catherine said, "The earl called on me a few days ago."

"My father?" Lord Kenelm's expression went momentarily blank with astonishment. He suddenly smiled. "I should have expected something of the sort."

"That's precisely what he said to me," Catherine said. She saw that Lord Kenelm did not quite follow her. "His lordship indicated that I should have expected him to visit, since I was so unexpectedly thrust upon his notice. He had a number of curious visitors, you see."

At that, Lord Kenelm burst into genuine laughter. He could well imagine the impotent fury the earl must have felt to receive well wishes on the betrothal of his heir to a lady unknown to him. His eyes danced. "I hope his lordship did not phrase it quite so baldly."

"On the contrary, the earl was most courteous and he was at pains to put me at ease. I think that his lordship and I came to an understanding of sorts before his departure," said Catherine. She did not enlarge on the understanding that was come to; she would hardly advance herself in the viscount's eyes if she were to tell him that she had dissected his character to his father.

"I am impressed, my lady. In the short time you have been in London, you have not only gained entry to society, but you have passed my father's critical scrutiny. Believe me, I would have heard before now if his lordship disapproved of your character or person," said Lord Kenelm, grinning down at her. He was back in charity with his betrothed. She was already proving a credit to him. He felt supreme satisfaction that his father had been won over by the lady of his choice. Lord Kenelm was once more certain in his conviction that he had chosen well. Miss Catherine Talbot would provide him with the easy, convenient marriage that he desired.

After the dance came to an end, Lord Kenelm suggested that they repair to the refreshment table. "I myself am parched. The hothouse temperature that is kept at these functions is ridiculous. It is no wonder that there is always someone who swoons."

"I, too, am rather warm. I should like an ice," said Catherine, agreeing. "Indeed, we saw a poor lady faint dead away just before you arrived. Henry and I did not know who she was until one of our new acquaintances told us that it was the Lady Albion. She was quite beautiful and yet there was a sweetness of expression in her pale face which made one wish to count her among one's friends. Are you acquainted with Lady Albion, my lord?"

To give himself a moment's respite, Lord Kenelm pretended that his concentration was all for negotiating their path around a large boisterous group of gentlemen. He mentally cursed himself for his shortsightedness. Miss Talbot was bound to meet Lady Albion sooner or later, and there was always at least one good soul who would consider it their duty to drop a hint in her ear. "What? Oh, Lady Albion and I were once quite close friends. I became her confidante, in fact. But lately we have grown somewhat apart," he said with an indifference which he hoped was convincing. "Here are the ices at last. Allow me to serve you, my lady."

"Justin! By Jove, but it is wonderful to find a friendly face in this press."

The viscount turned. The gentlemen shook hands. "Hugh, whatever are you doing at a gathering of this sort? I thought you never went near them."

Hugh Crofton shrugged and made a face. "The devil fly away with it all! It was my mother's doing, of course. She has some maggot on the brain that I must become more in fashion if I am ever to marry. She kicked up such a fuss over tonight, I was forced to come for fear she would die of a stroke." He became aware that there was a rather good-looking young lady on the viscount's arm and that she was regarding him with an amused look in her extraordinary green eyes. "My pardon, ma'am. I should not have spoken so before you."

"Hugh, I should like you to meet my fiancée, Miss Catherine Talbot," said the viscount with a certain pride. He had seen the flash of appreciation in Hugh Crofton's eyes as his gaze had fallen on Miss Talbot. "My lady, this gentleman is an old crony of mine, the Honorable Hugh Crofton."

Catherine held out her hand. "I am most pleased to make your acquaintance, Mr. Crofton. I do not know very many of his lordship's friends as yet, but I hope to meet them all quite soon."

Crofton bowed deeply over her hand. "Miss Talbot, it is indeed an honor. I last saw Justin in Dover, after he had won his race, and never a word did he breathe of the beauty which had engaged his heart. I shall tax him unmercifully for it, believe me."

"His race?" asked Catherine, casting a swift glance up at the viscount's face.

"Oh, has he not yet told you? Justin was challenged that he could not make Dover in less time than the record. He shaved off several minutes, setting a new record and, incidentally, winning me a substantial bet on the outcome," said Hugh Crofton.

"I did not know you were a gamester, my lord," said Catherine.

Both gentlemen laughed. "I fear that my sins are finding me out, Hugh," said Lord Kenelm, smiling.

"There shan't be another word from me then, I promise you." Hugh Crofton bowed again to Catherine. "My lady, it has been a rare pleasure."

"And for me as well, Mr. Crofton. I hope to see you again quite soon," said Catherine. As Hugh Crofton left them, she heard him murmur to the viscount, "Your angel of mercy, my lord?" Lord Kenelm's brows drew sharply together. Taking note of his frown, Catherine thought it best not to inquire into Hugh Crofton's soft aside, but in her mind, she filed away the incident as well as the discovery that Lord Kenelm was a gentleman of chance.

Lord Kenelm had again been caught off guard. He had forgotten that ludicrous tale he had spun for Lord Albion's benefit. First Lady Albion and now this. It appeared that it was to be more of a task to steer his betrothed through the Season than he had first supposed. However much Lord Kenelm had persuaded himself that Miss Talbot understood and accepted the terms of their betrothal agreement, it did not suit him that she should discover all of his secrets in one evening.

"My lord, here is Henry come to find me," said Catherine, breaking into her escort's obvious abstraction.

"I did not know you were also attending the rout this evening, my lord. How unfortunate! If we had but known, we would have prevailed upon you as an escort," said Henrietta, giving her hand to Lord Kenelm in a friendly manner.

"Is not Lord Talbot with you, then?" asked Lord Kenelm, surprised.

"Oh, Thomas!" Henrietta shrugged her plump shoulders. "He soon discovered some gentlemen who are as interested in trade as he is himself. It is a subject dear to his heart, as you may know, my lord, and I have not been able to pry him loose this last half-hour."

"I can well believe it," said the viscount dryly. He wondered what the respectable gentlemen interested in trade would say if they knew that they conversed with an actual smuggler. The thought frankly amused him. He chanced to meet Catherine's mirthful glance and a chuckle escaped him. It was all that was needed to set Catherine off as well and the two laughed heartily while Henrietta looked on in bewilderment.

"Things always seem to pass right over my head, and now I have missed a splendid joke," she said regretfully.

"Indeed, you have, Henry, but never mind. What did you wish to say to me?" asked Catherine.

"When?" asked Henrietta, again bewildered. As Catherine was opening her mouth, she belatedly recalled her errand. "Oh, yes. How silly of me to forget! I have requested that our carriage be brought 'round, as the hour is so late. Catherine, I have twice warned your father that we shall leave without him, but you know what he is when he is deep in conversation. He hardly hears a word one says. Do come and persuade him to come away."

"You are such a funny one, Henry. Papa knows that you are too tenderhearted to actually carry out your threat. I think you ought to teach him a lesson. Do you not think so, my lord?" said Catherine, turning to the viscount for support of her gentle teasing of Henrietta.

"Quite," said Lord Kenelm promptly. Henrietta appeared completely flustered then and he took pity on her. "Come, Miss Talbot. I shall myself endeavor to propel Lord Talbot into the street if that is your wish."

"Oh, it is indeed," said Henrietta, gratefully accepting his escort. Lord Kenelm and Catherine again exchanged glances brimful of amusement, but this time they were able to contain themselves.

The company at the rout had thinned considerably in the last hour and it was not difficult for Lord Kenelm to guide the ladies toward the end of the room where Henrietta indicated she had last seen Lord Talbot. They were speaking to one another and did not at first notice the gentleman who stepped into their path. "Miss Talbot, it is a pleasure to encounter you again this evening," he said.

Catherine looked around to meet the gentleman's cold blue gaze. "Lord Haversaw. Forgive me, I did not immediately see you," she said with a cool smile. There was an air about the gentleman that bothered her. Lines of dissipation marred his handsome face and bracketed his thin mouth. His white hands were long and almost too slender. Yet she found herself fascinated by him, and that disturbed her. "You have met my cousin, Miss Talbot, and I assume that you must be acquainted with Lord Kenelm."

"We have met," said Lord Kenelm shortly. His eyes had flared brilliant yellow.

Lord Haversaw smiled faintly, derisively. "I am indeed acquainted with the viscount. We once shared a mutual friend or two. But that was long ago, was it not, my lord?" He bowed to the ladies and sauntered away.

"Well! His lordship was a bit rude, do you not think?" said Henrietta.

"Lord Haversaw is not necessarily known for his court manners," said Lord Kenelm in a hard tone. He looked down at Catherine. "It would be best if you do not associate with that particular gentleman, ma'am."

"Is his lordship so dangerous?" asked Catherine curiously.

The viscount hesitated a moment. "He is mostly a danger to your purse. Lord Haversaw is a hardened gamester with no mercy for the young and foolish. He is what is known as a bad man."

"I see," said Catherine slowly, turning the information over in her mind. She did not know how as yet, but she had the feeling that she could put the viscount's obvious dislike of Lord Haversaw to good use.

Nothing more was said of Lord Haversaw. Lord Talbot was duly located and skillfully detached from his newfound cronies by the viscount, who then saw the Talbots to their carriage. Catherine leaned out the window to thank him. "And you must come to dinner on Wednesday next, my lord. We shall be at home then, just the family and one or two others, and—"

"What! A quiet evening at the fireside, Miss Talbot? I am astounded," said Lord Kenelm with mock-seriousness. She was laughing at his teasing as the carriage rolled away from the curb. The viscount turned toward his own carriage, a half-smile on his face.

Chapter 11

When Lord Kenelm reached home, he was met by his butler with the intelligence that Master William had arrived in his absence and was at that moment reposing in the best guest bedroom. Lord Kenelm groaned. "Allow me to venture a guess, Griffin. My brother drove up with a carriage filled with trunks, requested a poultice and a hot brandy, and disappeared into the bedroom complaining of drafts."

The butler could not disguise his appreciation. "Exactly so, my lord. Master William did pause long enough, however, to mention that he would be making an extended visit with us."

Lord Kenelm's eyes kindled. "Did he! He has very much mistaken the matter, Griffin. Master William shall be leaving for a hotel in the morning directly after breakfast. I wish rooms reserved in his name at the crack of dawn. Pray see to it that his valet has all the aid necessary to pack up those scores of trunks in record time. I shouldn't care to send my brother off without his belongings. He would catch his death without his shawls."

"Yes, my lord," said Griffin, his composure severely tested.

Satisfied that he had dealt with the matter of his unwelcome guest as well as could be that night, Lord Kenelm went up to bed.

The following morning while the viscount was taking breakfast, a rather stout young gentleman, attired in a lavender silk dressing gown, pushed into the dining room without ceremony. "Justin! What the deuce does Griffin mean by—"

"Good morning, William. I trust you slept well," said Lord Kenelm cheerfully. "Pray join me for some of this excellent kidney pie."

His younger brother glared with loathing at the offering. "You know very well that red meat does not agree with my constitution. I take gruel in the morning, with a teaspoon of milk only and perhaps a dash of salt." He was suddenly reminded of his grievances. "Yes, and that's another thing! My bowl was cold when it was brought to my room. I do not know what has come over your household, Justin, but it is the outside of enough when a man's gruel is cold."

Lord Kenelm leaned back in his chair, an appreciative gleam in his eyes. He really must congratulate Griffin on such a masterful stroke, he thought. "I quite agree, William. It is insupportable. What is it you wish to see me about, though I believe I may guess."

Mr. Avery seemed to swell with indignation. "Indeed, you might! Griffin claims to have acted upon your orders, Justin, though I cannot conceive of it being true. Even someone so lost to morality as yourself would not order a gentleman's wardrobe turned out of the drawers onto the floor. Or all his waistcoats and cravats thrown into a trunk so small that the top must be jumped upon to close it. Every article is undoubtedly crushed beyond repair. My valet is hysterical; he threatens to leave my service immediately or to slit his throat on the spot. I do not know which alternative is the worst, for I simply cannot do without him. He has such a particular way with the pressing iron that... Justin, Griffin claims in that wooden manner of his that this wanton destruction was undertaken at your orders. I demand to know if that is true!"

Lord Kenelm had listened to his brother's recital with a gratifying appearance of interest. His lips had twitched once or twice, but he gave no other sign of emotion. "I trust the accommodations at the hotel will be to your satisfaction, William," he said calmly.

Mr. Avery's eyes started from his head. His face was suffused with a choleric red. "You do not deny it! You do not even pretend! I am astonished, Justin; nay, I am aghast that you could be so lost to sensibility as to toss your own flesh and blood penniless into the streets. As the younger son I have endured much at your hands, but this outrage—"

The viscount jerked forward in his chair. His eyes were a brilliant yellow. "On the contrary, William. I have borne much from you. You prattle of the disadvantages of being the younger son, when your independence is such as would make most men bilious with envy. You descend on family and acquaintances alike like a damned locust, only to complain of inhospitality. I do not soon forget the six months that you made free with my household and home, William. I allowed you to stay so long only to satisfy my own curiosity in discovering the bounds of your selfish penuriousness. You are a leech and a penny-pinching hypochondriac, William. It is wonderful indeed that I should receive you at all."

The silence was unfriendly. Mr. Avery eyed his brother's hard expression for several moments. "On occasion you sound uncommonly like the old gentleman," he said sulkily.

Lord Kenelm laughed. "I shall accept that as a compliment." He leaned back in his chair, his humor somewhat restored. "Come, William. We are brothers, after all. Tell me what has brought you to London. I was not even aware that you had returned from the Continent."

"It became a tedious journey. I had letters of introduction, of course, but I discovered that ordinary Christian hospitality was in short supply and—" He caught the viscount's derisive grin and said hastily, "But that is neither here nor there. Imagine my astonishment when I arrived at Belchester and was told of your betrothal. I assure you, Justin, you could have knocked me down with a feather. Father approves of your betrothed, by the by. It seems he made a special trip to London specifically to meet Miss Talbot. I must congratulate you on accrediting yourself so well. I had never imagined that one of your tastes would settle on a respectable lady."

"Your approval must be the capstone of my achievement," said the viscount. His sarcasm passed straight over his brother's head.

"Yes, well, I was consumed with curiosity and so I came straight on here. I could not imagine the sort of young woman who would accept the suit from a renowned rakehell. But I suppose you shall not tell me anything regarding the lady," said Mr. Avery with a sniff.

"You suppose correctly, William. I shall allow you to judge for yourself. Miss Talbot is already well-received in society so you are very likely to meet her without my assistance. When you do, for my sake, pray do not go on about the indifference of your health and that you have inherited your various ailments from assorted ancestors. Miss Talbot might gather that we are a sickly family," Lord Kenelm said with a touch of humor.

Mr. Avery was affronted. "What do you take me for, Justin? I do have some regard for a lady's sensibilities. Despite what you think, I do not tout off my ill health. Besides, I shall be too interested in hearing what Miss Talbot has to say to—" He suddenly pulled his voluminous dressing gown closer about him as he glanced about suspiciously. "I feel a distinct draft, Justin. Are you certain there is not a window open? Justin, you really must become firmer with your staff." With that, he hurried from the dining room to escape its dangers.

Lord Kenelm sighed. He hoped that William would not take his usual time about his dress. The departure of his brother could not come too soon.

That same afternoon Catherine sat at an easel, her slender figure illuminated by the sunshine streaming from the sitting-room window as she painted. She was surprised when she received word that Lord Kenelm had called. She felt a flutter of excitement in her breast. She had not expected to see him again until Wednesday evening over dinner. After a moment's hesitation, in which she glanced toward the mirror to reassure herself of her appearance, she asked that Lord Kenelm be shown in.

She was setting aside her watercolors when Lord Kenelm entered the sitting room. The sun about her caught the glinting highlights in her unusual golden hair and bathed the cream color of her gown with soft shadings. The viscount was appreciative of the curves thus revealed, but he gave no indication of his thoughts as he approached her. "I see that I interrupt you at work, my lady," he said, taking the hand which she gracefully extended to him.

"Not at all, my lord. I am quite finished for today," said Catherine. She preceded him to the settee and gestured for him to join her.

He sat down beside her and gave a nod toward the easel, upon which was a simplistic and pleasing water-color of a vase of cream and yellow roses sitting before a mirror. "I am impressed, Miss Talbot. I did not know before that you were so accomplished."

Catherine laughed and shook her head. "I am the veriest dabbler, as you can well see, my lord. I was but humoring a whim to do something quiet this afternoon, but I was too restless to follow Henry's example and indulge myself in a nap."

"Then I shall confidently voice my reason for calling upon you, Miss Talbot. I have without my phaeton and I have come to request your company in a drive in the park," he said.

Catherine had not before taken particular note of his lordship's dress, except fleetingly to appreciate that he appeared very masculine. But now she observed his fawn coat, skintight buckskins and top boots, and the kid leather driving gloves he carried. His invitation greatly appealed to her and, her eyes alight, she said, "Oh, I shall be delighted, my lord. Give me but a moment to collect my bonnet." Catherine rose from the settee and Lord Kenelm escorted her from the sitting room into the hall. She smiled at him again before she quickly ascended the stairs.

Lord Kenelm resigned himself to a wait. His vast experience had taught him that the ladies invariably underestimate the time it took to change. He was pleasantly surprised, therefore, when but a few moments later Catherine came tripping downstairs. Her wide straw bonnet was well settled on her head, forming a delightful frame for her face, and she had put on a grass-green pelisse. She was in the process of pulling on her gloves as she joined him. "I hope I have not been too long, my lord. I know that it is not at all the thing to keep one's horses standing about," she said with a smile.

"On the contrary, Miss Talbot, you have been wonderfully prompt. My cattle will not have suffered one whit," said Lord Kenelm. He took her elbow and escorted her out to the carriage standing at the curb. A young tiger held the horses' heads while Miss Talbot and Lord Kenelm settled themselves on the phaeton's high seat; then, at a quiet word from the viscount, he released the horses and sprang up behind the carriage as Lord Kenelm flicked his whip.

The team moved swiftly into the traffic and for several moments Catherine watched the viscount's excellent handling of reins and whip as he guided the team swiftly to the park. "I had guessed from Mr. Crofton's mention of your race to Dover that you were a whip, my lord. But it is still quite a treat to see such skill in action," she said.

Lord Kenelm threw a surprised glance at her. It pleased him that she should compliment him on an accomplishment in which he took pride. "Your approval is gratifying, ma'am. I assume that you also drive?"

"You would find me the merest whipster, my lord. I do not pretend to drive to an inch as I have heard some of the ladies are able to do," Catherine said, laughing.

"I shall be the judge of that, Miss Talbot," he said and with a challenging grin, offered the reins to her.

After a moment's hesitation, Catherine accepted the ribbons and threw him a saucy look. "I have warned you, Lord Kenelm," she said.

He merely laughed and settled back against the seat squab, yet alert to any difficulty that she might encounter with the restive team.

Catherine did not speak again for several moments, but concentrated upon acquitting herself well. She guided the phaeton at a good clip through the other carriages and riders in the park. When at last she drew up the team and turned to hand the reins to him, she was becomingly flushed and laughing. "That was great fun! I must thank you for the treat, my lord."

Thinking that he had rarely seen such winsome sparkle in a lady's eyes, the viscount smiled. He discovered that he enjoyed having given her such a small pleasure. He found her hand and raised her fingers to his lips. "It is I who must thank you, ma'am. Rare has it been my good fortune to be in the company of such a pleasant companion," he said quietly, the expression in his eyes warm.

Catherine lowered her gaze, startled and thrown off balance by his sudden gallantry. Her heart pounded a little harder. She hardly knew what to say, but in the end, she was spared the necessity of a reply. The viscount released her hand and addressed an indifferent topic of conversation, thus enabling her to regain her equilibrium. Soon she was quite comfortable with him again.

The viscount had resumed driving and he now noticed two riders who trotted their mounts along the green hedgerows. The gentleman waved his whip in an expansive gesture that the viscount recognized, before putting spur to his mount and giving chase to his companion, who had set her mare into a gallop. "There is Hugh Crofton, but I do not know the lady with him," Lord Kenelm said.

Catherine glanced at the couple. The young lady rode superbly, her slender body completely in tune with her horse. A swift glance of the lady's face before she had swept past the phaeton left an impression of familiarity with Catherine. "Nor I, though for some reason I think that I should. I have probably met her briefly, but if it had been here in the park, I would surely have remembered her name. How I envy such skill!" The race was in full graceful flight, the two horses' thundering hooves churning great clods of turf into the air.

"Hugh lives for his horses. I am happy to see that he has at last discovered a lady who can give him a decent race. I shall no doubt hear much of this winged angel at the club," said Lord Kenelm with a laugh.

Catherine glanced at the viscount's profile, suddenly reminded of something that had once been said. "I recall that you, too, have an angel, my lord," she said.

Lord Kenelm was startled. "What?" He threw a quick glance at her face, but her demure expression gave nothing away. He wondered rather wildly what it was that his betrothed could possibly have heard. To his knowledge, none of his former mistresses lived up to that particular label. He was somewhat uncomfortable to have his betrothed bring up his past to him, for he felt certain that was what she referred to. It was inevitable that Miss Talbot should show some curiosity, he thought resignedly. There was not a lady of his acquaintance who would not, given the same position.

"Mr. Crofton mentioned an angel of mercy, in fact," said Catherine matter-of-factly.

The viscount stared, then he laughed. "Forgive me, Miss Talbot, but you have touched on an incident that I had quite forgotten. My angel of mercy was yourself, in fact," he said with deliberate intent to shock her.

It was Catherine's turn to appear startled. "My lord?"

Lord Kenelm grinned at her with a wicked light in his eyes. "Why, I had to explain my unexpected disappearance in some way, especially as it kept me from my appointed race to Dover. For the gentlemen's benefit I concocted a ludicrous tale of awakening to find an angelic lady hovering over me who insisted that I not move until fully recovered. Naturally, being who I am, I succumbed to the pretty distress in her eyes and all thought of the race flew out of my mind." That was close enough to the truth without bringing in any mention of Lord Albion or his lovely featherbrained wife, thought Lord Kenelm with satisfaction. For some unexplained reason, he still wished to shield Miss Talbot from the fact that it had not been so long ago that he'd had a mistress. He did not pause to examine this strange impulse of his, other than to briefly acknowledge it. It was only natural that Miss Talbot knew of his reputation, but it was quite a different thing for her to actually know who one of his mistresses was.

Catherine chuckled. "I did not know you before for a teller of Banbury tales, my lord. Though I suppose in a way it is quite true. If not for me, you might never have met such a desperate set of personages as we must have appeared."

"Then I am certainly in your debt, Miss Talbot. Truth to tell, I never enjoyed myself more," said Lord Kenelm, grinning. He added hastily, "That is not to say that I would wish to indulge in that sort of occupation every day of the week."

His betrothed gave a peal of merry laughter. "No, indeed, my lord," she said. Her green eyes glinted at him through her lashes.

The viscount was well aware that she was mocking him for his lack of adventure. "Do you know, I find myself with the oddest wish to thrash you roundly for impertinence," he said slowly. She but shook her head and laughed again. The rest of the drive was accomplished in great companionability.

Catherine returned from her drive with the viscount in glowing spirits. It had been a wonderful time, reminiscent of the halcyon hours she had spent in his company at Ravensclaw before he had made known his offer for her hand. As she removed her bonnet, she caught sight of herself in the hall mirror. Her cheeks were pink from the wind and the pleasure of the viscount's company, her eyes sparkled, and her mouth was curved in a faint smile. Catherine studied her reflection thoughtfully. She had never really noticed before how much color enhanced her fair skin and golden hair. It was a pity that one could not deliberately create such an effect, she thought. Then she recalled the ladies of the theater, who appeared so attractive and sophisticated on the stage. Certainly, they owed much of their beauty to the clever use of cosmetics.

Catherine's heart began to pound at a daring thought. She knew it was considered fast to use cosmetics, and few ladies in society made regular use of such artifice. But she was no ordinary debutante, after all. She was creating a reputation and already she was becoming known as the daring Lady Cat. What mattered one more step to ruffle the staid? It was Lord Kenelm whose interest she wanted to capture. "I shall do it," said Catherine aloud.

"My lady? Did you wish something?" asked a footman, who had observed her quiet reverie before the mirror.

"Yes. Pray send word to my maid that I wish her to accompany me on an excursion. And ask that the carriage be brought around. If anyone asks for me, you may tell them that I have gone shopping," said Catherine. She replaced her bonnet and tied the ribbons into a bow under her ear, and when Sadie appeared, she immediately left the house with the maid in tow.

At dinner on Wednesday evening Lord Kenelm noted that Miss Talbot had taken to darkening her fair lashes. He suspected also the becoming soft color in her cheeks and lips. It was a shocking innovation for a lady of quality. Cosmetics were used by common actresses and the *demimonde*. Lord Kenelm knew that very few ladies dared to defy the unspoken rule, except perhaps those who also defied the conventions by conducting discreet affairs of the heart. He had personally been involved with one or two such ladies and he had admired the enhancing power of the rouge pot and darkening brush. But he discovered that it was quite a different thing to see his betrothed so painted. He frowned, toying with his wineglass.

"Then we shall retire to the drawing room, gentlemen, and leave you to your wine." Catherine's voice penetrated Lord Kenelm's thoughts, and he looked up to find that the ladies were about to withdraw from the dining room as was customary after dinner. He rose just as Catherine was passing. She glanced at him, smiling, and he was struck by the enhanced allure that the light touch of cosmetics had given her. He was torn by conflicting emotions of appreciation and disapproval.

As for Catherine, she was well-satisfied with the impression she had made. She had wondered if her fiancé would even notice the artful addition to her appearance, but she had forgotten his reputation. As a connoisseur of women, he would not miss even the slightest change. She could see that he was perturbed, but there had also been a reluctant admiration in his eyes whenever he looked at her. With a slight catch of breath, she wondered if he would dare to question her on it.

Henrietta closed the drawing-room door with decided energy. "Catherine, I wish to know what game you are at. I was never more shocked in my life as when you came down to dinner tonight."

"Why, was my chemise showing?" Catherine asked, being deliberately obtuse. She went to the pianoforte and pressed a few melodious notes.

"You know very well that it was not! It is your face. I did not dare to glance at your father. What he must think to have his daughter appear before company brazenly painted, I do not know," Henrietta said.

"Papa is far too wise to allow any hint of his thoughts appear in his expression, Henry. Besides, I do not believe that he will protest overmuch. I have been very discreet, I think," said Catherine.

"You do appear lovely," said Henrietta with reluctance.

Catherine laughed and impulsively hugged her. "Dearest Henry, I am sorry you are upset, but I might as well tell you now that I intend to continue adding the merest hint of color to my face. I know that it is terribly fast and doubtless there shall be horrified whispers, but it is Lord Kenelm's reaction which interests me and I believe that he rather approved."

Henrietta sighed as she seated herself at the pianoforte. Her fingers moved with old familiarity over the keys. "You are too headstrong for your own good, dear Cat. Have I told you?"

Catherine laughed. "Once or twice you have mentioned it, Henry." She leaned against the instrument as Henrietta played and raised her voice in soft song.

That was how the gentlemen found them upon entering the drawing room. "What a pleasing picture you make," said Lord Talbot, coming over to kiss his daughter's brow. He murmured for her ears alone, "You have outdone yourself, Cat. Lord Kenelm has not stopped frowning." He stepped away to address their guest. "Perhaps you would care for a hand of whist, my lord? I know that my old crony Wesley here likes nothing better than to test his skills."

Sir George Wesley, a genial gentleman of portly stature, laughed. "Indeed, but it is more the opportunity to measure myself against you, my lord, than any particular pleasure in the cards. How well I remember our salad days when you were the sharp among us all."

"Of course, Lord Talbot," said the viscount agreeably, not allowing his discontent to show. He had wanted to speak immediately with Miss Talbot about her unexpected appearance, having come to the decision that it was entirely within his rights as her betrothed to do so. But he sat down to the card table with every sign of affability and for the next hour played at cards.

Despite his impatience, the viscount found his concentration centered on the game. Lord Talbot and Sir George were both formidable opponents, he discovered, and it required all his skill

to make a decent showing. At last the game was done with Lord
Talbot declared the winner amid loud amiable grumblings from Sir
George that he wished a rematch. Lord Talbot laughed and agreed.
He invited the viscount to enter a second game, but Lord Kenelm
gracefully declined. "I am totally outmatched, sir, and I know it," he
said with a smile.

Lord Kenelm rose from the green baize card table and
approached Miss Talbot. She had long since left her place beside the
pianoforte even though Henrietta had continued to play, and she
was now quietly embroidering. The viscount sat down beside her and
she flashed a smile at him. "Miss Talbot, I have waited all evening for
the opportunity to talk with you," he said.

"I am indeed flattered, my lord," said Catherine, not looking up
from her embroidery hoop.

"Perhaps you will not be so pleased after you hear what it is I
wish to say," said Lord Kenelm, dropping his voice after a glance
around to be certain that the others in the room were still occupied.

Catherine did look at him then, dropping the embroidery to her
lap. "Yes, my lord?" Her green eyes held a challenge.

Lord Kenelm regarded her thoughtfully. "I was frankly
astounded by your appearance this evening, my lady."

"Oh? Do I look too dowdy to you, my lord?" asked Catherine
coolly. She gave no indication that her heart was pounding as a result
of this confrontation.

"Not at all. Quite the contrary, in fact. However, I am well aware
that you have used cosmetics tonight. As your betrothed, I feel that I
am within my rights to insist that you dispense with such artifice in
future," said Lord Kenelm.

"Indeed! My dear Lord Kenelm, when you offered for my hand
it was my understanding that we entered upon a contract of
convenience, with each of us free to live our own lives as we chose. I
do not think that original agreement has changed," Catherine said.

The viscount was taken aback. Miss Talbot's steady gaze was dark with emotions that he could not readily decipher. He could hardly understand the mixed contradictions of his own feelings. He was furious with her for defying him and for using his own words against him. But because she had pointed out to him the basis of their agreement, he found that he could not rip up at her as much as he wished it. He had set the rules, after all, and he could not in all fairness change them to suit his convenience. It would jeopardize all that he had set out to gain in contracting for a marriage of convenience.

"I understand you, my lady. I shall in future consider that point most strictly," he said in a controlled voice. He rose and bowed to her stiffly, then walked away to rejoin the other gentlemen.

Catherine looked after him with a faint smile playing about her lips. Her stratagem had surpassed her expectations. Lord Kenelm had definitely taken notice of her. She hoped that her next efforts to goad him to response would be as successful. Humming, she picked up her embroidery and once more bent her head over the fanciful design.

A few days later Lord Kenelm, who was idly conversing with an acquaintance outside White's, was surprised to see his betrothed tooling a carriage down St. James's street. He uttered an incoherent exclamation, and his companion turned around to see what had so startled the viscount. The gentleman's jaw dropped.

"Oh, I say, Kenelm! Isn't that Miss Talbot, your betrothed? Frightfully daring of her to drive down St. James's, ain't it? I wouldn't want my sister to attempt it. Devilish bad on the reputation, you know." One glance at the viscount's frowning expression told the gentleman all that he was curious to know.

Lord Kenelm made an effort to appear bored. He was shaking with anger, but to his chagrin he found himself obligated to defend his lady's abominable action. "As to that, Miss Talbot is something of a rule unto herself. I do not myself censure a little harmless sport. One must give adequate rein to the ladies and indulge their whims, you know."

"Oh, certainly," agreed the gentleman hastily, but as he later told acquaintances, "The viscount was that beside himself, I thought he would pop. His eyes were that queer yellow, too, but he never once let on. I shouldn't wager against it that his lady is given a fine trimming."

But the gentleman was out on that score.

Lord Kenelm's first impulse was to snatch Miss Talbot from the seat of her carriage and give her a sound public thrashing. His reason won out, however, and by the time he had taken time to calm himself before seeking her out, he found that he no longer wished to confront her over her foolhardy trick. Her words at their last meeting echoed mockingly in his mind. He cursed himself under his breath for an idiot. He should have foreseen that his insistence on noninterference in each other's lives was a two-edged sword. But how could he have foreseen that Miss Catherine Talbot, unconventional in thought but seemingly so content with her womanly sphere, would cause such upheaval in his life? For this she had done. He heard everywhere of the daring Lady Cat, some comments admiring and others censorious. He had been surprised yet proud of her conquest of society and he had quietly laughed as she had set some people on their ears, but lately Lady Cat's exploits had begun to seem less amusing. And the viscount found that his hands were tied, for his own sense of honor would not allow him to interfere where he had himself set the boundaries for their relationship.

The Hon. Mr. William Avery was to make the acquaintance of Miss Catherine Talbot much sooner than either he or the viscount had anticipated. A few days after his removal to a hotel he took it into his head to put in an appearance at the theater. Unlike many other young gentlemen who attended the theater mainly to ogle the ladies in the boxes and the dancers on stage, Mr. Avery was a serious theatergoer. He was impressed by Mrs. Siddons' tragic performance in *Macbeth,* and the conversation of the smarts around him did not sway his concentration until he heard his brother's name.

"I say, isn't that Lord Kenelm's betrothed in that box?"

"Aye, that is Lady Cat. They say this is the lady's first Season and she was spoken for before she ever came to London, more's the pity. It's my opinion that the viscount is a devilish lucky dog."

"I should say! She is a regular dasher."

Mr. Avery had swiveled around in his seat and located the box at which the two gentlemen, oblivious to his sudden interest, were gazing. They soon turned their admiring eyes to other targets, but William continued to stare up at his brother's fiancée. He had told Justin the truth when he admitted to great curiosity about Miss Talbot, and now this glimpse of her across the theater thoroughly whetted his inquisitiveness. The thought formed in his head to visit Miss Talbot in her box at the intermission. She could not be other than pleased to be made acquainted with her future brother-in-law, he thought.

Catherine was oblivious to the interest her appearance had garnered or to anything else but the performance on stage. She had been enthralled by the magic of the theater on her first visit more than a month before, and each time she attended, it had not changed for her. Henrietta had called it unnatural that a young lady should be so engrossed in the performance that she should not even notice the salutes from acquaintances in the other boxes, but Lord Talbot had not agreed. "She is my daughter, Henrietta. Why should she not share one of my passions?"

"I remember well your passion for the theater, Thomas," said Henrietta with a sniff. "I recall that it began with a pretty opera dancer who possessed a nice turn of ankle, as you phrased it."

"Did it?" asked Lord Talbot with interest. He grinned wickedly at his cousin. "Then I am certain that I came to a fast appreciation of the finer points of the theater."

Henrietta smiled despite herself. "You are impossible, Thomas. And Catherine *is* like you. I never know what to expect of her these days."

"Expect what you like, Henrietta. Cat is my daughter and she will do as she wishes," Lord Talbot said, though with a shade of grimness.

Unaware of her father's unease, Catherine had indeed done whatever she wished. As an engaged woman, she'd had access to entertainments and acquaintances that any other debutante would have been guided away from. Catherine had attended a masquerade alone in the company of an admirer she knew would be certain to gossip; she had cultivated her acquaintance with Lord Haversaw and now met him quite frequently over the gaming tables that were set up at various functions as an alternative to dancing; and in order to win a bet put to her by a rather ramshackle smart, she had dared to drive down St. James's Street in the middle of the afternoon in full view of the gentlemen who frequented White's and Brooks's. Several correct society matrons were outraged and for nearly a week Catherine discovered herself met with a rather glacial reception at whatever function she attended, but she was the betrothed of Lord Kenelm, Viscount Kenelm, and the disgrace could not endure long against her social standing. However, it began to be said that the daring Lady Cat was a fit partner for a rakehell such as Lord Kenelm. Catherine had hoped that her growing reputation would come as an unpleasant surprise to the viscount, but he had said not a word to her. On those occasions that he escorted her to a function or came to call, nothing could have been more courteous nor more solicitous than his attentiveness toward her. Catherine had begun to despair of ever being able to shock him.

It was at this point that Mr. Avery made himself known to her. The play's intermission was always a jarring moment for Catherine, and she blinked, slowly coming back to herself even as the first visitors entered the box. Henrietta had accompanied her that evening—most reluctantly, since she did not particularly care for *Macbeth*. "It is such a morbid tale," she had explained, and she had managed to snooze through most of the performance. But Henrietta awakened at once when the curtain dropped and she was graciousness itself to those who stopped in to visit. There were a few old friends of her own, but most were admirers of Catherine's, and both ladies were engaged in lively conversation when Mr. Avery entered the box. He very correctly made himself known first to Henrietta, who immediately brought him to Catherine's attention.

Catherine held out her gloved hand to him with a warm smile. She was astonished that Viscount Kenelm's brother should present such a sober appearance both in countenance and in dress, but she hid it well. "I am very happy to make your acquaintance, Mr. Avery," she said with a warm smile. I hope that we may grow to be good friends."

Mr. Avery bowed, well-pleased by her graciousness. He took it as an appreciation of the sterling qualities that he flattered himself must be immediately evident in his person. "I am certain that we must, Miss Talbot. I have heard very good reports of you, I assure you," he said.

Catherine's eyes widened. "I beg pardon?" she asked, startled.

"My father, the Earl of Belchester, was quite impressed with you. He is a rather formidable man, you understand, and not easily pleased, as I am sure Justin must have intimated to you," said Mr. Avery with a comfortable glance that told her that he thought she would know to what he was referring. "Indeed, I was extremely surprised to find the old gentleman won over so thoroughly. I would have expected any lady of Justin's choice to have been disapproved outright, but such was not the case. I must compliment you, ma'am." He spoke in congratulatory tones and was totally unaware that he had insulted her.

Catherine stared at him, her temper ruffled. She had not expected to meet with such discourtesy at the hands of her fiancé's brother. She did not quite know how to respond and it was a relief when Lord Haversaw approached her. "My lord, how do you do? I shall not soon forget that you took my last guinea yesterday evening, and I promise you that one day I shall wreak my revenge."

Lord Haversaw laughed, his cold eyes lighting for just an instant. "I do not doubt it, ma'am. But recall that you were not the only one at the table whom I treated so ill. Your revenge may be forced to wait until others have a try at their luck."

Catherine turned toward Mr. Avery. "My lord, I do not know if you are acquainted with my future brother-in-law, Mr. William Avery." She was surprised by the stiff bow vouchsafed by Mr. Avery to Lord Haversaw, whose thin lips formed into a faint smile. The gentlemen did not speak and shortly thereafter Lord Haversaw took his leave of Catherine, again promising to meet her again over the gaming table.

The moment the door to the box had closed on Lord Haversaw's form, Mr. Avery turned to her. His plump face was filled with consternation. "Miss Talbot, I am shocked! Surely you do not acknowledge that fellow, let alone gamble with him!"

"Why ever not? Lord Haversaw may be a known gamester, but he is received in the most respectable houses," said Catherine, astonished by his vehemence.

"That is hardly the point. You must know the circumstances are such that . . . When I think what Justin's reaction must be to learn that you and Lord Haversaw are so familiar with each other, I am filled with trepidation. Why, he would be positively livid. There is no telling what he might do," exclaimed Mr. Avery. He drew himself up and said pompously, "You must break the connection at once, my lady. That would be the best thing; indeed, it is your only alternative."

Catherine stared at him coldly. "On the contrary, sir. I have no intention of breaking my acquaintance with Lord Haversaw. I find him an amusing companion."

Her unexpected attitude threw Mr. Avery into a fluster. "But Justin! I tell you, Miss Talbot, you have no choice in this matter. Once Justin discovers it, there will be a damnable dust."

"Lord Kenelm does not choose my friends. As for your concern, his lordship is already aware that I am acquainted with Lord Haversaw and he has voiced no objection to me," she said.

Mr. Avery was silenced, and while still held by open-mouthed astonishment, he quickly bowed himself out of the box. In the corridor he pulled out a voluminous handkerchief and mopped his sweating brow. He was stunned alike by Miss Talbot's formidable personality and by the intelligence she had conveyed that his brother knew of her link with Lord Haversaw. As he grew calmer and his thoughts settled, he slowly began to doubt the truth of Miss Talbot's assertion. He thought he knew his brother too well;

After years of sworn enmity toward Lord Haversaw, Justin would certainly not forgive him now. Justin must be told, and better by him than by a snickering scandalmonger, thought Mr. Avery. Suddenly having lost all interest in the play, he hurried off to hail a cab.

Meanwhile, Catherine was going over in her mind her conversation with Mr. Avery. Never had she disliked a personage more upon first meeting than she did Lord Kenelm's younger brother. She was incensed still by his supreme lack of awareness that he had offended her. The crowning insult had been for him to insist that she drop one of her acquaintances simply because Lord Kenelm disliked the gentleman. She remembered of a sudden that Lord Kenelm had warned her against Lord Haversaw. This, in conjunction with Mr. Avery's obvious fear of his brother's temper, gave her pause. Perhaps Lord Kenelm disliked Lord Haversaw enough that he would react if there seemed a closer relationship between Haversaw and herself. Catherine thought it worth the effort, and she began to devise various plans to accomplish her purpose.

Chapter 12

Mr. Avery drove immediately to the Kenelm town house and thought himself fortunate to catch the viscount, who was just on the point of going out. He leapt out of his hackney cab and hailed his brother. "Justin. I must speak with you. It is of the utmost importance," he said urgently.

Standing on the steps to his town house, the viscount continued to pull on his evening gloves. "Can it not wait until tomorrow, William? I have a rather pressing engagement this evening."

"I would rather we spoke tonight, and at once," said Mr. Avery. He threw a glance up at the porter, who had reopened the front door and now stood an interested spectator. "Can we not repair to your study, Justin? This is a most private matter."

The viscount sighed. "Very well. Come along, then. We shall at least have a brandy while you regale me. But I warn you, William, if it is about your newest ailment, I shall personally throw you from the house."

"It is no such thing," spluttered Mr. Avery as he followed the viscount upstairs and into the study.

Lord Kenelm closed the door and crossed to the decanter sitting on an occasional table near the desk. He poured but a generous measure of brandy for each of them, and as he handed a glass to his brother, he said, "Now what is of such moment that it cannot wait until tomorrow?" His tone was somewhat bored, which his brother's ear was quick to detect.

Mr. Avery laughed shortly. "Aye, you think me a nuisance. But you shall sing a different tune when I tell you that I have met your betrothed and that I am appalled by her loose propriety."

"What?" The viscount was at last looking at him with attention.

Satisfied, Mr. Avery nodded. "Indeed, you may well look taken aback. I was myself utterly flabbergasted when I learned with whom she spends her time."

"What the devil are you talking about? I warn you, William, I shall not take lightly any misguided criticism of Miss Talbot," he said, his brows lowering in a frown.

"I shall allow you to judge how misguided it is, my lord. I saw with my own eyes that Miss Talbot receives Lord Haversaw's attentions with every friendliness," said Mr. Avery. He nodded, satisfied that he must have set his brother back, and he took a sip of his brandy.

The viscount disappointed him by his calm reaction. "Is that all, William? Miss Talbot is aware that Lord Haversaw goes about in the same circles as we do, and naturally she shows him the usual courtesy. I have mentioned to her my personal dislike of the gentleman; I am certain that she respects my position enough to keep her acquaintance with Lord Haversaw just that, an acquaintance," Lord Kenelm said.

Mr. Avery was nettled that his sincere concern was brushed aside so easily. "There you are out, Justin! Your lady is gaming with his lordship, if you please. I heard her speak of it with my own ears; yes, and they have agreed to play again so that she may have her revenge." He laughed rather shrilly. "Her revenge! That's rich, by God. Haversaw shall not leave her a guinea to her name. If you do not take care, Justin, she shall end in Clarge's Street in the Jew's hands."

Lord Kenelm was no longer dispassionate. "That is quite enough, William. You have delivered your warning. Finish with your brandy. I have an engagement to keep."

Mr. Avery stared across at him. "Is that all? Do I not receive a word of thanks, Justin? I came immediately to you out of concern and—"

"You came to me carrying tales. You are no better than any other malicious gossip," Lord Kenelm said scathingly.

Mr. Avery clumsily set his glass on the desk, slopping the liquor in his agitation. "You do me an injustice, brother, and one that I shall not soon forget. I thought to do you a favor, to save your lady's reputation from a smear that could only be of particular repugnance to you. But you spurn my help. Very well, do not expect me to keep a still tongue in my head when she does go the way of—"

Lord Kenelm leapt toward him and grabbed his shirt-front. His yellow eyes were just inches from his brother's startled face. "Do not even dare to intimate such to me or anyone else. You would very much regret it. I hope you understand me, William." He released his brother with such abruptness that William staggered. Mr. Avery bowed jerkily to him and left the study with a slam of the door.

Lord Kenelm stood stock-still in the middle of the room. His fists clenched once, twice. He turned to his desk, calling harshly for candles to be lit. The footman who hurried in to do the task, after one glance at his formidable expression, did not dare to address him. The viscount was alone within seconds. He stared at the paper he had dragged to him and once more dipped his pen in the inkwell. All thought of that evening's engagement was completely forgotten as he composed a short note to Lord Talbot.

Upon reading it the following morning at breakfast, Lord Talbot's brows rose in astonishment. His eyes narrowed, then he carefully folded the note and put it into his coat pocket.

His daughter, who was nearly always attuned to his moods, was quick to discern that he was preoccupied by a worrisome thought. "What is it, Papa? Surely not another dun for one of my extravagant purchases," she asked with a teasing glance.

Lord Talbot returned her smile, but shook his head. "Not at all, Cat. Though there is one bill for a nightgown and robe that I must say I did find rather exorbitant."

Catherine laughed, her eyes gleaming mischief. "It is of the finest French satin, you see. One must pay to cover the cost of the smugglers' take, Papa."

"My sins are used against me," complained Lord Talbot.

His daughter laughed again and bent to kiss him before she left the breakfast room. "I must go up and hurry Henry. We are to call on Lady Augusta this morning, and I am determined not to go alone. Her ladyship is most formidable. Will you be going to your club as usual?"

"I shall later. I intend to clear my desk of bills first," he said.

"Then I shall not stay another moment, for fear that you will ring yet another peal over me," Catherine said. She waved to him as she went out the door.

Lord Talbot requested that hot coffee be brought to his study. "I am expecting Lord Kenelm. Pray show him directly in," he said to the butler. Hobson bowed his understanding, thinking that he could read Lord Talbot better than most, and his lordship was in an odd mood that morning.

When Lord Kenelm banged the knocker on the front door, Hobson wasted no time in taking the viscount to the study. Lord Talbot rose on the viscount's entrance and offered him some coffee, which was refused. Lord Talbot nodded to Hobson and the butler closed the door. Lord Talbot turned to the viscount with an unreadable expression. "Your note this morning was rather abrupt, my lord. Perhaps you would care to explain more fully your extraordinary request."

"I thought my note clear enough, but very well. I wish you to put a stop to Miss Talbot's gambling, in particular with Lord Haversaw. His lordship is a calloused gamester who thinks nothing of stealing the inheritances of the unwary," Lord Kenelm said shortly.

"I think you may rest easy about my daughter, my lord. She is neither unwary nor a pigeon for the plucking. I was once myself a formidable gamester and I taught both my children to play cards with a certain skill. Believe me, Catherine can well hold her own in a friendly hand," said Lord Talbot, smiling a little.

Lord Kenelm's expression hardened. "I do not think you understand me, Lord Talbot. Haversaw does not indulge himself in 'friendly hands.' I have personally seen what destruction he is capable of. It is extremely repugnant to me that my betrothed should associate with him over a card table."

Lord Talbot regarded him a moment. "I understand that your enmity for this man drives you to extraordinary lengths, my lord. I respect your concern for Catherine and I assure you that I shall guard over her. More than that, I shall not promise you, sir."

The viscount rose abruptly. "Then I must be satisfied, my lord. Pray relay my compliments to Miss Talbot. I shall undoubtedly see her later this evening." He bowed to Lord Talbot and took his leave.

Lord Talbot sat back in his chair. The sunlight coming in the window behind him gleamed off the silver of his hair. The interview with his future son-in-law somewhat disturbed him, despite the nonchalance with which he had dealt with it. He rather thought that he should inquire a little into Catherine's activities, even though he had every confidence in her. It would be best to discover exactly why Lord Kenelm so detested Lord Haversaw. Catherine would not know; that was evident in the fact that Lord Kenelm had chosen to approach him rather than his daughter. But Lord Talbot fancied that he had a few contacts who could be depended upon to discover the information he wanted. And if it proved that Lord Haversaw was indeed a threat to his dear Cat, he would deal with the gentleman himself.

That evening Lord Kenelm was engaged to escort Miss Talbot to the theater. Within moments of Lord Kenelm's entrance to the house, Catherine thought that he seemed more distant than usual. She hesitated to inquire if there was anything bothering him; she did not feel confident enough in their relationship to be able to presume such familiarity. Therefore, she said nothing about it and instead regaled him with a sprightly story of Henrietta's latest absurdity. "I dare not tax her with it, my lord. She would in all probability explain in that convoluted fashion of hers exactly how logical it was that she should come to do such a thing, and I do not think that I would be able to bear it without laughing," Catherine said, chuckling.

"Indeed. You have undoubtedly chosen the best avenue—cowardly but utterly understandable," said Lord Kenelm with a hint of his usual humor.

"I am complimented, I swear," Catherine said humorously. She was gratified when he laughed. She thought with satisfaction that Lord Kenelm was in a fair way to recovering his easy spirits.

The play was a farce, which further helped matters. At the intermission the viscount was again his former self. He smiled as he took her hand. "I hope you will not think me to be abandoning you, my dear lady, but I have seen Hugh Crofton below in the gallery. I mean to step out for a moment's word with him."

"Not at all, my lord. I shall be quite happy to remain here, for I usually see several acquaintances of my own in the box." She was startled when the viscount raised her hand to his lips and kissed her fingertips. A shiver of warm pleasure shot through her.

"I shall return with all possible speed," he said softly, and was gone.

Catherine was in a haze of happiness when the door of the box opened and a lady peeped around the corner. "May I come in, Miss Talbot?"

Catherine immediately recognized the small heart-shaped face crowned by dusky curls, though the violet eyes gazing at her stunned with their incredible beauty. "Lady Albion! Pray do join me." She indicated the chair beside her own.

Her visitor sat down, looking at her curiously. "Have we met before, Miss Talbot? I do not seem to recall—"

Catherine laughed and shook her head. "Oh, no, but once I was present when you chanced to swoon at a rout. I thought then what a sweet face you had and how much I should like to know you."

Lady Albion blushed with pleasure. "That is extremely kind of you, my lady. And especially since you are Justin's fiancée. I have hesitated approaching you before this because ... Well, you must know the reason as much as I."

Catherine thought she understood. It must be rare for a lady to meet the female confidante of her betrothed with any sort of friendliness. She hoped she was not so stupidly jealous. "But why should you let that trouble you? I assure you that I do not."

"Oh, you *are* kind! I was fearful that once you had heard of my and Justin's relationship you would be monstrously cold and unforgiving. But I see that it is not to be so, and I am so glad! Justin was my friend as well, you know, and it is very hard to give up one's friends," Lady Albion said, completely unaware that there was a slight stiffening in the lady beside her. "I must tell you at once, dear Miss Talbot, for I know that Justin will be so happy for me. I fainted at the rout for a reason quite other than the heat. As it turns out, I am in a most interesting condition. Oh, bother! I see that the curtain is about to rise again. I must return to my own box. Pray convey my warmest regards to Justin and tell him that I am very happy."

There was a queer look in Catherine's eyes. "Yes, of course I shall," she said automatically. She did not even notice when Lady Albion left the box. She was remembering that Lord Kenelm had acknowledged an acquaintance with Lady Albion and how coolly he had dismissed the importance of that relationship. "Damn him," she breathed.

When Lord Kenelm returned to the box, he was faintly surprised by the quietness of his betrothed. She hardly vouchsafed him a word before turning her gaze to the stage. He settled himself comfortably and gave himself up to the pleasure of the play. It was several moments before he realized that Miss Talbot was not laughing as she had over the first act, and he leaned close to her ear. "Catherine, is there anything wrong?"

Catherine started violently. She had been blind and deaf to her surroundings. "What? Oh, I have a touch of the headache. It is nothing. Pray do not regard it."

Lord Kenelm frowned at her. "You are pale, Catherine. Migraines come on just so suddenly. Come, I shall take you home immediately. I do not wish you to become ill." She did not demure, but allowed him to place her cloak about her shoulders and escort her from the theater. It was the only time she had ever left before the last curtain dropped.

The viscount handed Catherine over to Henrietta's care and said he would look in on her the following day. He held Catherine's hand a moment longer than necessary as he looked down at her with a frowning gaze. He seemed about to say something else, then changed his mind. Instead, he bowed to the ladies and left the house.

Henrietta escorted Catherine to her bedroom, exclaiming each step of the way. "My poor dear, you are fagged to death, and no wonder! Such fun as we have had. But you shall rest tonight and perhaps tomorrow as well. I shall tell anyone who asks that you have a touch of indigestion and they will well believe it. Everyone does at least once during the Season. It is all the rich food, of course. And some of it very ill-prepared, I may add."

Catherine stood it as long as she could, but when Henriette had dismissed the maid and they were at last alone, she burst out, "Pray do stop, Henry! Nothing is the matter with me at all. I do not wish to be coddled. I do not want a glass of warmed sherry. I simply wish to a little time to myself."

Somewhat taken aback, Henrietta looked at her. That odd intermittent intuition of hers chose that moment to come over her. Henrietta sat down on the bed. "It is the viscount, is it not? Now, do not pretend with me, Cat! I have eyes in my head and I can see the misery looking forth from yours."

Catherine suddenly found herself unable to retain her semblance of calm. She sank down beside Henrietta, who immediately put an arm around her shoulders. "Oh, Henry. My heart feels as though it is breaking."

"Tell me what has happened," commanded Henrietta.

Catherine gave a watery sniff. "I met Lady Albion tonight, Henrietta. I did not know it, but she is—or was—Lord Kenelm's mistress. She told me as much herself, with the assumption that I had already heard of their relationship. She also told me ... Henry, Lady Albion told me that she is with child."

"And did she tell you that it was the viscount's by-blow?" asked Henrietta sharply.

Catherine straightened with a startled look on her face. "Why no, not in so many words. But I assumed—"

"Then you are as foolish as this Lady Albion," said Henrietta forthrightly. "Think a moment, Catherine. The woman was stupid enough to tell you of her relationship with the viscount. Don't you think that she would have been as plain if the child were his?"

Catherine managed a little laugh. "You are right, Henry. I would vastly prefer to believe that Lord Kenelm was not to be father to a bastard. Dear Henry! Whatever would I do without you?" She threw her arms about the older woman.

Henrietta emerged from the fierce hug somewhat disheveled. "Indeed, I do not know. Only remember what I told you, Cat. Gentlemen will have their dalliances. You have had a hard lesson tonight, but you must learn to accept such things, and the sooner the better. Now I wish you to climb into this bed and go to sleep. You will feel much better in the morning. I have found there is little in this world that looks as bleak by day as it did by night." Within a very few moments she had Catherine tucked snug in her bed, and after whispering good night, she closed the door.

Chapter 13

It was all very well for Henrietta to assure her that things would look brighter by day, but Catherine woke to a bleak reality. She had known all along that Lord Kenelm had had mistresses. The knowledge had been supportable as long as those faceless women remained unknown, but Lady Albion, who was so beautiful, so exquisite of figure!

Catherine jerked her embroidery thread, knotting it for the thousandth time. It had been three days since she had met Lady Albion. She had seen Lord Kenelm twice since then and each time she could not stop a vision rising before her eyes of Charlotte Albion clasped passionately in the viscount's arms, her rosebud mouth clinging to his while her slender white arms entwined themselves around his neck. As a consequence, Catherine had been unable to help the slight stiffening of her manner whenever she had been with her fiancé. For the first time during their acquaintance there was a stiltedness to their conversation that was painfully apparent to both. Catherine had only herself to blame when the viscount took his leave of her with a puzzled frown.

She was vaguely aware that her father started to address her with a purposeful look on his face, but Henrietta skillfully intervened and drew his attention away. Dear Henry! Never had Catherine thought she could be so grateful to her sometimes vague cousin. But Henrietta had been a wonderful support to her, and not the least of her help had been devoted to keeping Lord Talbot occupied with other than his unusually quiet daughter. Catherine's thoughts returned to Lord Kenelm and she jabbed her finger with the needle. "Damn him," she muttered, putting the wounded finger in her mouth.

"What was that, Catherine?" Lord Talbot asked sharply.

"Nothing, Papa. I have merely pricked myself," she said calmly.

"You seem inordinately clumsy at your embroidery lately," he observed.

"As I was saying, Thomas, you need not escort Catherine and me to the soiree tonight if you had rather not," Henrietta said hurriedly. "It will be a friendly affair with several acquaintances known to us attending."

"Is the viscount attending?" he asked.

There was a short silence, which Catherine calmly filled. "He did not say so this afternoon, Papa. I expect he has a prior engagement."

Her father put up his brows in an incredulous expression, but he chose not to pursue the matter, for which Catherine was grateful. She did not know that Lord Talbot was resigning himself to letting her run her course, no matter what the outcome appeared to be.

Lord Kenelm was at cards when he looked up to find Lord Albion standing beside him. "Lord Albion! I have not seen you in the club for some time, my lord. I trust you have been well," said Lord Kenelm, surprised by his presence. Since the occasion when he had spun the absurd farrago on Lord Albion's behalf, he and his lordship had not spoken. When they had chanced to meet, they had merely exchanged civil bows and passed on their separate ways.

Lord Albion inclined his white head. "Quite well, thank you. Perhaps I could persuade you to a rubber or two of whist later, my lord."

Lord Kenelm glanced suspiciously at the nearly empty brandy glass beside his elbow. Surely it was the liquor he had consumed that made Lord Albion sound so friendly. "I beg pardon, but did you say whist?" he asked.

Lord Albion smiled, in his eyes an understanding of the viscount's confused state. "Indeed, my lord. Whenever you have done at the table, of course." He bowed and walked away.

Frowning, the viscount watched his lordship seat himself at a small card table against the wall. He was recalled to the game at hand by an irritated query from one of his opponents. "Yes, yes, Sheffield. I am at your disposal."

He turned his attention to the cards in his hand, but he found that he could not concentrate due to his curiosity over Lord Albion's odd invitation. Therefore, in a very few minutes the viscount withdrew from the game amid a few preoccupied protests, and sauntered over to Lord Albion's table. As he seated himself opposite Lord Albion, he said, "I must tell you, my lord, your invitation comes as a surprise."

"That hardly astounds me, Lord Kenelm," said Lord Albion, shuffling a deck of cards. He spread the pack facedown over the table. "Your draw, my lord."

Automatically Lord Kenelm chose his first card and Lord Albion did the same. There was silence as the gentlemen took up their hands one card at a time. Lord Albion turned up the last card to fix trump. "You did not actually request my company to play whist, my lord," said Lord Kenelm impatiently.

"No, I did not. You may felicitate me, Lord Kenelm. I am to be a father," Lord Albion said, looking at his cards.

The viscount was startled. Then a horrible suspicion came to his mind. "My lord, surely you do not think that—"

Lord Albion glanced up, his gaze somewhat wintery. "Pray do not finish that query, Lord Kenelm. I would find it somewhat insulting to my lady wife."

Lord Kenelm sat back in his chair, totally mystified. "I fear that I do not understand. Of all people in London, why should you then choose to announce such happy news to myself?"

"I was persuaded that such an announcement would come as a surprise to you. However, Lady Albion swore that it must be otherwise," said Lord Albion. The faintest of smiles crossed his face. "My lord, Lady Albion made the acquaintance of your betrothed a few evenings ago at the theater. It seems Miss Talbot was astoundingly broad-minded and my lady was encouraged to confide in her."

"Oh, my God." The viscount closed his eyes. He had wondered at the distant, almost bruised look that he had seen in Miss Talbot's eyes during their last meetings. Lady Charlotte Albion possessed a damnably foolish tongue! When he opened his eyes, the expression in them was somewhat hard. "I take your meaning too well, my lord. Pray accept my felicitations. I know that you will understand when I do not finish this rubber." He rose from his chair and Lord Albion followed suit. The gentlemen bowed to each other, then the viscount quickly strode out of the gaming room.

Outside the portals of the club, Lord Kenelm stood irresolute for a few seconds. He was not quite certain which function Miss Talbot might be attending. Surely there had been some mention of a soiree when he had called on her earlier in the day. He snapped his fingers, remembering. The viscount hailed a hackney cab and brusquely ordered the driver to carry him as quickly as possible to his own address. At the town house he leapt out of the cab, throwing the fare at the astonished driver, and took the steps two at a time. He had to change to evening dress before he could make an appearance at the soiree and seek out Miss Talbot.

The soiree's hostess was astonished but extremely pleased to discover that Lord Kenelm had chosen to attend her offering, after all. She was very obliging and quickly pointed him in Miss Talbot's direction.

Catherine was not aware of Lord Kenelm's presence until she felt a hand on her bare elbow. Startled, she looked swiftly around, and at sight of his face she felt quick pleasure, followed immediately by the guarded sensation which came over her now since she had met Lady Albion. "My lord, I did not expect you tonight," she said coolly.

"My plans for the evening have gone awry. I assume that Miss Talbot is somewhere close by and she will not be immediately alarmed if you are not where she left you," Lord Kenelm said shortly. As he spoke, he drew Catherine toward a draped window embrasure. Once inside he allowed the curtain to fall, thereby granting a measure of privacy to them.

"I do not understand you, my lord," said Catherine, with an eloquent gesture at the closed drape.

Lord Kenelm's gaze was unreadable. "I understand you met a new acquaintance when we were last at the theater. I am surprised that you did not mention her to me."

Catherine's fingers tightened on her fan. "Oh, do you mean Lady Albion? Yes, she stopped just a few moments. She wished me to convey her regards to you."

There was a short silence, then Lord Kenelm said quietly, "I know Lady Albion's conversational style too well, my lady. She did not end with those few words."

Catherine felt herself to be suffocating. She swiftly turned from him to stare out the paned window at the night. "I do not think that there was aught else of moment, my lord." She felt the warmth of his hands on her shoulders and she squeezed shut her eyes.

"Did you think the child was mine, Catherine?" he asked softly. He could feel her trembling. "Did you wonder if I had continued to see Lady Albion after you and I became betrothed?"

"Stop it, my lord!" Catherine put her hands over her ears. "I do not wish to hear any more."

He turned her then and forced down her hands, holding both slender wrists captive in one hand. With his other hand, he pushed up her chin so that he could see her deep-green eyes. "Listen to me,

Catherine. I have been with no other woman since you and I were betrothed," said Lord Kenelm, and it surprised him to realize that it was true. "My affair with Lady Albion was long past before ever I offered for your hand. Believe me, the child is not mine."

"Henry told me as much," said Catherine in a choked voice. The tears were swimming in her eyes and she prayed that she would not cry before him.

"Miss Talbot seems to hold an opinion on everything. Pray tell me what else she told you," he said, somewhat grimly.

Her lashes lowered and hid the expression in her eyes. Catherine's voice came almost too low for him to hear. "That I must learn to accept such things, that gentlemen will have their dalliances."

"Miss Talbot is extraordinarily insightful for such a gooseish woman. But there is one factor that she does not take into account. Your good opinion matters to me, Catherine. I would not lightly disregard it," Lord Kenelm said quietly.

Catherine's eyes flew open and she stared at him with a stunned expression. Surely, he did not mean what he had said. But she could find nothing but sincerity in his gaze.

Lord Kenelm reacted instinctively to the sudden light in her eyes. He lowered his head and gently, thoroughly kissed her. "My Catherine," he sighed against her soft hair as he gathered her close.

"Oh, Justin," breathed Catherine, feeling something wonderful happening to her heart. She lifted her face to his, inviting him to kiss her again.

He obliged her. She was willing in his arms and he felt himself becoming aroused. Reluctantly he released her. "We should return to the ballroom, my lady. There will be talk as it is."

Catherine quickly smoothed her hair and gown, then preceded him as he opened the curtain. She laughed at him over her bare shoulder. "What would be said but that Lord Kenelm and his betrothed were behaving with outrageous impropriety? I should not mind that in the least, my lord."

Lord Kenelm laughed with her. He took his place as her escort for the rest of the evening, and it was not until much later, when he was at home and remembering their conversation, that he realized he had virtually promised to be faithful to the woman he had chosen for a marriage of convenience. "Good God," he said blankly.

Catherine's world had come right again. Her sense of humor and her hopes were completely restored. Whenever she thought of the viscount's words, which had been followed so deliciously by his kisses, she could scarcely contain herself. He must finally, slowly, be coming to care for her.

The viscount, like most other gentlemen, did not escort his lady to every function to which she received an invitation. Catherine had hoped she might begin to see more of him now that he seemed more aware of her, but she soon realized that Lord Kenelm was still very much a part of the gentlemen's world. She decided that it would be in her best interest if she were not to request the viscount to escort her too often, for fear that he would begin to think of her as a demanding woman. Catherine did not fancy herself in such a role. During the week that a particular loo party was to be held she had already seen Lord Kenelm several times, so she did not ask whether he planned to attend. Instead, she went with a party of friends, which was chaperoned by one young lady's good-natured mother.

Catherine quickly established herself at the loo table. She had always been fond of any game of stakes. It excited her to pit her considerable skill against others, especially when the stakes were as substantial as they were that evening. She was soon so wrapped up in the turn of the cards that she hardly noticed the passing of the hours. The company gradually thinned as fatigue took its inevitable toll.

The matron who chaperoned Catherine's party bent close to her ear. "Miss Talbot, we are all agreed. It is time to go home," said the good lady.

Catherine looked around, dismayed. "Oh, no, no. Please let us stay a few moments longer. I am persuaded of my luck tonight. I cannot lose."

"You are sometimes so impossible, Miss Talbot," complained a young lady with an irritable toss of her head. "For myself, I am tired beyond belief of the pasteboards."

"But then you are such a poor loser, Mary," said her brother callously.

"I am not!" exclaimed the young lady indignantly, and a spirited sibling argument began to loom in the midst of the game room. The matron made distressed noises, to which neither of her progeny paid any heed, and the rest of the party began to appear uneasily unembarrassed. Loud protests for the unusual noise arose on every side from the gaming tables.

"I shall come at once," said Catherine hastily, throwing in her hand and beginning to rise.

"Pray do not feel constrained to go against your desires, my lady." Catherine looked around, startled, to discover Lord Haversaw standing near her. He bowed to the matron. "If you permit it, madam, I will myself endeavor to escort Miss Talbot safely home whenever she is satisfied of her luck."

The matron looked at him, wavering. "I do not know if that would be proper, Lord Haversaw, indeed I don't. Miss Talbot was consigned to my care, after all."

"But Lord Haversaw is known to me, ma'am. And it is not as though I am an unattached lady," said Catherine quickly.

The matron's troubled expression cleared. "Quite true, my dear. I had forgotten. Very well, then, if you do not think that the elder Miss Talbot will mind?"

"I assure you, ma'am, Henry is of the most placid nature," said Catherine truthfully.

After Catherine's friends had sleepily bid her good night and the matron had assured her for the fourth time that she would send a message to dear Miss Talbot to lay to rest any concern, Catherine was at last free to turn to Lord Haversaw. "I must thank you, my lord. It was good of you to step in on my behalf," she said with a smile.

"I well know the allure of the cards, my lady. Besides, I had an ulterior motive," said Lord Haversaw.

Catherine glanced at him curiously. "Indeed, my lord? I cannot think what it could be."

"It has been long since I promised you a chance to revenge yourself against me. I thought tonight as good a time as any," he said, offering his arm to her.

Catherine laughed as she accepted his escort. "Truthfully, my lord, I had quite forgotten. I shall be happy to sit down with you. But I warn you, I have not yet lost tonight. My luck is in."

"Is it? Then I must certainly take care," Lord Haversaw said with an amused twist to his lips. He led her to a small private card room, separated from the main gaming room by a heavy drape. Branches of candles burned in the wall sconces, throwing a glow over the green baize table and the unopened packs of cards. A decanter of wine and glasses stood to one side of the table's playing area. "I hope that you approve, ma'am. I thought that if we were to play a private game, it would be more discreet to do so here."

"Of course, my lord," Catherine said. She had wondered at how well-prepared the room appeared, but his lordship had satisfactorily explained it. She took her seat.

Lord Haversaw sat down opposite her and poured out a glass of wine for each of them. As Catherine accepted the glass, she inadvertently brushed his fingers on the stem. The coldness of his fingers startled her. Lord Haversaw raised his glass. "To your health,

Miss Talbot." Catherine accepted the toast and took a sip of wine. It was a pleasant bouquet, though somewhat sweeter than she was used to. "If you will permit, my lady, I shall open the first pack," he said.

"Certainly, my lord. Since it was I who challenged, what stakes do you choose?"

The expression in Lord Haversaw's eyes was unfathomable. "You have warned me of your luck tonight, my lady. Therefore, I would like to make the game more entertaining for us both. Shall we say a pound a point?"

Catherine's eyes widened, then narrowed. "That is indeed an interesting stake, my lord."

"Do you accept, my lady?" Lord Haversaw asked, pausing as he shuffled the cards.

"I hope I am not one to cry craven over high stakes, my lord."

Lord Haversaw smiled. The cards were dealt and thereafter Catherine was plunged into some of the deepest play she had ever encountered. She was a skilled player and she was rarely ruffled by reverses in luck. She had played against Lord Haversaw before, but never before in a private game, nor for such high stakes. She had thought that she had long since taken his measure; he was an addicted player, his eyes fever-bright and avid on every turn of the cards, and therefore he had a weakness that she herself did not possess. But Catherine was discovering that despite his obvious rapacity, he was a controlled and consummate opponent. She was hard put to match him, and the knowledge drove her to strive against him with a resolution that she had never before brought to a game.

Despite the brilliant heights she reached, Catherine gradually became aware that she was steadily losing to Lord Haversaw. No matter what inspired moves she made, he always seemed to forestall her. She began to gather the feeling that he was toying with her, much as a cat does a mouse. Finally, she sat back in defeat. "Enough, my lord. You have won every penny that I possess. I declare my defeat," said Catherine. She was flushed from the strenuousness of the game and fanned herself in the close air of the small card room.

"But you have yet to wreck your revenge, Miss Talbot," said Lord Haversaw.

Catherine eyed him with a slight resentment. "My lord, it is obvious that you are the better player. I am not such a fool as not to realize when the game is done."

"But I am such a fool, ma'am. Come, I cannot have this ungallant showing against you on my conscience. Give me the honor of one more hand, I beg of you," said Lord Haversaw. His long white fingers caressed the cards in his palm.

"But I have told you, I have nothing more to stake," said Catherine. She refilled her wineglass and fleetingly wondered at the low level left in the decanter. She did not recall imbibing as much as that.

"Then let us not stake coinage, my lady. Let it be something more personal. A private wager to be held only between us two," said Lord Haversaw softly. "Perhaps a lock of your golden hair against this very fine old ring. It is said that it once adorned the hand of a crusader." He extended his hand so that she could see the heavy gold circle crowned with an uncut stone.

The novelty of the wager enticed Catherine. She knew that Lord Haversaw was the better player and that she had shown poorly against him in the last hours. She glanced again at the nearly empty decanter and then met Lord Haversaw's slightly dilated eyes. She smiled faintly. Though she was not a passionate gamester, the temptation was there. Perhaps her luck could change. His lordship appeared much the worse for drink, she thought. "Very well, my lord. I accept your stake," she said.

The cards were dealt and within a few short moments Catherine was brought to the realization that she had made an error. Lord Haversaw was not in the least befuddled. If anything, his style of play was sharper and even less tolerant of mistakes. Catherine was close to tears when the last hand was played. Her smile wavered. "Well, you have fleeced me finely, my lord. I am all done up. Now if you please, I should like to go home." She rose from the table.

"You have forgotten our wager, my lady," said Lord Haversaw, not moving from his chair.

Catherine was startled. "Indeed, I have not, my lord. But I assumed that it would be claimed later. I do not carry a pair of shears in my reticule."

Lord Haversaw drew a small penknife from his coat pocket. "But I am hardly as ill-prepared, Miss Talbot." He smiled as he rose and stepped close to her.

"Very well. Do it quickly," said Catherine, disliking him immensely in that moment. She stood stiffly while he chose the promised lock of hair. His hands were cold against her neck and she could barely suppress a shudder. When it was done, she turned quickly. He stood staring at the gleaming lock of hair curled about his forefinger. There was a peculiar light in his cold eyes. "What is so intriguing, my lord?" asked Catherine.

With a low laugh Lord Haversaw folded the curl carefully in his handkerchief and placed it in his coat pocket. "It is a token of a most memorable game, my lady," said Lord Haversaw. He smiled twistedly at her. "I believe that you, too, will remember this evening, my lady."

"I should like to go home now," said Catherine coldly.

Lord Haversaw bowed and drew back the drape to the private card room. Those few who were still at the gaming tables did not look up as Catherine and Lord Haversaw passed.

Catherine did not address Lord Haversaw as they drove to Berkeley Street, but he did not seem in the least offended. He merely wished her good night as the porter opened the door. Catherine swept into the house without vouchsafing him so much as a nod.

Catherine was glad to find that her maid had not waited up for her, as she had half-feared that Sadie would. She had told Sadie several times that she would undress herself when coming in very late, but rarely had the maid paid her attention. As Catherine dropped her crumpled gown to the carpet and slipped on the satin negligee which Sadie had laid out for her, she grappled tiredly with the meaning of the odd expression in Lord Haversaw's eyes when he was staring at the curl of hair he had taken from her. She sensed there was something important in his reaction and it made her uneasy. But try as she might, she could come to no satisfactory conclusion and finally she rolled over on the pillow and slept.

She slept for several hours and wakened only after her maid shook her to consciousness to inform her that Lord Kenelm wished to see her. "I sent word down that you were still abed, but he declared that he would not leave until he had seen you," said Sadie.

Catherine sat up against the pillows. She could see the sunlight streaming into the bedroom and knew it was late. She thought a moment. Then she looked at the maid with a mischievous light in her eyes. "Thank you, Sadie. I shall receive the viscount in my sitting room."

"Very well, my lady. And what gown do you wish to put on?" asked the maid, opening the wardrobe.

"I will not be dressing just now," Catherine said. A smile danced across her lips.

The maid whirled, immediately taking her meaning. "Miss Cat! You're never receiving a gentleman in your bedclothes!"

Catherine laughed and stretched. "I am not wearing the sheets, Sadie. It is a negligee and it will cover me very well."

The maid implored her to change her mind. When Catherine remained firm, Sadie buttoned her lips to a disapproving line. "I shall be informing his lordship that you will see him in a few moments," she said stiffly.

Chapter 14

Catherine knew herself to be outrageously daring in choosing to receive Lord Kenelm in her sitting room. But she knew also that the sea-green and gilt walls and furnishings complemented her coloring admirably and she felt like being admired. Catherine looked at herself in the mirror. A faint, wicked smile touched her lips. Her gold curls were tumbled and the shoulder of her negligee slipped rakishly from one slender shoulder. Rarely had she felt so feminine; she looked the very picture of decadence. It was certain to generate a reaction from the viscount.

When Lord Kenelm entered the sitting room, he stood frowning, his gaze on his fiancée, who reclined on a settee with a cup of chocolate and a plate of toast at her elbow. He waited until the maid softly closed the door before he spoke. "What the devil are you about, Catherine?" he asked shortly.

"What do you mean, my lord?" asked Catherine innocently.

Lord Kenelm waved his hand at their surroundings. "This, my lady! Surely you know what the servants must think when you receive a gentleman in your private sitting room."

"How dull of you, Justin. We are betrothed, after all." She rose from the settee and for the first time he fully realized what she was wearing. A muscle twitched in his hard jaw. She was enchantingly *dishabille* in a creation of frothy gauze and satin. The negligee's décolletage was deep and the satin clung to her inviting figure as she moved toward him. He thought he had never seen her appear more beautiful. His voice was roughened when he spoke. "Betrothed or not, you should not receive a gentleman alone. And especially not attired as you are."

Catherine pirouetted before him, glancing mischievously over her shoulder as she did so. "Do you not like it, Justin? It was shockingly dear, but I could not resist. I shall order several more like it once we are wed if you should wish it."

Lord Kenelm took a hasty step forward to catch her about the shoulders, bruising her with the force of his grasp. Catherine gasped in shock. He gave her a hard shaking that rattled her. "Catherine, if your purpose is to irritate me, then you are succeeding! Pray stop playing the flirt with me."

Catherine put back her head. She gazed up at him with an odd expression in her green eyes. "Am I flirting with you, Justin?" she asked breathlessly.

"You know damned well that you are." The viscount breathed in the heady perfume she wore and his hands tightened on her. "Damn you, Cat," he muttered. He lowered his head and roughly took her inviting mouth. Her soft lips parted under his and a roar filled his head.

The force of his desire shook Catherine to the very core of her being. Yet she gloried in it. At last, at last, she thought incoherently. Her hands slid of themselves over his powerful shoulders. He crushed her close. His touch scorched her skin through the thin satin of the negligee. His hands roamed skillfully over her body until she was left weakened and pliant by the heat he raised in her. Catherine's breath came fast. She clung to him as he trailed kisses along her neck.

Lord Kenelm lifted her into his arms and Catherine's head fell back. His lips followed the line of her lacy décolletage to the soft hollow between her breasts. One of his hands slid down to her hip and pressed her closer. Catherine's fingers tangled in his dark hair. Unthinking, she whispered, "My love, my love."

The words acted like a dash of cold water on Lord Kenelm. He jerked upright. Somehow, he and Catherine had tumbled onto the settee and she lay beneath him. Her heavy-lidded gaze reflected passion, but now there was a growing hint of confusion. "Justin?"

The viscount drew a ragged breath, attempting to master himself. His hand trembled as he gently reached out to smooth her hair. "My God, Cat. What we have nearly done! I could have gotten you with child," he said hoarsely.

Catherine averted her gaze from the still-apparent hunger in his eyes. "I should like to sit up," she said in a small muffled voice.

The viscount obliged her by removing himself from the settee. He went to the mantel and grasped the edge with both hands. He did not look around at her as he spoke. "I apologize for my want of conduct, Catherine."

Catherine's face flamed. She pressed her palms against her hot cheeks. "There is really no need to do so. I suppose many betrothed couples make love," she said. She swallowed hard. She did not know what she should feel. Shame, perhaps, but instead she was confused and uncertain.

Lord Kenelm turned to look at her then. She sat on the settee, and as he watched, she dropped her hands from her face to clutch tight the top of her negligee. She appeared vulnerable and forlorn. Lord Kenelm felt a protective tenderness toward her that had nothing to do with the passion of a moment before. "Whatever others may do, Catherine, I know that it would not have been the right choice for us. I would not wish to expose you to the cruel judgments of society if we were forced to marry quickly in order to provide for a child," he said gently.

Catherine thought she would burst into tears at any second. "Please, my lord! Let us not discuss it any further."

Lord Kenelm agreed to it, then said with a wry smile, "But humor me in future and do not receive me in such tempting disarray, my lady."

Catherine colored once more as she took his meaning, but she nodded with composure. "Yes, my lord. I accept the wisdom of your request."

Her words reminded the viscount of his original reason for calling on her. The thought wiped some of the warmth from his gaze. "I have another request to make of you, Catherine. It is all over London this morning that Lord Haversaw won a certain token from you during last night's play. I have spoken to you before concerning this gentleman. I wish you to have nothing further to do with his lordship."

Catherine, who already infinitely regretted accepting Lord Haversaw's outrageous wager, was instantly put on the defensive by Lord Kenelm's arrogant, censorious tone. "Lord Haversaw is a skilled player and an amusing companion. He challenges me in a manner that I find quite stimulating. I may not wish to stop playing with him," she said coolly.

The viscount stared at her with an expression gone cold and stern. "Perhaps I have not made myself clear, Catherine. You have set yourself up in these past weeks as a source of gossip. I have no inkling why you have done so. Thus far I have allowed you free rein because you at least kept the line. But to go off for private play with Lord Haversaw was the height of folly."

Catherine was struck again by a strong sense of unease and unconsciously spoke her thoughts aloud. "I admit that my actions were ill-judged. Indeed, when I think back on it, I can scarcely comprehend how I—"

Lord Kenelm interrupted her with a short bark of laughter. "Ill-judged! My girl, you came off as a low and vulgar creature who cares nothing for her honor. I am told that Haversaw has delicately hinted in the clubs that the token he won is imbued with a meaning far other than the mere winning of a private hand," he said shortly. "In short, my lady, it is whispered now that Miss Catherine Talbot is the willing object of Lord Haversaw's desire."

Catherine turned white. "It is untrue, completely untrue!" She felt ready to sink. Surely Lord Haversaw could not have served her such a trick. But she could not help recalling the peculiar look of satisfaction in his eyes or his low laugh as he tucked away the curl of hair. Why would he do this thing to her? Then the enormity of her situation struck her. If Lord Kenelm were ever to learn that it was a lock of her own hair that Lord Haversaw had taken from her, it would damn her in his eyes as the wanton that Lord Haversaw was claiming her to be. She must somehow reclaim that lock of hair, but in her panic no obvious avenue presented itself to her. Her father's face rose before her eyes. She had always relied upon him, but she did not know if she dared go to him with this particular folly.

"Is it? I wish to God that those who matter may have the sense to reject the gossip. As for myself, I hardly know what to believe about Miss Catherine Talbot. She is talked about everywhere as 'the daring Lady Cat,' a lady always game for any outrageous folly," he said bitterly. "I have turned a blind eye to your gaming excesses and to your childish pranks, but this latest is for me the last straw. My own sense of honor will no longer support your determined pursuit of ruin."

Catherine felt her feelings exacerbated beyond endurance, and her temper flared. "I think that's the most idiotic thing you have yet said to me. Really, for you, of all people, to talk in such condemning tones of my excesses, my scandals! You possess the most shocking rakehell reputation in London. Your name is linked to every scandal that surfaces, and especially those involving the ladies. You are naught but a hypocrite, sir!"

"We are speaking of your reputation, not mine," said Lord Kenelm coldly.

"But we are not. You are saying in that insufferable fashion that my progress reflects on your sense of importance. Is that not the truth, Lord Kenelm? Is it not that I am so scandalous, but that you perceive my actions to reflect badly on you," said Catherine angrily. "When you offered for me, it was with the object of gaining a mouse of a wife, quiet and meek and unassuming. I am not that respectable nonentity, my lord. I never shall be, and I am glad that at last you have seen it."

"That is quite enough, Catherine. I am your betrothed and you will abide by my wishes now, even as you will when we are husband and wife. I demand that you immediately sever any connection with Haversaw and those others of his ilk. Further, you will no longer make yourself an object of gossip but conduct yourself in a fitting manner. I will not have the lady of my choosing expose herself, and me, to public censure and ridicule," Lord Kenelm said.

"And if I do not meet your demands?" she asked challengingly.

There was a short silence. The viscount's eyes were a blazing yellow. "I shall have no choice but to send you packing to Ravensclaw."

"I shall not go," Catherine said, actually trembling in her agitation.

"Oh yes you will go, my girl. You are betrothed to me and I can force you to accede to my will. I will myself put you into the coach and order the servants to carry you back to Ravensclaw." Lord Kenelm smiled unpleasantly. "Do not think that your father will protest on your behalf. He will recognize that I have the right to order my affairs as I will. And you, dear Miss Talbot, are very much my affair."

"On the contrary, my lord! I am not yours to order, nor ever will be. As of this moment our betrothal is at an end," said Catherine furiously, driven past her limits.

The viscount stared at her. Then he laughed. "You must do better than that, my girl. I am the heir to Belchester and to all the wealth and entitlements that position grants me. You'll not whistle me down the wind."

"Your insufferable arrogance is what I find most detestable in you," Catherine said thinly. She stripped the solitaire from her finger and flung it at the viscount's head. With a scathing look she turned away to pull on the bell rope. Her fingers were still on the rope as she said, "You will not be welcome in this house from this day forward, my lord." The sitting-room door opened and Sadie awaited her mistress's wishes. Catherine addressed the maid, though her steady gaze never left the viscount's shocked eyes. "Pray show Lord Kenelm out, Sadie. You may convey to the staff that his lordship will not be returning to this house. Do you understand me, Sadie?"

"Yes, my lady," stammered the maid, startled.

Lord Kenelm stood rooted for a long moment before he seemed to shake himself. He bowed to Catherine with bare courtesy. "You have made me a happy man, my lady. You have freed me from an entanglement which I regretted more each day. Miss Talbot, I bid you farewell." His voice and the expression on his face were cold. He turned on his heel and strode out of the sitting room.

The door was shut with what sounded to Catherine to be a note of finality. Catherine clutched the back of a chair for support. Her face was white and she could barely withstand the wave of sickness that assailed her. She had actually done it. She had jilted Viscount Kenelm, her dear Justin. She staggered around the chair to drop into it. Unseeingly, she gazed at the circle of gold that lay glittering on the carpet where the viscount had allowed it to fall. She had taken the gamble to win his love and she had lost. Catherine dropped her face into her hands and a shudder shook her body.

When Lord Kenelm left the house on Berkeley Street, he was in a state of shocked outrage. He, Lord Kenelm, Viscount, had actually been shown the door. Not content with that, the lady had had the audacity to instruct the servants in his presence that he was no longer to be given access to the house. The viscount fermented with rage. He was a matrimonial prize of the first water. There were ladies throughout London who would swoon at the thought of being his lady. But Miss Catherine Talbot had jilted him. That unknown country miss had had the gall—nay, the effrontery! —to throw his ring back in his face.

Lord Kenelm stood quite still on the sidewalk, his fists clenched, totally oblivious to the curious stares of passersby. He ground his teeth. Miss Talbot would rue the day she had ever dared to cross swords with him. He smiled grimly. She was in all likelihood having regrets even now. After all, Miss Talbot had thrown away the most eligible offer that was likely to come her way. Once it became known that she had callously jilted Viscount Kenelm, one of the most eligible bachelors on the town, Miss Talbot would quickly discover that scorn was reserved for those who so stepped past the boundaries of good *ton*. After the folly she had committed the night before in gambling with Lord Haversaw, today's action would be but the crowning blow to her social standing. She would not be immune from public censure as she apparently believed. Hostesses would be less ready to include her on their guest lists. Society matrons, those jealous guardian dragons of good *ton,* would be more critical and unforgiving of her daring social progress, and the more respectable gentlemen would be reluctant to pay her court. In short, Miss Talbot was shortly to taste public humiliation. She would have no choice but to run craven to Ravensclaw whether she willed it or not.

Lord Kenelm did not feel the satisfaction that he had expected to at the thought of the discomfiture which lay in store for Miss Talbot. In his mind, it was his right, and his alone, to punish Miss Talbot for her rash temerity. He came to several decisions in the space of a few moments. He had no intention of broadcasting the termination of his betrothal to Miss Talbot, or of inserting an announcement in the *London Gazette*. As soon as possible, he intended to meet with Lord Talbot and request him to persuade his headstrong daughter to the same silence. Lord Talbot would agree to it, not only because he was under an obligation to the viscount but because he could hardly be other than appalled that his daughter had acted so rashly. Surely Lord Talbot could be depended upon to curb Miss Talbot just once, thought Lord Kenelm.

Once he had completed his business with Lord Talbot, Lord Kenelm meant to pay a visit on Lord Haversaw. I should have confronted the dog years ago, thought the viscount grimly. If he does not publicly retract his diabolical untruths and restore my lady's honor, I suppose I shall have to kill him. The bloodthirsty thought unaccountably afforded him considerable satisfaction.

As for Miss Talbot, the viscount planned a particularly sweet revenge on her. He would woo her with every ounce of his much-vaunted charm and make her realize the foolishness of jilting him. Once she had fallen prey to him and she was his wife, he would punish her for the rest of her days. The form that this punishment was to take was hazy in the viscount's mind, but it seemed to involve much kissing and lovemaking. Lady Cat shall learn the folly of playing fast and loose with a gentleman's pride and honor, thought Lord Kenelm with grim satisfaction. On this laudable thought, he went home to compose a comprehensive letter to Lord Talbot.

Chapter 15

Lord Talbot was informed immediately of the rift between Catherine and Viscount Kenelm by his daughter's maid. He thanked the thoroughly upset maidservant and then prepared to bide his time. He knew that eventually Catherine herself would come to him, as she always had when she was distressed. He only hoped that she was not too disappointed at the outcome of her schemes. There was nothing that he could see that would mend such a breach. Lord Kenelm was a proud man and unlikely to accept his marching orders with grace, let alone be forgiving enough to wish a reconciliation.

Lord Talbot, having reached these conclusions, was therefore extremely surprised to receive the letter from the viscount, which was hand-delivered by a servant. As he read it, his brows rose. Lord Talbot was at once astonished and rendered thoughtful by the viscount's extraordinary request to keep the broken engagement a close-guarded secret. He was dubious as to the propriety of it; Catherine should be known as a young lady free to accept other suits if that was indeed the case. However, Lord Talbot was familiar enough with society to realize that Catherine would be the talk of the town for jilting Viscount Kenelm, and there were few respectable gentlemen who would be daring enough to link their name with hers until such notoriety died down. In all likelihood Catherine would find herself without another offer until after she embarked on her second Season in London. Lord Talbot was not opposed to saving his daughter the immediate social embarrassment she was bound to feel when the jilting became known. He would as lief not have it known until the end of the Season, when they were already on their return to Ravensclaw. But he was at a loss to deduce the viscount's motive in making the request, and that bothered him.

Lord Talbot again raised the letter and finished reading it. When he put the sheets down, his eyes were icy in expression. So, Lord Haversaw is making free with my Cat's good name. The gentleman has much mistaken his victim, as he will learn to his sorrow, thought Lord Talbot. He decided that he must know all of the particulars of this wager that Lord Kenelm mentioned in his letter. The viscount did not say, but Lord Talbot thought the stake won by Lord Haversaw must be something instantly recognizable as belonging to Catherine for the gentleman to be so confident in setting about such whispers. Lord Talbot rang the bell rope hanging beside his desk. The summons was answered by a footman, who was instructed to request Miss Talbot's immediate presence in the study.

Catherine wondered at the imperative tone of her father's summons and supposed that he had heard of the breach between herself and Lord Kenelm. He would naturally be upset and would demand an explanation, but Catherine thought that once he was reminded that she had actually warned him of the possibility, he would come around.

Prepared to deal with her father's disappointment, Catherine was completely taken aback when he showed her the letter from Lord Kenelm. "What do you make of his request, Catherine?" asked Lord Talbot, watching her face with keen eyes.

"I do not know, sir. I cannot imagine what his lordship is thinking," said Catherine, stammering a little. Unbidden, the thought rose to her mind that perhaps Justin regretted the breaking of their betrothal.

"Your face is like the page of a book, my dear. You hope that he wishes a reconciliation between you," said Lord Talbot gently.

Catherine flushed painfully. "You are too observant, Papa. Sometimes I wish you were not." Her fingers twisted together in her lap.

"I know that you are in love with this fine scapegrace. It does not take a great intelligence to carry that to its logical conclusion," said Lord Talbot dryly. "However, I did not summon you to discuss your wishes concerning Lord Kenelm. Those are already self-evident. I am more interested in Lord Haversaw and the wager he won from you. The viscount communicates in quite terse words that Lord Haversaw is bandying about that a love token was exchanged between you and himself."

"It is untrue! I have never exchanged more than polite conversation with Lord Haversaw, and that usually over a gaming table. How dare Lord Kenelm bring such lies to your ears. I thought him more honorable than that," said Catherine indignantly.

"Perhaps his lordship still has your interests at heart, Catherine," said Lord Talbot.

At his chiding tone, Catherine bit her lip and averted her gaze. "I do wish it were so, Papa."

"What was the wager, Cat?" asked Lord Talbot quietly.

Catherine swallowed. "I have been very foolish, Papa. I had thought myself a match for Lord Haversaw, you see, but it went all awry. He invited me to join him in a private game to give me a chance to revenge myself upon him for some paltry losses some weeks ago. And like the greenest fool, I accepted. He fleeced me of every pound, and then as I was on the point of declaring defeat, he offered a last final wager. I knew him by then to be the better player, but he had drunk so much wine that . . . The end of it was, I accepted the wager and I lost." Catherine was uncomfortably aware that the telling point had been reached. She barely managed to meet her father's steady gaze. "Lord Haversaw staked an heirloom ring of great antiquity. I staked a lock of my hair."

There was silence. Lord Talbot stared disbelievingly at his daughter. Catherine squared her shoulders to bear his certain explosion of anger. But when he spoke, it was quite softly. "Before this moment I had not known that you had inherited all of my greatest shortcomings, Catherine. It is my fault that you have come to behave so foolishly."

At the self-recrimination in his voice, Catherine involuntarily flung out her hand. "Papa!"

"No, Catherine. Hear me out. In my youth I was a gamester haunted and maddened by wine and the turn of the cards. I had mortgaged all that I possessed, and your good mother had died before I came to realize the destruction that I was bringing on myself and my beloved family. I taught you and Christopher familiarity with the pasteboards in the mistaken belief that if you understood them, you would be less likely to succumb to their seductive temptation. I see now that I have done you a grave disservice. By encouraging your natural skill at cards, I also instilled in you a mistaken arrogance in your own invincibility. I apologize most humbly, my daughter."

Catherine was in tears. She could not bear his obvious disappointment in her. "Oh, Papa! It is not that way at all. I am not addicted to gaming, truly I am not."

"I hope not, Catherine. Pray show me in future that I am mistaken and I shall be made a happy man."

"Indeed, indeed, I hope to do so," Catherine said, brushing her fingers over her wet cheeks. "But what is to be done about Lord Haversaw? He need only show that lock of hair and everyone shall believe the vile lie that he has told. And Lord Kenelm . . . Papa, what if he truly does wish a reconciliation? Somehow, I must get that curl back. It is by far too recognizable as my own."

Lord Talbot rose and put his arm about his daughter's slender shoulders as he walked with her to the door. "You must leave Lord Haversaw to me, Cat. I promise you that I shall not fail you."

Catherine smiled at him gratefully, but paused with her hand on the brass doorknob. "What puzzles me most is why Lord Haversaw would do such a thing at all. I cannot understand it, Papa. Why should he wish to ruin me?"

Lord Talbot's face hardened. "I should have told you before this, Catherine. Lord Kenelm requested some time ago that I forbid you to consort with Lord Haversaw. I thought it odd and I made a few discreet inquiries. It seems that years ago, in a card game, Lord Haversaw completely ruined one of the viscount's closest friends. Through the young gentleman's folly, his family was left penniless. The young gentleman could not bear the humiliation and felt compelled to take his own life. Since then the viscount has steered a number of young naives clear of Lord Haversaw's deadly orbit. It is my guess that Lord Haversaw nurses a hatred against the viscount for his interference, and entrapping you is his revenge on Lord Kenelm."

"How vile!" Catherine was white-faced. She understood now how ignorant and foolish she had been. "I have never in my life been angrier with myself. Indeed, I feel quite sick with rage that I fell prey to such a man. I hope that you punish him to within an inch of his life, Papa."

Lord Talbot laughed softly. His eyes glittered with a reckless light. "My dear Cat, surely you know by now that your father can be a very dangerous man when he so chooses."

Chapter 16

M r. Talbot returned to London at Easter as he had promised, bringing with him the last of the gowns that had been ordered from the village seamstress. He also brought from the good lady a delicately worded query regarding Miss Talbot's wedding gown, which needed to be started very soon if it were to be ready in time for a fine June wedding. Mr. Talbot teased his sister about the progress of her wedding plans until he realized that his sallies were not drawing the laughing response he had anticipated. Immediately he abandoned his levity. "What is it, Cat? You've said hardly one word and there sits Henry giving me the most frightful frown. Do not tell me that you and his lordship have had a falling out," he said, attempting to rally her with a smile.

Henrietta rose at once from her chair. "I shall take this gown upstairs to Sadie, my dear. She will be vastly interested to see it, I am sure." With that, she hurriedly exited the drawing room.

Mr. Talbot was utterly astonished. In his experience dear Henry had always turned a deaf ear to whatever was said around her, and she had never exercised a delicate tact on anyone's behalf. He closed his mouth and turned his gaze on his sister. Catherine seemed to be studying the pattern in her cashmere shawl with inordinate interest. Mr. Talbot said slowly, "I have put my foot in it, haven't I? Cat, what has happened between you and Lord Kenelm?"

Catherine laced the shawl's fringes with meticulous care. "I suppose Papa's letter did not have time to reach you before you left Ravensclaw. Christopher, I have jilted Lord Kenelm."

"What?" There was anger and disbelief in his voice. He shook his head as though to deny what he had heard. Christopher Talbot had always possessed a strong streak of respectability. Anything of questionable integrity was abhorrent to him; even though he had participated in the smuggling that his father had initiated and he had pragmatically accepted the need for it, he had nevertheless heartily condemned the undertaking. When Lord Talbot had declared that his smuggling days were done, he had felt as though a heavy burden had been lifted from his soul. He had hoped that his family would never be involved in anything as nefarious or as potentially scandalous again. But here was Catherine informing him with all the calm in the world that she had committed an act certain to make the Talbot name infamous.

"Are you mad, Catherine? Did you give no thought for the consequences?" he demanded. "You'll be whispered about and gawked at like some seventh-day wonder! Yes, and so will Papa and poor Henry. I especially feel for them. What the devil were you thinking of, Cat?"

Catherine had guessed that her brother would be shocked and disappointed. She had dreaded facing him with the news and she had been relieved when Lord Talbot informed her that he had written to Christopher for her. But her relief was short-lived as she realized that the letter had missed her brother and that she would have to break the news to him herself. She had not expected his utter condemnation, however, and it stung her to miserable anger. "I felt I had little choice, Christopher. From the first Papa supported me in the course I meant to take even if it should result in scandal, as I suppose it now will," she said.

"Naturally Papa would support you. He would support either of us even if it meant defying the devil himself. But do not play your tricks off on me, Cat. I am not such a soft heart as our dear parent. Of course, you had a choice in the matter. You've simply taken one of your freakish starts and just see where it has ended," said Mr. Talbot bitterly.

The unbearable tension that Catherine had been operating under threatened to overcome her. She beat her hands together. "But he doesn't love me! Oh, why can't I make you understand? He doesn't want me. He wants a marriage of convenience."

Shocked, Mr. Talbot stared at her. He could not doubt the sincerity of Catherine's surprising statement when she was furiously wiping the tears from her face. "My poor Cat," he said quietly, which only made her tears come faster. He put his large hands on her shoulders. His voice was grim. "I shall have his heart out for hurting you, Cat. I swear it. Our fine viscount will learn what it is to toy with a Talbot of Ravensclaw."

Catherine raised her head in alarm. "Oh, pray do not, Chris. I could not bear it. I love him, don't you see? And I could not bear it."

Mr. Talbot looked down into her tear-drenched pleading eyes. "It has happened at last, then. I would rather it had been a man worthy of you. The viscount has played an uncommonly mean trick on you, which I would never have suspected of him. On first meeting I took him for a man of honor."

Catherine shook her head in quick denial. "It is quite my own fault, Chris. I accepted Lord Kenelm's offer with my eyes open, knowing that I loved him and knowing that he did not love me," she said, her voice quavering at the last.

"But surely you realized that such an arrangement could only mean unhappiness. You have too much common sense for this, Cat," he said chidingly.

Catherine stepped away from him to lift the drape away from the paned window. Sunlight warmed her face; she wished it could do as much for her heart. "I thought I could win him, you see. I thought an engagement would be a tie of sorts, and I would have time to pique his interest. Perhaps I could even spark in him the beginnings of affection toward me. And indeed, I did think for a time . . . But that is all done with. It has come the reverse instead," said Catherine disconsolately.

Mr. Talbot took a quick turn about the room. "An experienced man like Lord Kenelm would hardly allow himself to be drawn in like a fish on a line, Cat. I wish you had applied to me for advice before you embarked on this nonsense." He stopped his pacing to settle a frowning stare on her. "And what was Papa thinking of to let you do this? He must have been as mad as you. For the life of me, at times I feel that I am the parent rather than him."

Catherine gave a watery laugh. She dashed the remaining tears from her eyes. "Dear Papa. You know he cannot turn me from one of my starts once I have set my course. But pray do not blame him, Chris. The fault is entirely mine."

"I do blame him. Cat. He should have given you the birch years ago. But well I know that there is not a dram of common sense to share between the pair of you," said Mr. Talbot roundly. He ignored his sister's indignant protest. "But what is to be done now? It is a pretty coil, 'pon my word!"

"I may have a thought or two to offer which, I flatter myself, might be found to be quite sensible." Brother and sister turned quickly to find their parent surveying them with an amused expression. Lord Talbot's gaze settled quizzingly on his son.

Mr. Talbot realized that his father had overheard his hasty words and he had the grace to flush. "Sir! I meant no disrespect, I assure you."

Lord Talbot waved a hand at him. "Well I know it, Christopher. Now, if you will both be seated, I shall tell you about the brief talk that I had with Lord Kenelm this morning when I visited him at his town house."

"Justin!" exclaimed Catherine. "But why should you ... What could his lordship possibly have to say? I hope he was not shockingly impolite to you, Papa."

Mr. Talbot growled agreement.

"On the contrary, daughter. It was a very civil meeting. The viscount said all that was proper under the circumstances and he exercised admirable restraint in pointing out your wayward nature. He magnanimously expressed his willingness to forgive your shocking breach of etiquette," said Lord Talbot blandly.

"He forgives me," gasped Catherine, her eyes kindling. "Well! I should like to know how I am to regard his cavalier behavior toward me. He threatened to pack me off to Ravensclaw, even promising to toss me into the coach himself! I should like to know—"

"Why should Lord Kenelm wish to send you to Ravensclaw?" asked Mr. Talbot, astonished.

Catherine tossed her head. "I was gaming with a gentleman who is Lord Kenelm's mortal enemy, as it turns out. But that is neither here nor there. Papa—"

Mr. Talbot was much struck. "I would have sent you packing, too."

Catherine threw him a dagger glance and turned her shoulder on him. "Pray tell me, Papa, does his lordship beg my pardon for his part?"

"He does not," said Lord Talbot. There was a gleam suspiciously like laughter in his eyes.

Catherine leapt to her feet. She turned to her brother, whose expression had grown thoughtful. "Christopher, you now have my permission to have out his lordship's heart. I shall not lift a finger to stop you, and indeed, I shall gladly hand you the sword myself."

Mr. Talbot settled himself deeper in his chair. "I believe Papa has yet to tell us the result of his interview with the viscount."

"What more need be said? The gentleman is arrogant and egotistical and absolutely certain of his own infallibility. He is obstinate and vilely proud. In short, he is impossible," Catherine said roundly.

"He sounds a fitting mate for a certain sister of mine," said Mr. Talbot.

"Oh!" gasped Catherine. "How dare you imply that I am obstinate and—"

Lord Talbot hastily intervened. "Kenelm is certainly all that you have said he is, Catherine. However, he is also surprisingly sensible. As you know, his lordship has proposed that the news of the severing of your betrothal be kept close the remainder of the Season. An announcement would be inserted quietly into the *Gazette* in June, thereby saving both parties the inevitable embarrassment that would be certain to arise while attending various functions," he said.

"I think that rather handsome of him," said Mr. Talbot with approval. He caught the eloquent expression in his sister's eyes. "You must own that it is the gentlemanly thing to do, Cat. It will save you from the worst of the scandal."

"Handsome! Rather, it is a stratagem for some purpose of his own. I can hardly credit that he cares a rush for my feelings," said Catherine hastily. Of a sudden, with her own words, the invigorating anger she had felt quickly dissipated to leave behind a hollow sensation of dejection. She turned to her father and said with a trembling voice, "I wish to be under no obligation to Lord Kenelm, Papa. I will myself insert the announcement that our betrothal is at an end and accept the consequences."

"That I will not allow, Catherine. In your own best interest, I must forbid you to make an announcement of any sort. Such an announcement would only serve to fuel the gossip concerning you and Lord Haversaw. I must also require you to continue to wear his lordship's ring." Lord Talbot spoke quietly, but it was with the compelling force of personality that proved him to be at his most formidable.

Catherine had rarely in her life met such implacability in her sire's eyes. Instinctively she knew herself to be balked. Tears pricked her eyes. "Very well, then. I shall do as you wish. I cannot think it other than hypocritical, however. But do not expect me to meet Lord Kenelm with any show of civility." With that parting shot, she whirled toward the door.

"Catherine!" Mr. Talbot attempted to detain her, but she was too quick for him and slipped out of the drawing room. He started to follow her, but Lord Talbot called him back. He reluctantly closed the door and returned.

"Let her be, Christopher. She will feel the better for a good cry," said Lord Talbot.

"But surely—"

"Your sister is a headstrong young woman who set her heart on a nearly unattainable prize. She feels herself scorned and yet she still loves the gentleman who has given her such pain. It is understandable that she is confused and unhappy at this time," Lord Talbot said quietly.

"It's just that I hate to see her in such distress," said Mr. Talbot with an unhappy frown. He wondered if he should not stay in town for a few days longer than he had planned. He had meant to return to Ravensclaw directly after Easter, but it would go against the grain with him to leave while his beloved sister was in such a state of upset.

"As indeed I do. But our Cat will come about, never fear. It will take a bit of time, however, before she comes to realize that Lord Kenelm and I have arranged matters between us in the best way possible," said Lord Talbot. He thought again about his interview with the viscount. He had no intention of confiding to his son all that was said, but if Mr. Talbot had been less preoccupied, he might have observed a certain stark cruelty in his father's eyes.

Catherine enjoyed a lengthy bout of tears. She did not go down for dinner, nor did she answer Henrietta's soft query at the door. She lay on the bed and stared at the white canopy overhead. Her thoughts were a maelstrom of confusion, but gradually they sorted and crystallized into an icy determination. Catherine was positive Lord Kenelm had a hidden motive for putting forth his suggestion of delaying an official announcement of their broken betrothal. She had initially felt a stab of hope that perhaps he did care something for her, after all, but reflection had brought her to the melancholy conclusion that it could hardly be so. Yet, no matter how she twisted and inspected the viscount's proposal, she could not puzzle out what was his true motive. She finally concluded that, whatever the viscount's game, she would never again allow herself to be vulnerable to his charm. She had foolishly fallen in love with him. She had hoped that he would come to love her in return; instead, she had been painfully hurt by the outcome of her gamble to win his love.

Since it was her father's wish, she would play out the farce of their betrothal for the remainder of the Season. Her heart would surely undergo further bruising under such ludicrous circumstances if she allowed it. But Catherine was determined to eradicate Lord Kenelm from her affections.

Chapter 17

Easter morning dawned bright and clear. The Talbot family attended chapel services, and their appearance was generously approved of by those who were interested in such things. Lord Talbot walked beside Henrietta, whose gray bonnet feathers amiably nodded with each step, to the cushioned pew. The elder Talbots were thought to be a distinguished couple, but most eyes were drawn to Miss Catherine Talbot and her tall escort.

"It is decidedly not the viscount. But who is the handsome creature?" whispered one dowager to her turbaned neighbor.

"I believe he must be Lord Talbot's son. There is a faint resemblance, as you see. I devoutly wish that I could get such a fine gentleman to my drawing room," responded the neighbor with a sigh as she thought of her five marriageable and very plain daughters. Her friend made commiserating noises.

Though a trifle paler than usual, Catherine appeared completely composed as she took her place in the pew. She knew that her brother had been anxiously watching her all the morning and now she smiled at him with a show of serenity. He responded readily enough and seemed to relax. Catherine hoped she had sufficiently assuaged Christopher's obvious concern so that he would not return to Ravensclaw still in a fret about her unhappy outburst the evening before.

Catherine had assumed that Christopher would leave Berkeley Street that same day. It therefore came as a surprise to her when over Easter dinner he announced that he had decided to remain in

London for a time. "I shall be taking lodgings at a hotel, so I shan't be putting anyone out in providing for my wants," said Mr. Talbot.

"But you wouldn't be putting us out, Christopher. Of course, you must stay with us here in Berkeley Street," objected Henrietta, and she embarked on all the reasons why he could not possibly stay in a hotel.

Lord Talbot met his son's gaze. Mr. Talbot gave a slight shake of his head. Lord Talbot said, "Henrietta, do pause for a moment in your exclamations and consider Christopher's position. He is a young gentleman wanting to be on the town. I do not think that our comfortable schedule would suit the irregular hours he is bound to keep, and only think how you would worry if he were not in his bed at a particular time."

Henrietta was much struck. "Indeed, I had not thought it out. How right you are, Thomas. I should very much dislike losing sleep over Christopher. Not that I won't in any event, Christopher, but at least I shall not know about your excesses the same evening."

Mr. Talbot laughed at her. "Thank you, Henry. I appreciate your concern and I shall try not to worry you overmuch."

Catherine, who had remained silent for some minutes, said with suspicion, "Why have you suddenly decided to stay in London, Christopher? It is very unlike you."

Her brother smiled disarmingly. "Why, I wish to taste a little of town life, dear Cat. I have little enough to do at Ravensclaw just now, what with the bailiff having everything well in hand for the moment. But if you must know the real reason, I am all curiosity to see how my little sister gets about in society. Henry has told me all manner of stories of outrageous follies and entertainments. I never took you for a gadabout, Cat, but from all Henry has said—"

Henrietta had steadily reddened through his explanation and she now slapped him smartly on the wrist just as he reached for the butter. "That will be enough, Master Christopher."

"What! It was just a little butter for my biscuit," said Mr. Talbot, startled. In the general laughter Catherine forgot for the moment her suspicions that her brother had remained in London for the express purpose of observing how she got on.

Mr. Talbot settled into Fenton's Hotel on the west side of St. James's Street. It was a small, elegant establishment that had been started as a fashionable lounge in the eighteenth century known as Perrault's and now catered to travelers to the city. He was well-satisfied with the comfortable accommodations given him, as well as the pretty chambermaid who dropped him a curtsy when she came into his room to bring fresh sheets for the canopied bed and half a dozen wide towels for the bath.

He sauntered downstairs to the dining room and passed on the way a sprinkling of officers of the army and navy home on leave from the Peninsular War who more and more could be seen in the high-class London hotels. In the dining room were several other guests who appeared to be travelers making a short stay in the city.

Mr. Talbot surveyed the crowd but unsuccessfully as the tables were all quite full. He suddenly espied in a corner a table occupied by a lone gentleman who appeared respectable, and he threaded his way across the room to address him. "I beg your pardon, sir, but if you are not expecting a party, I wonder whether I might join you?" he asked with his easy smile.

The gentleman looked up, startled, but then he motioned quickly to the chair opposite his own. "Of course, sir. Pray join me. It is quite a crush this evening, certainly."

Mr. Talbot seated himself, and after giving his order to an attentive waiter, he turned to his unknown companion. "From your statement, I assume that you have dined in this establishment before. I myself have but just arrived, but I am already favorably impressed with the service offered by the hotel."

"Indeed! I was most pleasantly surprised. Fenton's is quite unlike the accommodations one finds on the Continent, where one is given a single earthen or silver jug or basin to bathe in and a long strip of towel. I infinitely prefer our English tubs of handsome porcelain and the footbaths. I assure you, sir, that you will also enjoy the repast this evening, for the cook is excellent. I am able to complain only of the expense that living in a hotel entails," said the gentleman.

Mr. Talbot laughed, finding his companion's considered manner of speech somewhat droll. He took an immediate liking to the gentleman, whom he saw was much younger than the man's sober appearance and rounded build had led him to believe. Over dinner the two chance-met gentlemen discovered a mutual distaste for the bustle of London. He talked of Ravensclaw and all that the estate offered for someone like himself, who wished nothing better than to spend his days tramping through fields or sailing off England's coast. The gentleman expressed a wistful desire to experience just such quiet pursuits, saying that he was inordinately tired of the social round one was required to keep in town.

"Then perhaps I should invite you to visit me at Ravensclaw one day," said Mr. Talbot. He extended his hand across the table. "We have been conversing so pleasantly for an hour that I had quite forgotten that we have not exchanged names. I am Christopher Talbot."

The gentleman's round face altered to an expression of astonishment and he dropped Mr. Talbot's hand in surprise. "Talbot? But how extraordinary! Are you perhaps related to Miss Catherine Talbot?"

"My sister. Do you know her?" asked Mr. Talbot curiously.

"I have met her but once," said the stranger stiffly. He stared at Christopher with a hint of unfriendliness. "I must inform you, sir, that I am William Avery, younger brother to Viscount Kenelm, who is affianced to Miss Talbot."

"What an odd coincidence that I should meet you here, of all places," said Mr. Talbot with his generous smile. He could see that Mr. Avery was genuinely disturbed by their meeting. "I take it that your introduction to my sister was not encouraging. May I inquire why?"

Mr. Avery eyed him a moment, wondering how freely he could speak his thoughts. But Christopher Talbot's gaze was open, without suspicion or guile, and they had just spent a very pleasurable hour speaking together. It was not a common experience for him to strike up so fast a friendship, and he was reluctant to allow it to wither as quickly. Mr. Avery decided that he must make a clean breast of the matter. "I apologize if I seem less than enthusiastic about Miss Talbot. I am certain that she must be an engaging lady, and indeed upon first meeting I thought... But that was before our unhappy discussion about Lord Haversaw," he said.

His grimace was not lost on Mr. Talbot. "This Lord Haversaw is not known to me. Perhaps you could enlighten me." He sensed that he was on the verge of discovering something important that had to do with his sister's current unhappiness. It had been obvious to him that Catherine was still very much in love with Lord Kenelm and he rather thought that the viscount must hold some sort of regard for her in order for him to insist that the broken betrothal remain unknown. Mr. Talbot hoped that he might discover some way to aid Catherine in mending the breach between her and the viscount.

Mr. Avery was brutally blunt. "Lord Haversaw is my brother's mortal enemy. Miss Talbot is into deep play with his lordship, who is known to be a heartless and hardened gamester. When I warned her that Justin would not look kindly upon her close acquaintance with Lord Haversaw, she gave me the go-by with the coldest stare that I have ever encountered. It quite gave me a turn, I can tell you, when she had previously shown such gracious ways."

"I see," said Mr. Talbot slowly. He now understood how it had come about that Catherine had jilted the viscount. Obviously, Lord Kenelm had upbraided her for associating with Lord Haversaw, and Cat, being as headstrong and willful a female as he had ever met, had taken flying exception to the viscount's tirade. "You foolish, idiotic girl," he murmured.

"What?"

"I was but thinking aloud, sir. I hope that you do not hold my sister's coldness against her, for I assure you that she is usually the most pleasant of companions. But she is also headstrong and she will balk at the least interference," said Mr. Talbot.

Mr. Avery gave a short laugh. "Aye, and so I can attest. That will not suit Justin, let me tell you. He is used to the ladies clamoring to fill his least desire. Miss Talbot must lead him a pretty dance. I wish that I could see it!" He shook his head. "But I am not likely to see it if ever my father gets wind of Miss Talbot's gambling, and especially her unhappy connection with Lord Haversaw. He is a high stickler, you know. I am in the unhappy position of deciding whether I should not myself alert him. Though I detest carrying tales, I think he would far rather hear it from me than some malicious tabby who has it in for Justin. Indeed, it might be the best thing to pay a visit to my father at Belchester."

Mr. Talbot was appalled. Visions of the likely repercussions of such intelligence being carried to the earl, a gentleman whom his son so blithely termed a "high stickler," danced through his head. The viscount would be far less likely to pursue a reconciliation with Catherine if the match were frowned upon by his formidable sire. We would be in the suds then, he thought, recalling the unhappy expression in his sister's eyes.

"I think my sister and the viscount are well able thrash out their own concerns," he said hastily. He lifted his wineglass and contemplated the glowing color of the brandy. "It crossed my mind just now that I shouldn't be in London. I dislike town life so much, just as you have assured me that you do. Why do we not go down to Ravensclaw together? I can assure you of the finest hospitality. Frankly, I would not mind the company of a sober-minded gentleman to talk to in the evening while warming my feet at the grate and with a glass of good wine at hand."

The invitation was exactly suited to a gentleman of Mr. Avery's sedentary tastes. After much consideration, while Mr. Talbot began to despair of ever getting him to make the decision, he agreed to accompany him. "It shall have to be at the end of the month, though. I am committed to one particular engagement whose host may take offense if I were to cry off."

Mr. Talbot breathed a sigh of relief. He might be able to avert the catastrophe after all. "Good enough. We shall leave on the last Friday of the month then." And between now and then, my friend, I intend to stick as close as a burr to your side, he thought with his considering gaze on Mr. Avery.

Chapter 18

L ord Haversaw was at once surprised and wary when Lord Kenelm and Lord Talbot were announced and shown into his drawing room. He did not rise from his place beside the wide fireplace but contemplated them with narrowed eyes. "Gentlemen, I am honored. But you will forgive me if I express some astonishment to receive a social visit from either of you," he said. He inclined his head to Lord Talbot. "The viscount is known to me, of course, but I have not made your acquaintance before, sir."

"We have come on a matter of business only," said the viscount shortly. The firelight reflected yellow in his eyes.

"I did not think it otherwise." Lord Haversaw waved his footman from the velvet-draped drawing room. When the heavy door had closed, he gestured to the cream-silk-covered chairs opposite his own. "Pray be seated, gentlemen. I am curiosity itself and I promise you that you shall have my undivided attention."

Lord Talbot seated himself with relaxed grace. The viscount followed his example a bit stiffly, disliking to accept even this modicum of hospitality from the thin gentleman lounging opposite. "I am not one to stand on ceremony, my lord, so I shall come immediately to the point. Lord Kenelm and I have called on you regarding a certain token won by you from my daughter in a private card game," Lord Talbot said.

"Ah, now it becomes clear. Gentlemen, I regret to say that you have wasted this visit. The token in question is somewhat. . . special to me and it is not to be bought at any price," said Haversaw. He heard a sharply muttered oath and his eyes held a malicious triumph as he glanced at Lord Kenelm. "Indeed, I hold it in such esteem that I have toyed with the thought of wearing it in my lapel. Such an original ornament must excite interest, do you not think?"

Lord Kenelm's face hardened and there was no mistaking the cold intent in his yellow eyes. "I shall kill you, Haversaw, and enjoy doing so."

Lord Haversaw smiled faintly. "So you told me before years ago, on just such another unexpected visit to my home. If my memory serves me correctly, you were rather uncivil and I was forced to require the footmen to show you to the door. My dear Kenelm, I did not pay heed to your threat then; why should I now?"

"Lord Kenelm steps beyond the bounds of honor. I believe that my grievance has prior claim over his lordship's," said Lord Talbot. His terse statement broke the deadlocked stares of the other gentlemen.

Lord Haversaw turned to him with an assumption of polite interest. "Indeed, sir. Pray continue."

"My daughter's reputation is threatened by the broad hints that you have dropped concerning the token that you won from her. Lord Haversaw, you were bred a gentleman and therefore you must recognize the honorable course. I ask that the token be returned to me," said Lord Talbot.

"Unfortunately, that is not possible, my lord," Lord Haversaw said. He paid no heed to the sudden flare in Lord Talbot's eyes, but smiled. "I understand the difficulty of your position, however. May I propose a compromise? I shall wear the token as I have outlined and we shall allow society to judge the truth."

"You well know what would be the outcome, Haversaw. I will not allow you to besmirch my lady's name in such a way, even if I must choke it out of your possession," said Lord Kenelm savagely, half-rising from his chair.

Lord Talbot thrust out his hand and caught the viscount's arm in a surprisingly strong grasp for a man of his years. "You would not be so free with your hints, my lord, if you did not possess that curl," said Lord Talbot softly.

"But I do possess it," said Lord Haversaw with a low laugh. He thought he had never enjoyed himself more. It was a veritable treat to see the expression of naked fury and hatred in the viscount's yellow eyes. Gaming was the source of the sizable income Lord Haversaw required to maintain the style of living to which he was accustomed. Through the years the viscount had cheated him of what he thought of as rightfully his to take. He could hardly number the times that the viscount had maneuvered a ripe pigeon from out of his grasp. Lord Haversaw had waited long for an opportunity to pay back the viscount for his interference; he cared nothing that in the process he would destroy Miss Talbot.

"Suppose I was to wager my estate against that token, my lord?" said Lord Talbot quietly. He sensed rather than saw the viscount's abrupt movement of protest, but he kept his gaze on Lord Haversaw's face.

"A wager, my lord?" Haversaw's cold eyes gleamed and his tongue briefly touched his thin lips. There was a noticeable tensing about his shoulders. "You have captured my profound interest, Lord Talbot. Shall we set the contest here and now?"

"That is agreeable to me," said Lord Talbot.

"My lord," exclaimed the viscount.

Lord Haversaw rose from his chair and crossed quickly to the drawing-room door. Opening it, he thrust out his head. "Bring me candles and wine, quickly!"

While Lord Haversaw waited impatiently at the drawing-room door while his orders were carried out by hurrying footmen, Lord Kenelm sought to convince Lord Talbot of his folly. "My lord, I understand why you have issued this challenge to Lord Haversaw.

But you must not go through with it," he said urgently. "Haversaw is a hardened gamester. He has crushed several men of skill in just such a manner. Believe me, sir, it would be far better if I were simply to force him to a duel."

"What, and have Catherine scolding me for allowing you to place yourself in danger? I did not voice my reservations at our meeting when you announced your determination to face Lord Haversaw on the field of honor if his lordship would not listen to reason, but I hoped even then to see the matter resolved otherwise. Actually, I believe my way to be the more fitting, do you not think? I shall be giving the devil a bit of his own," Lord Talbot said. He smiled at the very real concern in the viscount's eyes. "You need have no fears for me, my lord. I was toying with the pasteboards while Lord Haversaw was still in short skirts."

The viscount opened his mouth, prepared to point out with brutal force that Lord Talbot had so nearly ruined himself by gambling that he had had to turn to smuggling to reverse his fortunes, but he was not given the chance.

Lord Haversaw returned to his guests. He was rubbing his palms together and there was a fever-bright light in his eyes. "I presume that you are ready, Talbot."

Lord Talbot bowed. "I am at your service, my lord."

The three gentlemen sat down to a large card table that had been dragged to the middle of the carpet. Several branches of candles had been set about the table and the drawing room seemed ablaze with light. The principals agreed on whist and the stakes were set. Four or five new decks of playing cards were stacked ready for use on the corner of the table. Lord Haversaw broke the seal on one of the decks and shuffled the cards with precise flicking movements of his fingers.

The viscount watched with a feeling of frustration and helplessness as the cards were dealt out. He could not interfere once the challenge had been agreed to by both parties. At this point he was but witness to the game. He picked up the full wineglass that stood at his elbow, but his concern was such that he did not even taste the wine he swallowed.

The first few rounds the opponents appeared to be taking each other's measure, and the points were spread roughly even between the gentlemen.

Lord Haversaw's smile did not quite reach his cold eyes. "You have played before, my lord."

"Whist was once a favorite of mine, but I rarely play these days," said Lord Talbot with a shrug. He took up the cards to shuffle them.

"Indeed." Lord Haversaw's eyes glittered. "Shall we increase the stakes for the next rubber, my lord?"

Lord Talbot seemed to hesitate fractionally as he shuffled, but he agreed to it and the new stake was set. With a flip of the wrist, as though he was tossing back a long cuff of lace, Lord Talbot dealt the new hand. As Lord Haversaw received his cards he refilled his wineglass. His glance fell on Lord Talbot's full wineglass and he frowned. "You do not drink, my lord?"

Lord Talbot appeared almost embarrassed. "I fear I have been too intent on the play, Lord Haversaw. You are a remarkably fine player."

Lord Haversaw gave the veriest ghost of a laugh. "It is my lead, I believe," he said.

Lord Kenelm gathered several impressions as the contest progressed. Lord Haversaw was tense of body, seemingly coiled to strike each time he laid down a card, his hot eyes never wavering from the business at hand. Lord Talbot sat at his ease with one arm stretched along the edge of the table beside his silver wineglass, which remained untouched. His cards were held carelessly in one hand so that an observer might gather an impression of insouciance, until glancing at his lordship's eyes. The expression in those eyes was hard, calculating, keen; but what startled the viscount was the cold cruelty that entered them whenever Lord Talbot gazed across at his opponent. Lord Kenelm could not doubt what he saw, and he comprehended that Lord Talbot meant to do more than win back a simple token.

As the hours passed and the points taken mounted, Lord Haversaw slowly realized that he had at last met his master. The cards were going steadily against him even as the stakes were raised with each hand. He snatched at his wineglass for a hurried drink, then set it down so hastily that the remaining wine slopped onto the green baize tabletop. Unaccountably his head was spinning. Lord Haversaw pulled at his cravat to loosen it, thinking that the heat had become unbearable in the drawing room. Again and again, his eyes were drawn across the table to what was there.

Disaster loomed, personified by the untidy heap of coins and hastily scrawled IOUs which sat in front of his silver-haired opponent. Lord Haversaw recognized it, but even though his intelligence screamed enough, his dangerous appetites proved too strong for him. One more hand, he thought. It is against all odds that the old bastard will win every rubber. I must—I will break him. With bloodshot eyes, Lord Haversaw looked across at Lord Talbot. "I've the deed on this house and my estate, my lord. I will stake it all against what stands before you," he said hoarsely. His long fingers were twitching on the cards face down in front of him.

"Bring them out. But I'll have the token from my daughter as well, sir," said Lord Talbot, his eyes steely.

Lord Haversaw was about to refuse, then he shrugged. He rose from the table and went to the desk set against one paneled wall. Unlocking the desk with a key taken from his pocket, he withdrew from a drawer two parchments and a closely tied square of linen. Returning, Lord Haversaw threw the parchments and the linen packet onto the table. "There, my lord. You see before you the last of my once substantial assets," he said with an attempt at humor.

Lord Talbot nodded curtly. "It is your call, my lord," he said softly.

Silent and watchful, Lord Kenelm felt himself tense. He knew that it was the pivotal hand. Lord Talbot could win or lose all on what happened in the next few moments. Lord Haversaw played his hand with a maniacal skill and concentration, but it was all for naught. The points went to his grave-faced opponent. Lord Talbot reached out for the linen packet and opened it, satisfying himself that it was indeed the curl taken from his daughter.

Defeated, Lord Haversaw slumped limply in his chair. His hair was disarranged, as though it had been raked through many times, and the points of his starched white neckcloth had wilted. He watched while Lord Kenelm and Lord Talbot silently gathered the winnings. He could barely grasp the significance of what he saw. The disaster was so complete, so devastating, that it threatened his grasp on sanity. When Lord Talbot picked up the deeds and slid the crinkling parchments inside his coat pocket, the full horror burst upon Lord Haversaw. He had lost everything he had once possessed. He straightened abruptly in his chair and placed his hands flat against the table. "Lord Talbot! I should like a chance for revenge," he said, his voice rough.

At Lord Haversaw's loud statement, the gentlemen paused at the door and turned back toward him. Lord Talbot stared coldly at his erstwhile opponent. "I fear that is out of the question."

"But as a man of honor—" began Lord Haversaw desperately.

"Honor? Where was honor when you cared nothing for the ruination of my daughter, sir?" Lord Talbot said sharply. His expression altered, smoothed to one of urbanity. "My lord, you must have played this scene far too many times not to realize that the one who does the fleecing never gives his victim another chance." He opened the door and went out without a backward glance.

Lord Kenelm continued to stand a moment, unsure of what he should say. But Lord Haversaw was not looking at him, but at his hands. Slowly Lord Haversaw raised his hands, with his long white fingers extended, up before his dilating eyes. On his face was such a naked expression of horror that it froze Lord Kenelm's blood. The viscount left quickly, not even giving a nod to the footman who handed his hat and cane to him.

He found that Lord Talbot had waited for him on the sidewalk in front of the house. "Remind me, sir, never to run afoul of you," he said quietly.

Lord Talbot laughed, his eyes remaining shadowed even under the street lamp. "It was a close night's work, my boy, and one that I never intend to repeat. His lordship could have had me more than once, but his greed constantly caused him to overreach himself." He paused, then said, "The grip of the cards is a horrifying thing, Lord Kenelm. Once, I felt it as acutely as Lord Haversaw – at least I did so when the fumes of wine pervaded my brain. I no longer touch wine."

The viscount recalled suddenly that not once had Lord Talbot touched his wineglass during the long contest. He had vaguely wondered at it at the time, but it had not seemed important. It was borne in on him with blinding clarity exactly what sort of temptation Lord Talbot had courted for himself in issuing the challenge to Lord Haversaw. Lord Kenelm thought with tempered respect that he had never met a more daring or more reckless gentleman.

Lord Talbot held out his hand and in his palm was the linen packet, once more closely tied around its precious contents. "I believe this belongs most appropriately to you, my lord. When you approach my daughter, be certain to browbeat her a little. My Cat is proud and not likely to show a scrap of remorse to you unless you do."

The viscount took the soft packet and put it in his pocket. "I shall remember that, my lord." He espied a hackney cab and hailed it to the curb. He and Lord Talbot climbed into it and the cab moved off down the dark street with the hollow clopping of horse hooves.

Chapter 19

T he startling news that Lord Haversaw had shot his brains out with his own dueling pistol after losing all his possessions in a mysterious card game was a seven-day wonder, but there were few who actually mourned his disappearance from society. His cronies shook their heads and mouthed regrets, but each held private thoughts that Lord Haversaw's death was all to their gain. He had been a dangerous man, who on a whim was as likely to fleece those whom he called friends as he would any green stranger. By others it was thought to be poetic fate for a gentleman who had driven so many others to the brink of despair.

Talk dwelled more on the curious story, supposedly gotten from some footman or other, that it had been Lord Talbot and Lord Kenelm who had participated in the ill-fated card game that had ended in Lord Haversaw's ruination. But it was in the end thought to be rather unlikely. Lord Talbot was known to be a very correct gentleman who never played for more than a penny a point, if he sat down to a card table at all. He was therefore an unlikely candidate for Lord Haversaw's peculiar brand of attention. The fact that Miss Catherine Talbot's name had been so recently linked to Lord Haversaw's raised some speculation that perhaps Lord Talbot had tried to intervene with his lordship on behalf of his daughter and had perhaps issued a threat to him. But this was discounted almost immediately. Lord Haversaw had been known as a cold, compassionless man. No amount of angry parental blustering could have breached his defenses, let alone driven him to suicide. As for

Lord Haversaw being visited by Lord Kenelm, the very idea was absurd. The viscount's well-known distaste for Lord Haversaw precluded a social visit of the sort the footman supposedly described.

Lord Haversaw's house and holdings were quietly disposed of in private sale. No one knew who his heirs might be, and the solicitor who handled the business was not likely to be forthcoming. Within a matter of days Lord Haversaw ceased to be a topic of conversation and indeed his very existence seemed to pass from society's memory. It was the oddest thing, however. Now and again a tale would surface of a family, reduced to penuriousness by Lord Haversaw's unmerciful rape of the family fortune, which suddenly came into a substantial bequest. But no one seriously considered that the vague stories which were circulated to be more than curious coincidences.

The manner and suddenness of Lord Haversaw's ruin was shocking to Catherine, especially as the suspicion flashed through her mind that her own dear father had perhaps supplied the motivation for that gentleman's death. She knew that Lord Talbot had at one time been an extremely skilled gamester, but though Catherine wondered whether her father had somehow been instrumental in the entire business, she knew better than to ask. Lord Talbot did not welcome prying into what he considered his affairs, and in this instance, Catherine preferred ignorance. All Lord Talbot ever said to her about Lord Haversaw was that he had regained possession of the token she had so foolishly lost at cards.

Catherine was therefore relieved of her greatest fear, which was that Lord Kenelm would somehow discover what manner of token it had been, and she was able to turn her mind once more to the Season's entertainments. Invitations had been accepted for nearly every evening of the two months remaining to the Season. These included routs and balls, two masquerades, and a moonlit dinner al fresco set in the gardens of a hostess well-known for her originality. Catherine managed to squeeze in several outings to the theater, which never failed to enchant her. Her days were equally filled, with morning calls, shopping expeditions, and afternoon teas. As the weather had grown warmer, so had the number of forays into Hyde Park. Though Lord Talbot had sometimes to be practically dragooned to act as escort for Catherine and Henrietta, he never failed to accompany the ladies to the park, riding tall and distinguished beside their open carriage.

Occasionally the ladies had been able to persuade Mr. Talbot as well to join them, but he more often than not declined. "I can withstand only so much of the polite buzz of gossip before I feel myself suffocating," he said. "Besides, I've discovered a jolly set of fellows who care as much as I for the sort of gadding about that you do."

"But if you do not go about socially, what then do you do?" asked Henrietta.

"Oh, we have famous discussions on crop drainage and the proper breeding of animals and such. I have become a member of what is known as a scientific society, Henry," said Mr. Talbot with a broad grin.

"Crops ... the breeding of animals . . . how very interesting, to be sure," stammered Henrietta.

Henrietta's two young cousins laughed at her appalled expression. Catherine reached over to comfortingly pat her arm. "It will all come about, never fear. One day Chris will discover a perfectly marvelous young woman who is an enthusiast of drainage, and once wed, they will be very content inspecting the fields together."

"Oh, dear," said Henrietta, depressed further. She rallied herself to smile brightly at Mr. Talbot. "I wish you every fortune in finding just the sort of bride you wish. I only hope that she comes of good stock, whoever she might be." She blinked in utter confusion when her companions fell into fresh whoops of laughter. "Whatever have I said now?" she wondered.

Lord Kenelm called frequently on Catherine and was in every way more devoted than he had been before their estrangement. Catherine could not stop wondering at it, particularly whenever she chanced to catch a peculiar, watchful expression in his glance that instantly vanished the moment he became aware of her observation. For Catherine, Justin's manner had become extremely odd and she guessed that it was somehow connected to her ill-fated wager with Lord Haversaw, but with the token safely in her father's possession Catherine felt herself able to face the viscount's suspicions.

"But why should he say anything? We are not betrothed, after all," she said aloud one night while plumping her pillow and preparing to sleep. Her hand paused in its activity. "And why is he so attentive and so charming toward me?" She gave the unoffending pillow an unnecessarily vigorous thump. It would be so very much easier to fall out of love with Lord Kenelm if he did not smile at her just so, if he were not there to hand her into a chair at dinner or aid her out of a carriage, if he were not so solicitous in placing her cloak about her shoulders when they were to go out, if he did not hold her so close when they danced.

Catherine's defenses against Lord Kenelm were slowly crumbling, and she knew it. She had found increasingly that she could not behave with an impersonal civility toward him. His company was too entertaining, his glance too friendly, his clasp when he placed her hand through his elbow too warm. It certainly did not aid matters when more and more frequently acquaintances remarked on what a handsome pair they made. Lord Kenelm nearly always agreed with the flash of a smile and a charming word about her. Catherine had begun to hear rumors that the viscount had at last succumbed to a devoted passion. And in the deepest recesses of her heart, she had begun to hope that it might possibly be true. But then there were those queer looks that she had caught, as though he were but waiting to pounce on her. Catherine did not know what to make of it, except that he was playing a dark game of his own and she was the objective.

"Drat him! What does the horrid man hope to accomplish?" she said with irritation as she turned restlessly once more in the bed.

Lord Talbot requested that a dinner party be planned for the family, which was to include Lord Kenelm. Catherine still had not decided what Lord Kenelm's motive could be in insisting upon no announcement of their broken betrothal. His attentiveness was beginning to drive her mad with inner questionings, and she welcomed the private dinner party as an opportunity to discover the reason behind Lord Kenelm's wooing of her, for she could call it nothing less.

Henrietta expressed open amazement at Catherine's calm at the prospect of actually having Lord Kenelm in the house. He had escorted them about town and had made several morning calls, of course, but that certainly was not the same as having him as a guest at a private family gathering. Even though Henrietta accepted the pretense of an engagement for the appearance of things, she thought that this was carrying the matter too far. She was appalled at Lord Talbot's utter lack of consideration for Catherine's feelings. "I am certain your father does not intend to be so insensitive, dear Cat. However, it certainly seems to me that—"

Catherine interrupted her cousin. "Pray say no more, Henry. I am not at all distressed. My father wishes all to seem the same between myself and the viscount, and of a certainty it would be thought odd if Lord Kenelm were never a guest in our house. As a dutiful daughter, I have agreed to abide by his wishes, which must include receiving the viscount with civility. There is no cause for astonishment in that."

Henrietta had her own thoughts on Catherine's surprising declaration on duty, which had not seemed to weigh with dear Cat overmuch in the past, but for once she held her peace. Henrietta began to anticipate a rather interesting evening and she bustled off to the kitchen to consult with the cook on the preparation of the repast.

When Mr. Talbot sent word that he would be bringing a friend to the dinner, Henrietta threw up her hands. "I do wish he had consulted us first. You know how robust Christopher's gentlemen friends can be. Besides which, we are already short on ladies, and how we are to be seated at table is what I should like to know. But it is mostly family and hopefully should not matter too much in the end. I shall simply have to tell Cook that there will be another gentleman sitting down to dinner and perhaps an extra meat pie can be made up. I am persuaded that if the unknown gentleman does not indulge himself overmuch, then we shall have sufficient quantities of the currant pudding."

"And if we do not, I shall cheerfully give up my portion," said Catherine. She held out Christopher's hastily scrawled note for Henrietta's inspection. "But see here in the corner, Henry. Chris says that he is shortly leaving London. I wonder why, when he told us only days ago that he meant to stay awhile."

"Oh, but I am not at all surprised. He is always more at home at Ravensclaw than anywhere else. Indeed, I am astonished that he remained in town as long as he has," said Henrietta comfortably. "Cat, I am thinking of my watered silk for this evening. I have donned it so many times that it appears to me very nearly worn out, but it is my favorite blue and we are only entertaining the viscount, after all. And Christopher's friend, of course. What is your opinion?"

Lost in thought, Catherine gave her a somewhat abstracted answer. She had suddenly realized that she had not planned her own toilet. Even though she was determined to show Lord Kenelm that he no longer had the power to disturb her, she also wanted to present the most attractive appearance possible. She suspected that Lord Kenelm was beginning to sense that her defenses were shaken and she hoped to reverse that impression. His lordship was to be made aware that she was not a watering pot, sighing with tearful regret over the loss of his exalted name and person. She excused herself to Henrietta and went up to her bedroom to consult with Sadie.

The dresser was enthusiastic when she was told what was required. Ever since Catherine had sent the viscount away, Sadie had cherished hopes that her mistress could somehow regain his lordship's regard. She had interpreted their continued social contact as a hopeful sign, but Catherine's request seemed a heaven-sent opportunity and she used every ounce of her considerable skill to bring out the best in her mistress's appearance. The gown she chose for Catherine had never before been worn; it was a confection of rose satin with lace insets, a swooping décolletage, and elegant puffed sleeves. Tiny seed pearls trimmed the bodice and insets.

Catherine wore pearls in her ears and a simple string of the lustrous beads about her neck. When she glanced at herself in the mirror, she knew that she had rarely appeared more beautiful. She was not aware that the soft glow of anticipation in her wide green eyes had more to do with her beauty than did the gown.

Chapter 20

Catherine returned downstairs only moments before dinner was announced. When she opened the drawing-room door, she paused briefly in the entrance. She knew that her and Sadie's efforts had been successful when the gentlemen's eyes lit with startled admiration. Lord Talbot came to meet her and lifted her hand to his lips. "You are magnificent tonight, daughter," he said.

"Thank you, Papa," she said, smiling warmly at him. Her gaze wandered to Lord Kenelm, who stood at the pianoforte with Henrietta to aid in looking through the sheet music. Catherine's glance met and clashed a moment with the viscount's, then deliberately she turned her eyes to her brother. "Christopher, I am always glad to see you," she said, walking up to kiss him on his cheek.

"Have I told you recently how nicely you have turned out? Quite different from the hoyden I grew up with, in fact," said Mr. Talbot softly, looking down at her with a grin. Catherine laughed and shook her head. Her brother drew her hand over his arm as he turned with her to the gentleman behind him, who rose hurriedly from the settee. "Catherine, I believe you have met my guest before this, the Honorable Mr. William Avery."

"Your servant, my lady," said Mr. Avery, taking her free hand.

Catherine's expression had chilled even as he bowed to her. "Mr. Avery. Indeed, how could I forget our first meeting? I believe that you were quite free with your opinions."

Mr. Avery reddened. "I beg your pardon, Miss Talbot. I realized some time later that I was perhaps too free."

There was an amused chuckle at Catherine's shoulder. "I apprehend that you are a trifle discomfited, William. Pray allow me to rescue you," said Lord Kenelm. With a nod to Mr. Talbot, he led Catherine off to an unoccupied settee at a distance from the rest of the party.

Catherine did not know what she should do. She did not in the least wish to be private with the viscount, yet it was so hard to resist his masterful manner without appearing insufferably rude. She directed a glance of mute appeal in Henrietta's direction, but that lady seemed suddenly very much preoccupied in showing Lord Talbot the selection of music in her hands. "Drat Henry!" muttered Catherine under her breath.

"Did you say something, my lady?" Lord Kenelm asked. His eyes laughed at her.

"It was nothing, my lord," Catherine said shortly. She felt herself to have been neatly trapped and it was intolerable that he had so obviously guessed it.

"What a pity. I had hoped it was the beginning of a sparkling conversation between us." Lord Kenelm picked up her hand and turned it over to trace her palm with his finger. "We used to speak so comfortably together, Catherine, did we not?"

Catherine felt her heart begin to race at his touch. She hastily withdrew her hand from his gentle clasp. "But then we were betrothed, my lord. Surely you do not expect the same ease between us now."

"Then let us begin again. Cat, I am willing to leave our past misunderstandings behind us." His voice was low, his gaze incredibly warm, and Catherine wondered wildly how just a glance could turn her to molten gold. She tried to gather the tattered rags of her determination, but it was impossible to steel her heart against him when he slowly caressed the sensitive inner side of her bare arm.

It was all the more sensual because it was done so scandalously in public.

"My lord, pray stop," begged Catherine, throwing a speaking glance toward her father and the rest of the party.

"I am a rake, my lady, do not forget. And you are very much the object of my desire."

Catherine's face flamed. "My lord!"

The viscount laughed softly, but eased himself slightly away from her. "For the moment only, sweet Catherine. But I warn you, I am not yet done storming your defenses." He reached into his coat pocket and withdrew something. He held out his hand, palm up, and there lay a golden curl of hair. "I believe this once belonged to you, my lady."

Catherine stared at the curl, so undeniably and damnably hers. Her thoughts tumbled; the token was supposed to have been in her father's possession. She could not imagine how Lord Kenelm had got it, or why he should choose to wait so long to confront her. She remembered the odd waiting expression in his eyes that she had now and again surprised and she felt quite ill. Her face had whitened when at last she looked up at him. "I suppose you have come to denounce me," she said, a strained quality in her voice which Lord Kenelm heard at once.

"Take it, Catherine. It belongs to you," he said quietly.

She searched his face. She did not see the condemnation she expected to in his expression. "But why?" she asked, more to understand him than anything else.

"You made a foolish wager, nothing more," he said gently.

Catherine felt tears start to her eyes and she averted her face. She had not expected charity from him and least of all understanding. "I cannot. I am sorry, my lord."

Lord Kenelm raised her hand to his lips. "As I am, Catherine, for every cruel word that I have uttered and for every thoughtless action. I hope most humbly that you can forgive me, my lady."

Catherine turned quickly. She could hardly believe what she had heard. "Oh, Justin!" Her green eyes were bright with unshed tears.

"If we were anywhere else but here, I would snatch you up in my arms and make passionate love to you," he said, his head bent close to her ear. "I mean to marry you yet, Lady Cat. And when I do you shall not be allowed out of bed for a fortnight."

Catherine felt herself blushing. She did not again draw her hand away when he clasped her fingers between his own. A part of her mind questioned the happiness that she was feeling, jibing at her for losing herself so quickly to the viscount's charm. But she did not care. Justin meant to marry her after all. He must care for her, and that was all she had ever wanted.

"I beg pardon if I am *de trop,* but dinner has been announced this past five minutes," said Lord Talbot in his blandest tone.

Catherine looked up, startled, and the color deepened in her face.

"Of course, sir. We shall be with you at once," said Lord Kenelm, rising from the settee with Catherine on his arm. She was embarrassed to discover that she and the viscount were the object of great curiosity from everyone else in the room, but she pretended that she did not notice as they joined the others before the open drawing-room door.

Suddenly, on the threshold, appeared the Earl of Belchester. His gold-flecked brown eyes were hard as he surveyed the surprised company. When his gaze fell on Lord Kenelm, Catherine standing beside him, his thin-lipped mouth tightened.

"My lord!" gasped Henrietta. "If I had but known you would be joining us, I am sure we would have waited dinner a few moments longer."

"I have not come for dinner, madam." The earl's voice was clipped. He directed a bow toward Lord Talbot. "I realize that I intrude, sir, and I proffer my apologies at this time. However, I feel it is imperative that I speak to you, Lord Talbot, and the viscount."

"Lord, but the old gentleman is in a flaming temper," muttered Mr. Avery for his friend's ear. "What has set him off, I wonder?"

The earl's steely gaze swept over his youngest son. "I am not yet deaf, William. Be so good as to confine your comments until such time as they are required." His son blenched.

Lord Talbot came forward. "I apprehend that you are operating under sizable upset, my lord. Pray reveal to us the trouble."

"I prefer privacy, my lord," said the earl haughtily.

"What is it that should demand such immediate, private consideration, sir?" Lord Kenelm asked slowly. His eyes were on his sire's wrathful face. He felt himself tense and unconsciously he drew Catherine closer to his side as though to shield her.

The earl slapped his leather gloves forcibly against his thigh. "I see that you will have it before all the world, Justin. You were always one to thumb the conventions, were you not? Very well, this once I lower myself to your level. It has been brought to my attention that Miss Talbot is the talk of London. She consorted openly with that rubbish Lord Haversaw and even saw fit to bestow a love token upon him. I will not have it, sir, and so I tell you! I will not have one of your same ilk as the next Countess of Belchester."

There was a gasp. Catherine did not know if it was Henrietta's or her own, but she found herself falling back in the face of the earl's unutterable contempt. The viscount's fingers tightened painfully on her elbow and dragged her back to his side. Startled, she looked up to find that his face was flinty with anger as he stared with blazing yellow eyes at his father. "You have gone too far, sir!"

"Have I indeed! I told you once before, Justin, that I would no longer allow scandal in our family. I thought that requiring you to wed would slow your race to ruin, but I see it is not so. You have found just such a one as yourself—a rake and a gamester!" said the earl bitterly.

Catherine swayed as though she had been struck. The color drained from her face, leaving her eyes dark pools. She had the oddest sensation of falling swiftly down a deep well.

"Now see here!" exploded Mr. Talbot, his fists bunched as he took a hasty step toward the Earl of Belchester. Mr. Avery made an ineffectual gesture of protest as he saw his friend's threatening advance, but he found that he was rooted with horror.

Mr. Talbot was stopped in his tracks by Lord Talbot's outflung arm. "It is not for you, Christopher. His lordship insults me first in maligning our Catherine," said Lord Talbot harshly. His eyes were cold as winter ice as he stared at the Earl of Belchester. "You are wrong about my daughter. I shall demand a retraction of you before you leave this house."

"That will not be necessary." All eyes turned to Catherine, who had drawn apart from the viscount and stood alone, her eyes incredibly dark against her white face. "His lordship voices strong doubts of my suitability as the next Countess of Belchester. He no longer need concern himself. My betrothal to Lord Kenelm is at an end."

"Catherine!"

She shook loose Justin's hands and turned on him such a look of loathing that he drew back. "How dare you, sir! All your talk of respect and your lovemaking were naught but a mask. You were *required* to find someone to marry. I never mattered at all. If I had refused you, you would have gone on to another with the same fine words, the same kisses. I despise you!" Catherine flew past the Earl of Belchester out of the drawing room.

As he started to follow, the viscount's furious gaze chanced to fall on his younger brother, who was appalled by the scene. Lord

Kenelm's eyes narrowed unpleasantly. "I see your hand in this, William. You carried the tale, did you not?" he said harshly. "Damn you!" He strode out of the drawing room, intent on catching Catherine.

Aware of the look of dawning disgust in Mr. Talbot's eyes, Mr. Avery shook his head violently. "I never said a word, I swear it. I decided not to. It was Justin's affair to do with as he saw fit."

"I abhor your judgment even as I admire your loyalty to your brother," said the earl. "In this instance it would have been best if you had come to me at once. When I learned of Miss Talbot's involvement with Lord Haversaw—"

"Lord Haversaw does not figure into it. He is dead," said Lord Talbot sharply.

The Earl of Belchester stared frowningly at him. "You are mistaken, sir. I heard but a day ago of his scandalous play with your daughter."

"Lord Haversaw committed suicide this week. My daughter was never involved with the gentleman in the manner you have so plainly inferred. Once only was her name linked with his lordship's, and that was over a foolish wager," said Lord Talbot, his voice hard. "Your information was both deceptive and malicious."

The Earl of Belchester stood silent for some minutes. There came an oddly pained expression into his eyes, almost one of embarrassment.

By Jove, the old gentleman is mortified, William realized with amazement. He had never beheld his thoroughly correct sire in greater discomfort.

"Perhaps I have acted in error. If that is so, pray accept my profound apologies," said the earl stiffly. He bowed in Henrietta's direction. Then he turned on his heel and left quickly. The front door closed decisively behind him.

"Well! I concluded weeks ago that the Earl of Belchester was an odd man, but I never dreamed him capable of such a freakish start," said Henrietta faintly.

It struck Mr. Avery as an exquisitely funny observation and he began to laugh uproariously. The three Talbots turned to find him doubled over the back of a chair. Tears streamed down his cheeks. He gasped, "Forgive me, ma'am. But the mortification in his face! And then to hear the proud old gentleman described as odd or—or freakish! It is wonderful, I swear!"

When Lord Kenelm burst into the hall, he caught a glimpse of Catherine's gleaming skirt whisking past the banister posts above. "Catherine!" Unheeding of the openmouthed footmen, he took the stairs three at a time. But he did not succeed in catching up with her before the door to her sitting room slammed shut. Lord Kenelm wrenched on the knob but it did not turn. He pounded on the door panel. "Cat! Unlock this door at once!" There was no response from within. Thoroughly losing his head, he threw his shoulder against the door with force enough to rattle the hinges.

"My lord! I pray you—"

Lord Kenelm shook off the restraining hands on his shoulder. He directed a blazing stare at the elderly butler who had followed him and the two footmen who hovered close behind. Their expressions of shock brought him to a realization of how his actions must appear. The viscount stepped back and took a deep breath. He said, "I shall be downstairs. Pray convey my deepest regards to Miss Talbot and my request that I be granted an audience." He strode back down the way he had come. His eyes glittered as he thought of what he would shortly say to his father.

Catherine was actually disappointed when Justin stopped beating on the door. A moment longer and she would have flung it open simply to give him a thoroughly deserved raking-down. Lord, what a fool she had been! It was all clear to her now—Lord Kenelm's request to postpone an announcement of their dissolved betrothal and his subsequent attentiveness. None of it had meant a thing to him. He was required to have a bride, and bride he would have. She had been his original choice and the only reason he still meant to have her was because she had once dared to spurn him. The arrogance of the man knew no depth.

"How I despise him!" breathed Catherine. He had used her from first to last. His sweet words of reconciliation had been but more of the same, she thought furiously. Her eyes flashed. But Lord Kenelm would not so use her again. He would not be granted the opportunity.

Chapter 21

Lord Kenelm found the Talbots and his brother still in the drawing room, but there was no sign of the Earl of Belchester. Balked of his original prey, his furious gaze settled on Mr. Avery. "My dear brother, I warned you once of carrying tales, did I not? It is a pity that you did not heed me." He advanced menacingly on William, but the younger man moved with a surprising swiftness for one of his build.

Mr. Avery put the occasional table between himself and the viscount. He stammered, "Justin, you mistake! I did not breathe a word to the old gentleman, I swear it. I thought of it, but I did not."

Lord Kenelm did not appear to hear him.

Mr. Talbot deliberately placed himself in the viscount's path. "William speaks the truth, my lord. The earl himself denounced your brother for not coming to him," he said.

Lord Kenelm stared into Mr. Talbot's steady eyes and read the truth in them. He passed a hand briefly over his face and sighed. "I must have been mad." He smiled wearily over the table at his brother. "I had no right to leap to the conclusion that I did. I hope that you will accept my apology, William."

Mr. Avery eyed him somewhat askance, but he nodded. "I willingly do so, Justin. Lord, but you gave me quite a turn just now. I am still queasy to the stomach."

"And I do not wonder at it, as upsetting a time as we have had, and no dinner to speak of. Mr. Avery, I insist that you sit down to the table at once. You will feel much more the thing after a little barley soup and a claret cup. Come, Thomas, we shall all go in. I only hope that dinner is not quite ruined," said Henrietta, firmly taking control. She linked her hands through Lord Talbot's and Mr. Avery's elbows and urged them out of the drawing room. Over her shoulder she said, "Christopher, pray show the viscount the way, for I do not believe that we shall have poor Cat joining us this evening, after all."

"No, I do not imagine we will," said Mr. Talbot with the ghost of a grimace. He slid a glance at the viscount's frowning face. "You have at last run headfirst into my sister's perverse temper. What think you? Will you still have her?"

The viscount was startled. Then he said evenly, "I think the question is more whether she will have me. It was a damnable piece of work that was done this night."

"Aye, it is as bad as it can be," agreed Christopher. He eyed the viscount with a change of expression. "I knew of the estrangement between you and Catherine, but earlier this evening it appeared that it was well-nigh put aside."

"As I had hoped, Miss Talbot was not entirely immune to my persuasions. But that is of no moment now. My father has seen to that all too well," said Lord Kenelm with a flash of bitterness.

"My lord, do you love her?" asked Mr. Talbot softly.

Lord Kenelm did not answer at once. He stared unseeingly at the butler who appeared in the drawing-room doorway. "I do not think that I could now live without her," he said quietly. He glanced at his companion, a fleeting smile crossing his face. "I am in the deuced of a fix, my friend. The lady of my heart will have none of me."

"I would not be too certain of that, my lord. Your proposal of a marriage of convenience deeply wounded Cat. I shall allow you to guess why. As for tonight's drama, you are a man of polished address. Perhaps if you but found the right words, she may yet come about," said Mr. Talbot. He looked at the butler. "What is it, Hobson?"

"I have come with a message from Miss Talbot for his lordship," the butler said reluctantly. There was a pained expression on his normally wooden countenance.

Lord Kenelm threw up his hand. "Pray do not convey it, Hobson. I can well imagine the lady's response. I doubt if my pride could withstand another beating this night. Christopher, let us join the others at dinner. If what I gather from your broad hint is true, I shall need proper sustenance to carry me through the next battle."

Mr. Talbot laughed, and the two gentlemen left the drawing room.

Catherine did not go down for dinner, nor for breakfast the following morning. Instead, she requested that a pot of chocolate and a plate of toast be brought to her room. When Henrietta heard of it, she said, "At least that is an encouraging sign. She is apparently not going into a decline."

Lord Talbot stared at his cousin. "I believe that is the daftest thing you have ever uttered, Henrietta," he said, before rising with his paper still in hand. "I shall be at the club if I am wanted."

With her mouth agape, Henrietta watched him stride out of the sitting room. She turned to Mr. Talbot. "Well! I have never received such a look! What have I said to upset your father so?"

"He is simply anxious on Cat's account. Pay him no heed," said Mr. Talbot. Restlessly he moved around the porcelain figurines on the mantel. "I am supposed to journey down to Ravensclaw with William Avery this afternoon. I had hoped to see Cat before then."

Henrietta smiled and held out her hand to him. "Come to luncheon, Christopher. Your sister is not one to skip more than one or two meals, you know. I should not be at all surprised to find her down then, especially as I have instructed Cook to prepare all her favorite dishes. And Sadie has promised me faithfully to mention the menu to her."

"You are a complete hand, Henry. I do not know how we would go on without you. I only hope you are proved right," said Mr. Talbot, giving her frail fingers a brief, grateful squeeze before he let them go.

"So do I," sighed Henrietta, taking up her embroidery hoop once more.

Catherine did indeed come down to the dining room for luncheon, but she only picked at her food. Henrietta and Mr. Talbot exchanged an eloquent glance. They each attempted to carry on a sprightly conversation, but it was made all the more difficult by Lord Talbot's refusal to be drawn into it. Instead, he glanced frequently in the direction of his unusually withdrawn daughter. As for Catherine, nothing appeared to make the least impression with her, not even when her brother announced that he was leaving London within the hour.

"Indeed? I suppose that you will be returning to Ravensclaw," she said indifferently.

"Yes, I am taking William Avery with me. He expressed a fondness for the country and I hope to show him a splendid visit."

At last Catherine showed some interest. Two bright spots of color appeared in her pale cheeks. "I hope that you do not mean to make a friendship with that gentleman, Christopher. I would take it in extreme bad form if you were to associate with any of that particular family."

While her brother still stared at her in stupefaction, Lord Talbot said, "Catherine, that is quite enough. We are all aware of your unhappiness, my dear, but you need not think that gives you the right to order whom Christopher does or does not befriend. One cannot order a loved one's actions to suit themselves."

"But is that not exactly what you had me do, Papa? On your order, I agreed to pretend that my betrothal to the viscount was still existent. I even continued to wear his ring. It has brought me nothing but humiliation. But yet it is not seemly for me to request that Christopher refrain from associating with those who have wounded me so gravely," said Catherine. Her father had an arrested hurt in his eyes but she paid no heed. She placed her napkin beside her unfinished plate and rose. "I believe it is quite past the time to think of my own life once more." She swept out of the dining room.

"Oh dear, oh dear," said Henrietta worriedly. "Thomas, what do you think she means to do?"

"I am certain we shall discover it soon enough," said Lord Talbot grimly.

Though Mr. Talbot was now even more disinclined to leave London, after luncheon he reluctantly said his farewells and went to meet William Avery. He was therefore not present when Catherine tripped down the stairs dressed to go out. Henrietta espied her from the drawing room and came quickly into the hall. She spared a quick glance for the wooden-faced maid who stood beside Catherine and at Sadie's slight shake of the head her heart sank. "Why, Catherine! Wherever are you going? I was not aware that we had a call to make today. Do but wait a moment while I put on my bonnet and pelisse and I shall accompany you."

Catherine finished drawing on her kid gloves. "That will not be necessary, Henry. Sadie will be accompanying me." With that, she nodded to the porter to open the front door, and she left the house.

Henrietta saw that a carriage was waiting at the curb and she watched with misgivings as Catherine and her maid entered it. "I wonder what she is about?" she murmured. A footman asked if she required anything and Henrietta waved him away irritably as she went in search of Lord Talbot.

It was some hours before Catherine returned. Lord Talbot and Henrietta were preparing to sit down to dinner. Catherine took her usual place at the table, appearing calm and completely composed. For once at a loss for words, Henrietta rolled her eyes in an urgent appeal to Lord Talbot. "I trust that your outing proved beneficial, daughter," he said.

"Indeed, it was." Catherine looked up from her soup. The expression in her green eyes was cool. "I have spent a most interesting afternoon with our solicitor, Papa. Once I convinced him of my determination to do so, I learned all the details of my independence. You should know immediately that I have requested him to procure for me a residence in Bath."

Henrietta froze with her wineglass halfway to her lips. "Bath! Your independence! Whatever are you talking about, Catherine? I understand none of it," she said in liveliest dismay.

Lord Talbot did not remove his eyes from his daughter's face. "I believe I do understand, however. Are you certain you do not wish to return to Ravensclaw, Catherine?"

"Not return to Ravensclaw! Cat, I demand to be told what it is you have done," exclaimed Henrietta sharply.

Catherine ignored her agitated interruptions. "I am quite certain, Papa. At least, not yet. I wish to have some time to myself. I know that you do not approve, and indeed you probably wish that you had never set up the independence at all. However, I hope that you will understand," Catherine said.

"You are correct on all three counts, Catherine," Lord Talbot said, smiling tiredly.

Henrietta set down her glass with a snap. "I have finally realized what this is about, and I tell you to your head, Catherine, that I will not allow it. Even though your father will not lift a finger to prevent it, you are not going off to racket about Bath. It would be the crowning straw to a horridly uncomfortable Season," she said forcibly.

"I am sorry if it has been horrid for you, Henry, but there is nothing you can say to change my mind. Indeed, I have quite burned my bridges behind him. This afternoon I inserted a notice in the

Gazette that my betrothal to Lord Kenelm is no longer an item. I have also returned the viscount's ring to him by the post. I shall doubtless be a social outcast before the week is out. So you see, I really have no wish to remain in London," said Catherine.

"As if I care for any of that," exclaimed Henrietta. "My dear Cat, *I* know what it is like to lose a gentleman. You need not think I will attempt to prevail upon you to stay here when it is so very painful. But I will not have you unchaperoned in Bath. Therefore, I intend to accompany you. And only try to dissuade me!"

Catherine was startled into laughter. "Why, Henry, I had no inkling that was what you were thinking! I thought . . . But never mind. Certainly, you may accompany me. I would like it of all things."

"That's settled, then," Henrietta said with a nod. She turned to Lord Talbot. "I hope you do not mind it overmuch, Thomas, but I shall look after her, I promise you. And I shall be certain to depress any who would dare look down their noses when wind of this affair reaches Bath."

"You relieve my mind of its most pressing concerns, Henrietta," said Lord Talbot. There was an amused note in his voice, yet he also managed to convey sincere appreciation and gratitude toward his cousin. He lifted her hand and lightly kissed it. Henrietta flushed with pleasure; she was more used to his lordship's tolerance than his approval.

It was weeks before Catherine heard anything positive from the solicitor concerning the search for a suitable residence. In the meantime, Henrietta managed to fill the days with all sorts of planning and shopping activities.

Catherine refused to decline the invitations that came to Berkeley Square even after the whispering and the stares started. She simply ignored the avid looks and smilingly turned aside the catty remarks that were made to her face. Henrietta did her utmost to squelch the pretentious, and each day the light of battle grew brighter in her usually placid gaze. Lord Talbot always accompanied his ladies, making a strong unspoken statement that he stood in full support of his daughter. The Talbot defense was such that eventually public opinion slowly turned more fully on Lord Kenelm. It was wondered what he could possibly have done to create such a breach between himself and his betrothed. He had always been at the center of scandal, after all. Why should this occasion be any different? Those who sided with the Talbots said that it could hardly be wondered at that Miss Talbot had reconsidered her decision to wed the viscount.

For Lord Kenelm, the weeks since the disastrous evening at the Talbots' became a lesson in humility and frustration. He had sworn in fluent and colorful language when his ring was returned with no note to accompany it. He had thought he knew then the depth of Miss Talbot's anger. But he had taken Mr. Talbot's words to heart, and believing confidently in his own powers of persuasion, he had set out to rewin his lady's heart. But Catherine refused to see him when he called at Berkeley Street. His notes were returned to him unopened on the same day they were sent. He ordered flowers to be delivered every other day, certain that Catherine could not return those. And I have never yet known a woman whose anger could not be softened by a few fragile blooms, thought the viscount. His complacency was shaken when he learned that Catherine was giving away his offerings to whoever chanced to admire the dainty bouquets and sprays. "Damnation! What is to be done with such a woman?" he said explosively.

His valet jumped. "My lord?"

"It is nothing, Simmons. Hand me another cravat. I have ruined this one," said Lord Kenelm, wrenching the offending silk tie off his neck. Without a word the valet gave him the new cravat. Frowning, his mind still only partially on the task, the viscount's nimble fingers folded and creased the fine silk to a satisfactory appearance. Lord Kenelm thought over his dilemma for the hundredth time. His prospective brother-in-law had hinted that Miss Talbot was in love with him and that he could yet win her if he could but find the right words. But how was he to get the opportunity if she would not even grant him a moment or two? Lord Kenelm broodingly inspected his finished cravat in the mirror while Simmons waited with inheld breath.

The notice in the *Gazette* had created quite a stir, but Lord Kenelm had gone about in society just as he always had. He neither avoided the Talbots at the functions at which they all happened to be guests nor sought them out either. He had merely exchanged civil bows with Lord Talbot and the ladies before continuing on his way. He had not wanted to give the gossip tattlers any more food than necessary. But he thought that he had little choice now except to approach Miss Talbot in public. Surely, she could not refuse to speak to him with hundreds of eyes watching them. Though he disliked it, it was still the best alternative that he could think of. "It will have to do," he said. He turned to the relieved valet to collect his gloves.

The ball that evening was at Carlton House. Lord Kenelm could not think of a better place to approach Miss Talbot if he must do so during a public affair, for the Prince Regent's residence had several sitting rooms that he knew of where he could take Miss Talbot for privacy. And he fully intended that Miss Talbot was going to hear him out, even if he was obligated to force her to accompany him.

Chapter 22

Catherine had been to Carlton House only once before during the Season and her initial impression of unexpected simplicity had never quite left her. The Prince Regent's residence was in the very center of the fashionable world in Pall Mall. Inside the palace a Parisian influence could be seen in its octagon-shaped hall and handsome double staircase. The principal apartments were decorated with gilding, brass, and ormolu to create a harmonious effect throughout. Countless mirrors reflected blazing candlelight and the large company that mingled with much laughter and talk. The Prince Regent himself was still a handsome man, ruddy of complexion and possessing bright-blue eyes that admired the ladies who came within his vicinity.

Lord Talbot had grumbled when he learned that they were to attend a ball at Carlton House, and Henrietta scolded him roundly for his lack of enthusiasm for an invitation to the Prince Regent's hospitality. "I beg pardon, Henrietta, but I do not particularly anticipate an evening spent in a hot house," he had said. As she looked about her, Catherine could not help sympathizing with her father's comment. It was extremely hot in the rooms. Most of the ladies had had the good sense to attire themselves in their lightest gowns, but the gentlemen suffered in their coats and high cravats. Fans were much in view and their eddying offered the only relief attainable since the Prince Regent was known never to open his windows to the dangers of the night air.

Catherine had just finished a set on the dance floor and her partner had gone to procure a lemonade ice for her. She fanned herself, her face slightly pink with her recent exertion, and wished longingly for an open window.

"Well met, Miss Talbot," said a too-familiar voice beside her.

Catherine shut her fan with a snap and turned to face Lord Kenelm. Her one thought was to be rid of him as quickly as possible. "My lord, how fortuitous that you have found me. My throat is parched. Pray, could you find for me something cool to drink?" she asked.

Lord Kenelm smiled at her. He shook his head. "Coming it too strong, my lady. I am too experienced a hand to be taken in by such sudden friendliness. You wish me to the devil; I read it in your eyes."

"Indeed. Perhaps you should take heed, then," Catherine said.

"Not I. I am a persistent rogue, as you are well aware by now. Miss Talbot, I beg an audience of you. You cannot gainsay me forever," he said with the hint of a smile.

"I do not wish to talk with you, my lord, and indeed you shall soon find yourself quite *de trop*," said Catherine. "I am expecting a gentleman to join me at any moment."

"And undoubtedly he will be bringing an ice to you," said Lord Kenelm, nodding. "I see that I was wise in not playing the gallant. That was very unkind of you, my lady."

"Do go away!" begged Catherine.

"I shall, and with great speed, if only you will accompany me. I must and I shall talk to you, Catherine. And I am quite capable of doing so here, surrounded as we are by countless ears," Lord Kenelm said.

"You would not dare," said Catherine quickly.

"You forget, my lady. Viscount Kenelm is no stranger to scandal. I flaunt the conventions most blatantly," he said suavely.

Catherine looked at him with a frown. She thought that he probably spoke the truth, and much as she disliked the thought of talking privately with him, it was infinitely preferable than to have avid listeners hanging over her shoulder. She in no wise wished to have the details of their broken betrothal known; it was private humiliation enough. Lord Kenelm was holding out his arm to her. Catherine reluctantly slid her hand through his elbow and allowed him to guide her through the throng to a door giving onto a hall. She hung back then. "Is this not a private way, my lord?" she asked.

"There is a sitting room directly before us that is often used by guests who find themselves overcome by the heat," said Lord Kenelm. "We shall not be trespassing in the least, my lady."

Though still dubious, Catherine allowed him to lead her into the hall a few short steps. Lord Kenelm opened a door and courteously waited until she entered the sitting room before him. There was a fire in the grate, but the room was noticeably cooler than the overcrowded apartment that they had just left. Catherine breathed a little freer and began to recover from the wilted feeling that she had been suffering. She turned to the viscount. "Well, my lord?"

Lord Kenelm gestured for her to seat herself on the settee, but Catherine did not deign to notice. He sighed resignedly. "I see that we are to be antagonists. I wish it were not so, Catherine."

"Indeed? I cannot think why it should matter," she said coolly.

"But it matters a great deal, my lady. I have learned that what I had thought of little consequence has now become very precious to me. I speak of your respect and liking for me, Catherine. I know that I have handled the situation between us in an abominable fashion. I should have been more frank with you concerning the reason for my wanting to marry. Most of all, I should have been more aware of your sensitivities," said Lord Kenelm.

He looked at her a moment and thought how lovely she was. She was attired in a white gown with a silver overdress of gossamer lace.

Her slender shoulders were concealed only by the daintiest of puff sleeves and her slim throat by three strands of pearls. The brilliancy of her green eyes was startling against the pale tones of her skin and dress. She was a vision of cool beauty, distant and unattainable. He ached to take her into his arms and kiss her as he had that long-ago morning in her private sitting room.

"I can appreciate the effort that you have gone to in presenting this speech, my lord. I do not know how I am to respond, however," said Catherine.

"I had hoped that you might forgive me, ma'am," Lord Kenelm said quietly.

Catherine shrugged elaborately. "I can tell you only that I am not one to hold bitterness for slights given. Rest easy, Lord Kenelm. We can be as friends when we meet in society." She gathered her skirt and turned toward the door.

Lord Kenelm detained her by placing his hand on her arm. "Miss Talbot, I hope for more than a social friendliness between us. I wish to reinstate our betrothal and—"

"Pray say no more, my lord!" Catherine stared at him coldly. "I am aware that you must marry, sir, but I pray you to turn your sights on some other lady. I am not a fool. I do not put my hand twice into the same flame."

The viscount's breath was coming rather faster. "Catherine, pray heap no more coals upon my head. I am humbled and chastised—yes, and sick at heart for what has passed. I ask only that I be given another chance to prove the worth of my feelings for you."

"My lord, I wish I had two pennies to rub together to count the worth of your feelings," flashed Catherine. She gathered hold of her unraveling composure. It had been a mistake to agree to this private interview. He had still the power to cut through the shield she had erected between herself and the hurt he had inflicted on her. "I am certain my presence has been missed. I must return to the ballroom at once, my lord."

Instead of making his bow and escorting her from the sitting room as Catherine had expected him to do, the viscount suddenly gathered her roughly into his arms. She had little more time than to gasp before his lips descended upon hers. His mouth moved hungrily, seeking a response from her. The speed of his onslaught left Catherine motionless from shock for perhaps two seconds. Then her intellect came alive and she wrenched her head to one side. "No!" she choked. She struggled against the strength of his embrace, but his arms only tightened like iron bands about her.

"Catherine!" breathed the viscount. He drew back to look down with a passion-hooded gaze into her dark angry eyes. "You are mine, Cat. You are still in love with me, and so you will admit."

"Never! I detest you, do you hear? I detest you with all my being," exclaimed Catherine, twisting against his imprisoning hold. She panted with exertion and the tumult of emotions within her.

Lord Kenelm gave a low laugh. "My lady, I think I understand a woman's passions too well to believe you." One of his hands roved caressingly down the curve of her back.

Catherine slapped him with all her might. The hard crack of her palm against his cheek left a mottled red imprint. The viscount bit down on an oath. "That is how well you know me, my lord!" she hissed.

"We shall see," he said with grim purpose. His eyes had turned an odd yellow. He swung Catherine up in his arms and carried her to the settee, where he set her down with a thump. Catherine flung herself to one side, attempting to flee him, but he caught her back. Deliberately he pressed her captive against the cushions until she was half-reclining. He slowly let his glance pass over her face to follow the contour of her throat, to the pulse that beat wildly at its base, and down to the swell of her swift-rising bosom.

"I shall scream," said Catherine warningly.

"No one will hear you over the loud talk and music," said the viscount. He was no longer looking at her, but instead his head lowered to her neck. His lips trailed sensuously over her throat, found the intriguing pulse.

Catherine bit her lip. She glanced desperately about. Just past the viscount's shoulder was a blue porcelain vase on a stand. She stretched out her hand and her fingers closed about its neck. With all the force she was capable of, she brought the vase crashing down on the viscount's skull. He gave a kind of a grunt and half-fell off the settee to sit ludicrously on the floor, shattered porcelain all about him. His hand went gingerly to his head.

Quick as a bird, Catherine flew up from the settee and had crossed the sitting room before the viscount thought to look around. She opened the door but paused before she went through it. Her eyes held an expression of contempt for him. "Rakehell that you are, Lord Kenelm, I had thought you at least a gentleman." She swept out of the room and the door crashed shut.

Catherine paused before a hall mirror to glance at her reflection. She smoothed her hair with quick fingers and adjusted the left sleeve of her gown, which had slipped off her shoulder. The white carnations pinned to the front of her gown were sadly crushed, telling their tale all too plainly. With a grimace, Catherine unpinned the corsage. She glanced about for somewhere to rid herself of it, and her eyes fell on a Grecian urn in a wall recess beside the mirror. Quickly she dropped the bruised flowers out of sight and then calmly walked back into the ballroom. She found her father near the place she had vacated some minutes before while in the viscount's company. "Hello, Papa. Why are you not mingling with your friends?" she asked, reaching up to kiss his cheek.

"Even I tire of talk on the lack of proper trade," said Lord Talbot. He gazed at his daughter. She was all cool composure, but there was the faintest telltale rose in her cheeks. He did not think that her high color was due to the dancing, for he had not seen her on the floor the past several minutes as he had stood looking about him. "Do you enjoy yourself, daughter?" he asked.

Catherine shrugged and opened her fan to lazy movement. "It is a ball like any other, Papa. One is initially excited, but after a while it begins to pall. The buzz of conversation becomes much like the drone of bees and makes as much sense. But I find the heat tonight is particularly irritating."

Over her head, Lord Talbot caught sight of Lord Kenelm. He had emerged from a hall and stared in their direction. When his gaze met that of Lord Talbot's, he bowed slightly and turned away. "Yes, I can understand how the heat may strike one as annoying," said Lord Talbot, tongue-in-cheek. He laughed silently. "Shall we collect Henrietta and make our escape, Cat? I for one am quite willing to call an end to the evening."

Catherine closed her fan with force. "Indeed, nothing could be more welcome to me. I should like to experience the quiet of our own residence."

"You seem inordinately put out, Catherine. One could almost wonder whether you are irritated at more than the temperature," murmured Lord Talbot with a sliding glance at his daughter's face as he escorted her through the crowd.

Catherine managed a light laugh. "Do I? Then I am more tired than I knew. We have kept such a pace these past several weeks that I do not know if I am on my head or my heels. Oh, there is Henry. Who is that gentleman with her? He looks quite devoted to her. It astonishes me at times how many old beaux she has collected since returning to London. After our visit to Bath, I do not know if she will want to return to her same quiet life at Ravensclaw."

"And what of you, Catherine? Society is a heady wine, even in staid Bath. Will you ever be content to pick up your old life again?" asked Lord Talbot.

"Of course, I shall," Catherine said stoutly. But she felt the force of his question. There was some doubt in her mind, and she was bothered by it. Surely, she could not wish to continue the sort of life that she had experienced this Season. It had been all too hectic and frantic for a country miss such as herself. The debacle with Lord Kenelm had contributed inordinately to the overall feeling of frenzy. Yet, despite it all, there had been something peculiarly exciting about town life. At Ravensclaw life revolved about the seasons and for a short time the smuggling. Though Catherine had always been happy with her life at Ravensclaw, she knew how very unlike Christopher she was. Her brother lived and breathed the land. He found complete contentment in submerging himself in the affairs of Ravensclaw, whereas she had wondered from time to time if there was not something different to experience. There was a restless part of her heart that had never quite found its place—at least, not until she fell in love with Lord Kenelm. It had proven to be an unfortunate happening.

While Catherine was lost in her own thoughts, she and her father and Henrietta had made their way out of Carlton House onto Pall Mall, which had recently been furnished with the controversial new gas lamps. Henrietta had addressed her several times since they had left the ballroom, but had yet to elicit a response. Concerned, she asked, "Catherine, are you quite all right?"

Catherine was startled into awareness. "What, Henry? I am sorry, but I was woolgathering. What was it you said?"

"I merely asked if you had seen the viscount tonight. I am certain I caught a glimpse of him earlier," Henrietta said.

"Yes, I believe that his lordship was here. But his appearance or nonappearance is really of no significance to me, Henry," said Catherine, a little sharply.

"I did not think that it was, my dear," said Henrietta, glancing at her face. She had a thought, which she took care not to voice. It would wait for another time. Catherine was not at all amenable to suggestions at the moment. "Thomas, I thought you sent a servant after the carriage, but here we are, still standing on the walk."

"Patience, Henrietta. Give the driver a chance to thread his way through this appalling traffic," said Lord Talbot with a sigh. He thought that he understood human character better than most, but he was at a loss to explain why his ladies should both of a sudden become unaccountably snappish.

Chapter 23

When Lord Kenelm stepped out the door of his town house he was the very picture of a fine gentleman. Attired in a tight-fitting coat tailored by Weston and black pantaloons, he carried white gloves, a silver-headed cane, and wore a silk beaver. He paused on the steps to draw on his gloves before continuing down to climb into the carriage waiting at the curb.

Through the grapevine Lord Kenelm had learned that the Talbots would be attending the theater performance at Drury Lane that evening. He stared unseeingly out the carriage window as it wended its way to the Theater Royal. He hoped to be able to speak to Miss Talbot in her box between acts. His thoughts were occupied with what he wanted to say to her.

At the theater, Lord Kenelm awaited his chance. As soon as the curtain went down on the first act, he left his own box to saunter down the hall toward the Talbots' box. When he saw that the Talbots momentarily did not have any other visitor in the box, he walked in.

Catherine saw him immediately and stiffened. "My lord, you are not welcome here," she said coldly.

"How well you make that clear, Miss Talbot. You could undoubtedly teach a thing or two to an iceberg," said Lord Kenelm dryly. "However, I am made of stern stuff and I am not frosted so easily." He saw the flash of anger in her eyes. "Catherine, I beg a moment only to plead my case. Is that so much to ask?"

Catherine turned her shoulder on him. Lord Talbot and Henrietta were interested observers, and Catherine addressed her father. "Papa, pray show the viscount the door. He appears to have forgotten where it is located."

Before Lord Talbot could reply, Henrietta plucked at his sleeve. His lordship glanced at her inquiringly. "I think that the viscount should at least be given the courtesy of a hearing, Thomas," said Henrietta quietly. She did not glance at Catherine, knowing what her reaction might be. But she had given the breach between Catherine and Justin some thought after the ball at Carlton House, and she had decided that Lord Kenelm deserved a chance to right things if he could.

"Henry!" exclaimed Catherine, outraged by her cousin's betrayal. She was even more put out when Lord Talbot nodded in agreement.

"Perhaps you are right, Henrietta. My lord, I shall grant you the few minutes you desire. Henrietta and I are in need of refreshment. We shall step outside to the foyer until the next curtain rises," said Lord Talbot. So saying, he and Henrietta rose from their seats and left the box. After bowing them out, Lord Kenelm locked the door to the box.

Catherine observed his action with indignation. She was flushed with both anger and a sort of dread. "Is it to be another seduction scene, my lord?" she asked with irony as she nodded at the locked door.

Instead of approaching her, Lord Kenelm remained close beside the door. He leaned one broad shoulder against the patterned wall. "I shall not come near you, since that is your wish, Miss Talbot. See, my hands are in my pockets. You are safe from my lovemaking."

"How very amusing, sir," she said. She made a point of glancing over the edge of the box to the stage below. The curtain was not yet rising on the next act, and she frowned. Lord Talbot and Henrietta would not be making their way back, then. She was made uncomfortable to be alone with the viscount. However much she wished to deny it, she was still attracted to him. Shall I not ever be free of him? she wondered while her eyes absently followed the comings and goings in the gallery seats below.

As though he read her thoughts, Lord Kenelm's voice cut into her brown study. "Catherine, you shall not dismiss me so easily. I will not allow it, you see. I am determined to make you understand that I care for you, so deeply that I am willing to humble myself at your feet, if that is your desire."

She did not turn. After a tense moment Lord Kenelm went toward the front of the box until he stood but an arm's length away from her. He made no move to touch her. He said, "Catherine, I made a terrible error at Carlton House. I had thought only to speak to you. But you were so beautiful and distant that I lost all sense of propriety."

"It is an overweening fault of yours, sir," Catherine said coolly.

Lord Kenelm forced himself to laugh. The interview was going badly against him, and he did not know how to retrieve it. "So you made me profoundly aware, my dear lady. I beg your forgiveness for the offense I gave you."

Catherine swept him with an indifferent glance. "It is of no moment, my lord," she said. She yawned delicately behind her gloved hand.

Lord Kenelm felt his opportunity to be slipping inexorably away. He captured her hand in a desperate attempt to break through her obvious lack of interest. "Catherine! I appeal to what you once felt for me. Surely you can understand the torment that I now undergo. Catherine, I have fallen in love with you."

Catherine looked at him with unfathomable eyes. She recalled a time when she would have given all she possessed to hear just such a declaration from him. But she thought she now knew what value to place on such words coming forth from Viscount Kenelm. He was a rakehell; tender words and half-truths were his stock-in-trade. There must be a legion of women in his past who had succumbed to just such an appeal. Catherine did not intend to make one of their number. She pulled free her hand. "You have always reserved a pretty phrase for me, Lord Kenelm. But I have learned to my past sorrow that the words meant nothing. I do not intend to be taken advantage of so easily ever again, my lord, so you may spare yourself this effort. I shall not listen to a word you utter."

"I shall have no choice, then. I mean to haunt you at every function until you do condescend to listen to me, Lady Cat," said Lord Kenelm with an attempt at a smile.

"How thankful I am that I am shortly to leave London! I shall not then be forced to endure such unwelcome persecution," Catherine said hastily. She was breathing very fast with her tumbled emotions. "You speak of love when you do not know the meaning of it. What you feel is wounded pride, my lord, nothing more. I am but the woman who escaped your infamous charm. It galls you, does it not? Rest easy, my lord. I am certain that there are many others who will succumb to you. But as for me ... How I have come to despise you, my lord!"

Lord Kenelm stood very still. His eyes were blank with shock. He said finally, "I see, ma'am. I did not before appreciate that my presence had become so wretched a burden. I beg that you forgive my obtuseness. It was certainly never my intention to persecute you, Miss Talbot. I shall not insinuate myself upon your notice again." He unlocked the box door and opened it without looking again in her direction.

Even as he stepped out of the box, Catherine swiftly put out a detaining hand. But too late. Lord Kenelm was gone. She gazed unseeingly over the edge of the box and did not know when an acquaintance in a neighboring box waved to gain her attention.

Lord Kenelm blindly made his way down the hall to the foyer and descended the curving staircase to the lower foyer. All that he could think of was that he had lost the only woman he had ever truly loved. She was gone to him forever. He was seized by an almost overwhelming grief. Without being aware of it, he emerged from the theater's portico and stumbled down the steps to the sidewalk. Lord Kenelm wandered aimlessly, finally stopping to lean against a lamppost. He was oblivious to the stares of passersby.

Several moments passed during which he was in deep despair. Gradually Lord Kenelm became aware of increased activity about him. He was an island in a sea of hurrying individuals of all classes. There was an excited quality in the shouts he heard. Of a sudden Lord Kenelm realized what was being said.

"Fire! The Theater Royal is afire!"

He swung around to stare over the bobbing heads on the sidewalk in the direction he had just come. Horror engulfed him when he saw the billowing black smoke, visible against the vivid flames that shot forth from the windows and doors of the theater. Figures stumbled out of the blazing building to be lost in the growing crowd of exclaiming onlookers in the street.

"My God! Cat!" Lord Kenelm began to thrust his way through the crowd, heedless of the protests and oaths generated in the wake of his rough passage. Somewhere along the way he lost his beaver and cane. He reached the portico. The pungent smoke caught in his throat and stung his eyes to water. Coughing, he pulled up his coat in an effort to protect his face before he plunged into the building. The foyer was a scene of mad panic. Screams and urgent shouts rent the air as ladies and gentlemen alike climbed over those who had fallen in the mindless scramble to safety. A few brave souls did their best to aid those no longer able to help themselves, but it was a pitiful effort. Crashes could be heard as parts of the roof began to give way.

Lord Kenelm stared about, intent on finding a familiar face in the eddying smoke. But he did not see the one face above all others that he wanted desperately to find. He slowly fought his way through the mill and started up the curving staircase to the boxes above. Halfway up a hoarse voice hailed him.

"Lord Kenelm! My lord!"

Despite his watering eyes, Lord Kenelm peered closely to his left. Lord Talbot stood on the stairs, one hand clutching the smooth banister. The other arm was clamped tight about an unconscious Henrietta. She dragged heavily on him and his face was white with strain. Lord Talbot shifted slightly and his supporting arm came into view. Lord Kenelm was appalled by the deep stain that soaked his sleeve. "Lord Talbot! You are hurt!"

Lord Talbot glanced down at his arm almost with surprise. He said matter-of-factly, "Aye, we were in the foyer when one of the lamps broke free. The blood spurted and Henrietta fainted dead away, damn her eyes." He was suddenly seized by a paroxysm of coughing that nearly doubled him over.

Lord Kenelm glanced swiftly about them. "What of Cat? Where is she? Is she out?"

Lord Talbot shook his head. There was a terrible fear in his eyes. "I do not know. We did not have time to return to the box before everything went up in flame. I beg of you, Justin, find her."

Lord Kenelm hardly heard his lordship's last words as he plunged upward. At the top of the stairs he became momentarily disoriented by the thick smoke. But he got his bearings and took the hall at a run, crouching to stay below the worst of the pall of smoke. The heat was worse. Here and there tongues of red flame ate at the walls. Close to where he knew the Talbots' box was, Lord Kenelm stumbled over some beams that had fallen through the ceiling to the floor. He was on the point of moving on when he suddenly espied a pitiful heap lying half under one of the beams and squeezed up against the wall. His heart came into his mouth. He knew without doubt that he had found her.

With maniacal strength he lifted the beam from off her, then went to one knee to pull her into his arms. With the greatest fear, Lord Kenelm wrenched aside the cloak that she had wrapped about her head. She coughed wretchedly in the smoke and he had never heard a more welcome sound.

Her hand came up to clutch his lapel. She blinked up at him and tears streaked her smoke-blackened face. "My leg is broken," she said hoarsely.

Without a word Lord Kenelm lifted her over his shoulder and retreated at a fast crouch back down the hall. Behind them more beams crashed through the ceiling, and under his feet the floor shivered. Breathing shallowly, Lord Kenelm staggered down the stairs. The sweat poured from his brow. He could feel time growing short.

He burst out of the theater door onto the portico and heaved a gasp for air. His lungs expanded gratefully, reinvigorating him. Lord Kenelm did not stop, but went on until he was a comfortable distance from the burning theater, which had now become but a blazing inferno. He was able to hail a hackney cab and carefully deposited his precious burden on the seat inside. After directing the driver to Berkeley Street, he climbed in and fell onto the seat close beside his lady. She had begun to recover from the stupefaction caused by the quantities of smoke she had inhaled, and her first thought was for her family. She tried to reach the latched door. "But we cannot go! Papa . . . and Henry!"

Lord Kenelm took hold of her wrist gently. "I have already seen them. They are safe," he said soothingly. Catherine's wild-eyed expression slowly dissipated and her body slumped. He put an arm about her and with a sigh Catherine allowed her head to rest against his shoulder.

After a moment, she said, "It hurts abominably, you know. How odd that I should not have noticed before."

"I expect that your mind was otherwise occupied," Lord Kenelm said grimly. He thought he would never forget the sight of her curled tight inside her cloak, trapped beside the blackening wall. Catherine agreed to his observation and thereafter fell into silence.

The drive to Berkeley Street seemed to take an inordinate amount of time, but at last the carriage swayed to a stop. Lord Kenelm roused himself and eased a half-asleep Catherine upright. "We are here," he said quietly. She nodded and with what struck him as an ironic gesture she instinctively reached up to smooth her hair. It apparently struck Catherine the same way, for she laughed throatily.

"I fear that I am a sad sight," she said, still smiling.

Lord Kenelm looked at her for a long, long moment. Her hair stood up in brittle dirty spikes; her brows had been singed off; her face was black from smoke except where her tears had smeared muddy tracks. "You are beautiful, my love," he said with all the sincerity of his heart. His gaze captured and enmeshed Catherine's wide questioning eyes.

Then the carriage door was opened and the timeless moment was gone. Lord Kenelm rejected the footman's offer of help and himself carried Catherine up the steps to the house. The front door stood open and Lord Talbot awaited them. His left arm was bound up in a white sling and his face had been reddened from the heat, but otherwise he appeared much as usual.

Catherine smiled at him. "Papa."

Lord Talbot acknowledged his daughter with a tender touch on her cheek. Then he requested that one of the footmen carry Catherine on up the stairs to her room; the doctor was waiting to examine her. He turned to Lord Kenelm and wrung his hand. "Thank you! When I saw you in that terrible place, I knew that you would bring her safely home."

"I intend to marry her yet, my lord," Lord Kenelm said quietly.

"And with my blessing. But we will talk of that happy event later. Come, you are exhausted. I shall have a bed made up for you," said Lord Talbot.

Lord Kenelm shook his head. "I should like to return home, I think. I will call on you and your daughter later this evening, my lord."

His lordship nodded and saw him to the door.

Lord Kenelm requested that the hackney cab carry him to his town house. His household was relieved to see him alive and well, having known that he meant to visit the theater. Lord Kenelm was very tired when he arrived, and his valet swiftly saw him to bed. He fell immediately into a deep dreamless sleep.

Lord Kenelm awakened hours later, refreshed and with but one thought. An hour later, bathed and suitably attired, his locks freshly barbered to remove the singed ends, Lord Kenelm presented himself in Berkeley Street. The porter opened the door to him immediately and a footman took his hat and gloves. The butler showed him into the drawing room with great ceremony and closed the door.

Lord Kenelm stood at the door and looked across the room to the lady who sat demurely on the settee. "Miss Talbot, I bid you good evening," he said formally.

"And I you, my lord," said Catherine, her voice still husky. She gestured for him to seat himself beside her. She waited until he had done so before she looked at him again. "I must thank you for coming to my aid tonight. I do not think that I would be sitting here otherwise."

"I could have done no less, Catherine," he said quietly.

She looked quickly away from the vulnerable expression in his eyes. She was having difficulty breathing. Never had she thought to see such a look in his eyes. She began to play with the sticks of her fan. "I behaved abominably to you. I am sorry."

"It is rather I who must apologize, ma'am. You were hard-pressed and but spoke your true feelings," Lord Kenelm said.

"Not my true feelings," murmured Catherine, still not looking at him. He was very still beside her and at last she dared a quick glance up at his face. There was a strained quality about his mouth, as though he was restraining some strong emotion. Catherine's hand stole into his open palm and his fingers closed on hers almost painfully. For a moment there was no need for words.

Then Justin gently raised her face. "I love you most distressingly, Lady Cat."

"Distressingly, my lord?" Catherine asked.

"Quite distressingly," he said firmly. "I had planned a marriage of convenience, you see, and now I must rethink what I am to do. Any rakehell worth the name cannot properly be in love with his own wife."

"It is assuredly an awkward position. Perhaps a fortnight in bed could ... Justin! *Justin!*" He had caught her up to kiss her with thorough passion, and it was several minutes later before Catherine emerged from his embrace, disheveled and breathless. She was bright-eyed. "I do adore you, Justin."

Author's Note: The theater at Drury Lane did not burn in 1807, but in 1808. The Theatre Royal in Covent Garden and the Theatre Royal in Drury Lane burned to the ground within months of each other. Covent Garden reopened in less than twelve months, but Drury Lane did not reopen until 1812.

By Gayle Buck

*The Righteous Rakehell Mutual Consent
Willowswood Match The Demon Rake*

Love's Masquerade The Fleeing Heiress Cassandra's
Deception Belle's Beau
Magnificent Match Honor Besieged
Lady Althea's Bargain Love for Lucinda
Frederica's Folly Chester Charade
Cupid's Choice Lord Darlington's Darling
A Chance Encounter The Waltzing Widow
Tempting Sarah Lord John's Lady
Lord Rathbone's Flirt The Desperate Viscount Hearts
Betrayed The Hidden Heart
Miss Dower's Paragon Lady Cecily's Scheme
<u>Regency Tales</u>
Old Acquaintances Holybrooke Curse
Christmas Cheer Season of Joy
Regency Christmas: Christmas Collection

Don't miss out!

Visit the website below and you can sign up to receive emails whenever Gayle Buck publishes a new book. There's no charge and no obligation.

https://books2read.com/r/B-A-AISJ-LDUEB

BOOKS 2 READ

Connecting independent readers to independent writers.

Also by Gayle Buck

Tempting Sarah
The Waltzing Widow
The Holybrooke Curse
Season of Joy
Hearts Betrayed
Chistmas Cheer
Old Acquaintances
Mutual Consent
The Chester Charade
The Desperate Viscount
Lady Althea's Bargain
Fredericka's Folly
Love for Lucinda
Lord Darlington's Darling
The Demon Rake
Lord Rathbone's Flirt
Miss Dower's Paragon
Belle's Beau
Cassandra's Deception
Love's Masquerade
The Righteous Rakehell
A Magnificent Match

www.ingramcontent.com/pod-product-compliance
Lightning Source LLC
Chambersburg PA
CBHW030141180626
46812CB00002B/787